BLUEBERRY BLUNDER

Also in the Amish Candy Shop Mystery series by Amanda Flower

Assaulted Caramel
Lethal Licorice
Premeditated Peppermint
Criminally Cocoa (ebook novella)
Toxic Toffee
Botched Butterscotch (ebook novella)
Marshmallow Malice
Candy Cane Crime (ebook novella)
Lemon Drop Dead
Peanut Butter Panic

And in the Amish Matchmaker Mystery series

Matchmaking Can Be Murder
Courting Can Be Killer
Marriage Can Be Mischief
Honeymoons Can Be Hazardous

BLUEBERRY BLUNDER

Amanda Flower

Kensington Publishing Corp.
www.kensingtonbooks.com

KENSINGTON BOOKS are published by

Kensington Publishing Corp.
119 West 40th Street
New York, NY 10018

All Kensington titles, imprints, and distributed lines are available at special quantity discounts for bulk purchases for sales promotion, premiums, fund-raising, educational, or institutional use.

Special book excerpts or customized printings can also be created to fit specific needs. For details, write or phone the office of the Kensington Sales Manager: Attn.: Sales Department. Kensington Publishing Corp., 119 West 40th Street, New York, NY 10018. Phone: 1-800-221-2647.

First Printing: June 2023
ISBN: 978-1-4967-3463-1

ISBN: 978-1-4967-3464-8 (ebook)

10 9 8 7 6 5 4 3 2 1

Printed in the United States of America

For Dan, Melissa & Jonah

ACKNOWLEDGMENTS

Many thanks to my readers who have read and enjoyed every one of my Amish mysteries set in Harvest from both the *Amish Candy Shop Mysteries* and the *Amish Matchmaker Mysteries*. These series would not be still going if it wasn't for you. Jethro sends his thanks as well.

I also thank the people who make this series possible: my agent, Nicole Resciniti, my editor, Alicia Condon, and my publicist, Larissa Ackerman. You are all the very best in the business to work with. Thank you.

Thanks too to Kim Bell for reading and commenting on the book.

Love always to my family and friends for their support, but especially to my husband, who is my number one fan.

And finally thank you to God in heaven for allowing me to tell these stories set in the Amish world.

Chapter One

My heart was racing faster than the little pig that zoomed around the factory as if his curled tail were on fire.

"Jethro! Jethro!" I shouted at the polka-dotted black-and-white pig, but it was no use. He flew by me in a squealing blur. The sound of his squeals could break glass and grated on my very last nerve.

The blunt ends of Jethro's hooves clicked on the concrete slab like a tap dancer on Broadway, and the sound echoed through the hollow shell of Swissmen Candyworks. The candy factory that I had thought was such a wonderful idea months ago had now turned into a bit of a nightmare. When construction began in winter, I'd been excited and optimistic about the future of the candy-making business I shared with my grandmother, Clara King. Six months later, we were knee-deep into construction and I was beaten down by never-ending bills and delays.

At the moment, I had little more than the foundation and frame to show for my efforts to build the factory and open in record time. The project should have been much further along at this point. I had been told it would be all but done by now, the end of June. How wrong that was. The plan was for the factory to open at the end of August, so we could work out all the kinks in production before the busy holiday season, but since it was already summer and the interior walls still weren't up, it wasn't looking good.

Jethro buzzed around the cavernous space, and then around and around the multilevel scaffolding in the middle of the room as if it were a Maypole. The top platform was easily ten feet long and six feet wide. The Amish framers had used the scaffolding to raise the building's rafters, and even though I'd been told it would be removed a week ago, there it sat. It wasn't hurting anything by being there, I supposed, but it was just one more thing to deal with. I wondered if the workers installing the insulation could use it. Any forward motion at this point would be more than welcome.

"Jethro, stop!" I said, for what felt like the tenth time.

"This is great! This is great! Are you getting this?" Devon Cruz asked her cameraman as she brushed her bright frizzy hair out of her face and adjusted her glasses.

The cameraman, who just went by the name of Z, grunted in reply as he adjusted his large video camera on his shoulder. By the way he moved, it was apparent that he was used to the weight. It didn't hurt that he was six-foot-three either. I supposed the grunt meant that he was in fact "getting it."

I winced. My behavior didn't evoke the professional candy entrepreneur that I wanted to present on the show. "Are you sure this is good for the reality show? I'm not sure it gives the image we are looking for."

"Of course it is. Stuff like this is perfect for when the storyline slows down. Who doesn't want to watch an adorable pig on the screen?" She glanced around the room. "I have to record something. Nothing else is happening here."

She didn't even bother to hide the criticism in her voice.

As if I didn't have enough stress with the build, I had to deal with Devon's small film crew too. Devon and Z were there to capture the construction of the building for a new reality show on Gourmet Television that I very much regretted agreeing to.

I had worked with Gourmet Television and executive producer Linc Baggins, who did in fact live up to his name and look like a hobbit, for several years on my popular cooking show *Bailey's Amish Sweets*.

The show was inspired by recipes from Swissmen Sweets, the Amish candy shop in Harvest that I ran with my grandmother. She and my grandfather had opened the shop decades ago and lived in an apartment over the shop for the majority of their lives. When my grandfather passed a few years back, I left behind my big city job as chocolatier at world-famous JP Chocolates in New York City and moved to Ohio to help my grandmother.

I'd never thought for a moment when I left New York that the big city would come to Holmes County looking for me, but it had. A few months after my move, I was approached by Linc Baggins to film a candy-making show, and the rest was history.

When he had asked to make a show about the new factory, I'd been hesitant, but I hadn't felt that I could say no. This factory—which would take our family business to a global market—would never have been possible without *Bailey's Amish Sweets* because of the money and exposure I got from the show. Against my better judgment, I'd agreed, thinking at least I knew what it was like to work with Linc. The issue was that on the first day of filming, Linc hadn't been the one who'd knocked on my door. It'd been Devon, an eager young producer with neon-yellow hair, baggy jeans, and a driving hunger for her big break.

I had nothing against a person wanting to fulfill their dreams; I was certainly a dreamer myself. I wouldn't have been standing in an empty building at the moment if I wasn't a dreamer, but Devon was a tad more aggressive than I would have liked. She wanted to be with me every waking moment to catch every last second of my life. I suspected if it had been an option, she'd record me sleeping at night.

Now that I thought about it, I wondered if I would have better luck convincing the contractors to do their jobs if I was as aggressive as Devon.

"Don't worry. The running pig is B roll," Devon said. "It's always good to have filler when on a shoot. Lots of it ends up on the cutting room floor, but it's better to have too much than too little. When is Wade supposed to show up?"

Wade Farmer was my general contractor on the candy factory build. I had booked him because of the excellent construction work he'd done across the county, his glowing reputation, and to be honest, his low quote, but at this point, I was wondering who had been lying. When the project started, Wade had been on point. He answered my thousands of questions and seemed enthusiastic about the idea of building a factory from the ground up. It was true he could be a little rough around the edges at times, but that was something I expected from an English contractor who had almost solely Amish employees. The Amish could be direct and blunt when it came to work. This was especially true with Amish men, so it was no surprise to me that Wade had taken up that manner of speaking to his men and his clients.

Overall, we had a good working relationship until about three months into the project, when everything started to slow down. He claimed that it was materials delays and issues with employee retention. He told me that if I advanced him more money, he'd be able to continue the work. He claimed that the men he hired wanted higher wages, and the price of materials had skyrocketed.

I hadn't been a business owner for years without the ability to sense when something was off. I told him "no" and that we were going to stick to our original payment agreement. I would allow his next draw when the insulation was put in.

Apparently, it had been the last straw with him because work had come to a screeching halt. During April and May there'd been no movement on the building. Devon and Z had arrived the first week of June in the belief they would be documenting the end of the construction project, only to find we hadn't even made the halfway point yet.

To my credit, I'd warned Linc, the executive producer, that the building wasn't as far along as I'd hoped it would be by June. However, he said he was sending Devon and Z anyway to "capture the drama" or my nervous breakdown, whichever came first.

I touched the dark circles under my eyes. I hadn't slept a wink the night before as I worried over what I would say at this meeting with Wade. I had also worried over the fact he might not even show up, which was the root of the problem. With so many other things going on in the candy shop, my cooking show, and my personal life, I'd let the candy factory project get out of hand. I'd ignored the delays and assumed that Wade would take care of it. He hadn't, and when I finally got around to asking him about it, he avoided my calls, text messages, and countless emails.

I was at the end of my completely frayed rope and felt that he'd left me very few choices as to how I could deal with him.

"He'll be here soon," I said, forcing myself to sound positive even though I wasn't feeling that way in the slightest. Wade was already forty minutes late.

Jethro circled the scaffolding for what seemed like the fiftieth time.

Devon grinned at him. "Have you thought of taking the pig on call?"

"On call?" I asked as Jethro zoomed by.

"Yes, on audition in New York. He really has the potential to get a lot of parts, especially in press and media commercials. You should try it. There's a lot of personality in that little oinker."

She had no idea.

"He's not my pig," I said, praying she wouldn't mention this idea to the pig's real owner, Juliet Brook, the local pastor's wife, and my boyfriend Aiden's mother.

Juliet was already trying to make Jethro a star, and I saw nothing wrong with that. My problem was that Juliet would most likely expect me to take him to auditions. But I couldn't add anything more to my to-do list; it was already overflowing with endless details concerning my candy shop, building the factory, *Bailey's Amish Sweets*, and now this reality show I regretted.

"What is going on in here?" a man bellowed.

My heart sank. I hated how I cringed every time I heard Wade's gravelly voice. That alone should've told me it was time to cut my losses and find a new general contractor.

Jethro stopped running and flopped over onto the concrete floor as if he'd been shot. Perhaps the little pig thought Wade was a grizzly bear, and playing dead was the best option for survival. I couldn't say I blamed him. Wade *did* resemble a grizzly with full salt-and-pepper beard, angry growl, and fierce glare.

I scooped up the pig before he recovered and started running around the building again. The last thing I wanted was Jethro misbehaving in front of Wade. The little pig wasn't wearing a hardhat. It was against protocol.

Wade stepped into the factory from what would be the loading area. At this point, there was a concrete ramp there and little else. He was followed by a young blond Amish man, Naz Schlabach. Naz was lanky and seemed to be all arms and legs. He was constantly Wade's shadow on the job, so I wasn't surprised he was there. He held a clipboard and pencil in his hands. Naz smiled at me; Wade did not.

Wade scowled at Devon and Z. He then turned to me. "You think so highly of yourself that you actually believe someone will watch the construction of this building?" He glared at Z. "Get that camera off me."

Z stumbled back a couple of feet, but Devon put her hand on his shoulder to steady him. "Keep recording. He agreed to be part of this project, and he can't change his mind now."

She was right. Wade had signed the release form to be included in filming. He'd done it of his own volition. My guess was because his contracting business would receive free publicity. However, not all press was good. Z had caught on camera dozens of times how rudely Wade had spoken to me and how slow progress had been. I believed anyone who saw the show would think twice before hiring Wade Farmer.

Wade turned his angry expression to me. "Why did you drag me out here this morning? I'm a busy man and have several projects I'm working on. I can't run to an owner's side to coddle them every time they are bellyaching."

As he spoke, I knew this wasn't going to end well, but I decided to give him one more chance. I took a breath. "I'd like an update as to what is going on with the building. There's been no progress in weeks, and the target completion date is August twenty-seventh."

"Construction takes time. Ask anyone. There are always delays. Things go wrong. I could speed up the process if you were willing to put more money into it, but since you're not . . ." He shrugged as if it were my fault.

Naz made a note on his clipboard. I had no idea what he could have been writing. Perhaps, "Client is being a pain."

"We agreed on the estimate and the fund draw schedule. We have a contract. I shouldn't have to put more money into the project than was agreed upon."

He removed his ball cap and used it to wave away my concern. "When was the last time you built anything? This is my area of expertise. If you won't listen to what has to be done, the delays are on you."

I shifted Jethro under my arm and hoped I looked intimidating, even though I was holding a small pig like a football. "I understand delays, but there's been no movement for two months. This project has to be ready for the grand opening in August. We agreed to that. It's also in the contract."

"I agreed to try, but I can't make materials appear out of thin air. There are delays on all building materials now. Your loading dock door, for example, is on a three month back order. There's nothing I can do about it."

"I understand delays, but there must be a way to work around them. Cancel the order and get the garage door from another supplier."

He slapped his cap back on his head. "You don't tell me how to do business. I don't tell you how to make your little candies."

I squeezed Jethro tight.

"Anyway, you should never have scheduled the grand opening until we passed all the rough inspections."

"And when is that going to happen?" I asked.

"I don't know. We have delays," he shot back.

I was no longer trying to be nice. It was time to be firm. "You told me on more than one occasion that eight months was plenty of time. In fact, you said this project would be done in six months, not the eight I requested."

He shrugged as if it was none of his concern. "Things change. You have to be flexible. Not everyone is going to be able to move at the pace you need. Money makes business run better. You're holding back on that, and now you can see what's happened."

"What materials are we missing? If I knew what they were, I could help you look for other sources."

Naz opened his mouth as if he was about to answer my question, but after glancing at Wade, he snapped his mouth closed.

"You don't work in construction. You can't help."

"Making calls, asking if a company has something for sale, is not the same as driving a nail home. I do it all the time for my own business."

"This conversation is insulting," he spat. "I don't have to put up with it. When I say there are material shortages, you need to believe there are. I'm the general contractor."

"I need evidence. Can I see some evidence of these shortages?"

"Excuse me?" His face morphed to bright red.

"If it's really true your suppliers are experiencing such terrible delays, you must have an email, a letter, or something from them telling you so. I'd like to see that evidence."

He opened and closed his mouth as if he could not believe I would have the audacity to question him or to ask for corroboration like that. I couldn't believe I was the only client who had ever asked, especially if something was missing.

"I'm sure other things can be done while you wait for materials. What about the electrician? Can he begin to work on the wiring?" I asked.

"When a building is under construction, the work has to be done in a certain order. I don't expect you to understand. It's why you hired me. If you knew what to do, you could have built this place yourself."

"Burn," I heard Devon whisper.

I shot her a look. Weren't reality television producers supposed to be quiet and just capture the events unfolding in front of them?

I let out a breath. This conversation was going nowhere, and I knew there was only one thing left to do. "I'm sorry, Wade, but this just isn't going to work. I have a firm deadline for this project, and I need to get it done. If you can't make it, I have to find someone else who can. I'm going to have to let you go."

His eyes went wide. "You can't do that."

"I can. I've already called my bank and asked them to put a pause on any more draws to you until they receive my permission. I'm about to call now and tell them to remove your name altogether."

"You can't do that!" He shouted it this time. "We have a contract."

"We do, and it includes a termination clause. The lack of progress is grounds to end the contract. I'm going to have to ask you to leave." I sounded calm and in control, but on the inside I was shaking. Wade was unpredictable, and despite how hard he was to work with, I felt a little bit guilty over firing him. I really hadn't wanted it to come to this. I'd given him every chance I could, but I was out of options. I had to get this building up and running by the end of August.

Devon whispered something to Z, and the cameraman zoomed in on Wade's reaction, which was something to behold. His face flushed from bright red to purple to red again.

I took a couple steps back from him. Had I been alone with him, I might have been frightened. This was one time I was happy Devon and Z were present with their microphone and camera. If Wade tried anything, it would be on tape.

"This is so good," Devon whispered behind me.

"Thank you for what you have done so far on the job, but I need to go in a different direction," I said with finality.

He opened and closed his mouth as if he couldn't believe this was happening. Finally, his voice returned. He shook his fist at me. "I will sue you for breach of contract!"

Naz wrote so furiously on his clipboard that his pencil tip might've broken at any second.

I straightened my spine. "You can try, but I already had an attorney look over the contract, and he said I'm within my rights to let you go. I have plenty of documentation proving there's been no action on the jobsite in weeks. If anything, I could sue you . . ."

He glared at me. The sound of a racing engine filled the docking area, and a moment later we heard a car door slam shut. Margot Rawlings ran into the factory. Her short, curly brown hair bounced as she moved, and she was wearing her summer uniform of jeans and a solid-colored T-shirt. In the winter she switched out the T-shirt for a sweatshirt.

"Bailey! Bailey!" she said in a frazzled voice. "We have a blueberry emergency. A blueberry 911."

Of course, we did.

Chapter Two

"We're in the middle of a conversation," Wade snapped at Margot.

She put her hands on her hips. "I'm sorry to interrupt, but I have a blueberry catastrophe on my hands. Bailey King is the only one who can fix it."

I wrinkled my brow. When had I become the go-to for blueberry emergencies? I didn't remember signing up for that. I had never been involved in a blueberry-related incident before. Leave it to Margot to appoint me to such a position. She was the community planner for the village of Harvest, and over the last several years, she'd been on a mission to make Harvest the number one tourist destination in Holmes County, Ohio.

Currently, the popular stops were Berlin with its extensive shopping, Sugarcreek, and Charm, but Harvest was getting there. A lot of our growing popularity was due to the weekend celebrations and events that Margot hosted on the village square, which was just two blocks from the candy factory.

Swissmen Sweets, my candy shop, was across the

street from the square, which was the most prized and coveted location in Harvest. Up until the launch of *Bailey's Amish Sweets,* a lot of the candy shop's success could be credited to location. And my grandparents' delectable confections, of course.

I turned to Wade. "Thank you for coming in for this meeting, Wade, but I think our conversation is over. Please deliver any materials I have already paid for to the jobsite."

"This isn't over." He spat the words. "You will pay for this. This place will never get finished. I'll make sure of that! Let's go, Naz!" He stomped past Margot and out of the building.

Naz gave a little wave and hurried after his boss.

Margot stared after him. "What's his problem?"

I sighed. "I had to let him go. I need to find a new contractor. It just didn't work out."

"That sounds rough." She clapped her hands as if she was ready to move on to another topic. Her topic, of course. "I have something that will take your mind off that. Blueberries."

I shook my head. Margot had the uncanny ability to laser focus on one thing. It was really quite impressive. But she was right; I did want to get my mind off of firing Wade. It wasn't going to be an easy task finding a new contractor to work in the middle of summer. Because Ohio's winters could last from November to April, there was urgency to get things done in the summer, and it was the busiest construction season. I certainly was feeling the pressure. To make matters worse, I had a firm deadline for the August grand opening. It might be prudent to change my opening plans. The only problem was the reality show. I glanced at Devon. I couldn't see her letting me delay the event. However, it was possible neither of us would have any choice in the matter.

"What's the blueberry situation?" I asked.

"I'm glad you asked, because it is most definitely a situation. The blueberry princess has the stomach flu! Can you believe that? The flu in the middle of summer? I have never heard of such a thing." She folded her arms. "It's really terrible timing!"

"Is she okay?" I asked.

"She's fine. She needs to drink tea and stay in bed." Margot grunted with little sympathy. "The real problem is how this will impact the First Annual Blueberry Bash. Now, I have to find a new blueberry princess by five o'clock tonight for the opening of the celebration. I'm left with very few options."

It didn't take a lot of detective work on my part to realize I was one of those few options. It seemed Margot always came to me when there was a village-related crisis.

I began shaking my head even before she could start her pitch, a pitch I knew was coming. I had been roped into Margot's wild ideas to promote Harvest for years. She claimed since I was a business owner in the village, I should have an interest in the village's success. She was right up to a point. But perhaps I would feel differently if I wasn't asked to resolve something every single week, or so it seemed.

"We can make you work," Margot said, sounding self-assured.

"Make me work? Work on what?" I yelped.

She didn't answer, but I was afraid I knew what she was thinking. This conversation was reminiscent of the time when Margot had strong-armed me into playing the Virgin Mary at the village live nativity on the square. I'd been new to the village and really hadn't known what I was getting myself into. This time I knew better.

She looked me up and down. "You're a bit taller and thicker than the previous princess, but it can't be helped. You're the closest person in size to her, and I think you'll fit into the dress. It might be a bit snug, but we can sew you in. Goodness knows there are enough Amish seamstresses in Harvest who can do the job."

Thick? Did she really call me thick and think I would do her a favor?

I stared at her. "You want me to dress up as a blueberry princess?" I paused. "*Tonight?*"

"Yes. You're the only one dum—destined to do it."

Dumb was what she was going to say. I was smart enough to know that. I set Jethro on the dusty floor and was relieved when he sat at my feet instead of racing around the factory again. I was also acutely aware of Devon and Z, who were eagerly filming my conversation with Margot.

I took a breath. "Margot, as much as I want to help—and you know that I have helped the village a lot over the years and you, in particular, with these events—I can't. I just can't do this. I'm in the middle of a huge construction project and being followed around by a film crew. It's just not going to work."

"Are you kidding? This is reality TV *gold!*" Devon jumped in. "I think your dressing up like the blueberry princess will give the show the small-town authenticity we're looking for. And it will be a lot more exciting than watching you walk around an unfinished factory with resting sad face."

I touched my cheek. "I don't have resting sad face."

"You do. Trust me. I'm talking to special effects to find out if there is a way to make you look happier."

My brow knit together. Could it be true that I appeared unhappy to everyone around me? It had never been like this before. I think, on the whole, people would say I was a happy person. I rubbed my forehead. I must've been really stressed out if I looked sad all the time.

Margot clapped her hands. "Brilliant! Yes! Oh, yes, this is a brilliant idea. What a wonderful way to kick off the First Annual Blueberry Bash, with its being televised. Do you know what this will do for the village?" she cried. "This will be the event that will change everything for Harvest. Tourists will flock here in droves." She narrowed her eyes. "Berlin will wish they were us." She ended her speech with what only could be described as a triumphant grin.

Devon elbowed Z. "Tell me more about Harvest's relationship with Berlin. I think we can make something out of the rivalry between the Amish towns in Ohio."

I frowned. "I don't think Berlin knows there is a rivalry."

"Bailey, you are not taking this seriously. The Blueberry Bash will be *the* event to catapult Harvest to the number one destination in the county, if not all of Ohio! We will no longer be seen as a sleepy little Amish village, but a vacation destination to rival Disney."

I kind of liked the sleepy little Amish vibe, but I knew better than to say that to Margot.

"I can see it now." Margot stared up at the scaffolding as if she were having some sort of vision. "Your reality show will clinch our victory. We will be on national television. Can Berlin or Charm say that? I wouldn't be surprised if all the local television stations wanted to cover the bash too. They won't want to be scooped by a reality show." She clapped her hands. "I'll start a press release. Even more people will want to come to the bash because of the filming. I should tell the newspapers and the village council." She shook with excitement and turned to me. "I have the blueberry princess dress in my car. I'll drop it off at Swissmen Sweets on my way to the village hall." She glanced around the construction site. "I gather the candy shop is cleaner than this place. I can't have dirt on this dress. It has to be perfect. It can't have one speck of dust on it." With that, she hurried out of the factory.

"This village was made for television," Devon said cheerfully. "Z! Let's go back to the B&B and regroup. We need to prepare for a long stretch of filming so we don't miss one minute of the Blueberry Bash."

The quiet cameraman followed her out of the factory.

I looked down at Jethro. "How do I get myself into these situations?"

He snorted, but I thought it was a chuckle at my expense.

Chapter Three

On the walk back to Swissmen Sweets, I had time to think about my predicament. The Blueberry Princess Situation wasn't ideal, and it certainly wasn't something I had time for or wanted to do, but it wasn't nearly as upsetting as my last conversation with Wade Farmer. I felt a mix of relief and frustration that I'd had to let him go. However, the overarching emotion was anxiety. Could he really stop construction of my building?

I shook away the thought. I was a businesswoman, and I wasn't going to let Wade push me around. The first thing I needed to do was to find a new general contractor as soon as possible and get the project moving again.

I prayed that my *maami* would have some idea of people I could ask. Perhaps there was a builder in her church district who would take on the job. Honestly, I should have hired an Amish general contractor from the start. My reluctance had stemmed from all the technology I wanted for the candy factory. We would be using my family's hundred-year-old Amish recipes, but making them with modern techniques. I liked the idea of twenty-first century technology making nineteenth century recipes.

Jethro walked ahead of me on his yellow-and-blue polka-dotted leash. Juliet, his owner, loved polka-dotted everything, from her clothes to her accessories to her pig. To be honest, I was surprised she didn't dye her hair with polka dots. I supposed the only thing that stopped her was the fact that her husband was the pastor of the largest English church in Harvest. That and the whole Cruella vibe such a hairstyle might suggest.

Juliet's large white church sat right across from Swissmen Sweets on the other side of the square. Usually, when the square was a hive of activity, the church was as well, because Reverend Brook, Juliet's husband, generously allowed the community to use the building. He saw it as important outreach to the village.

Before I could cross Church Street to cut through the square on the way to my shop, my phone rang. I fished it out of my jeans pocket, knowing who it was before I even answered because of the distinctive ring tone. "Aiden?" I said breathlessly.

"Bailey," he said, and a calm fell over me. It was certainly what I needed after my confrontation with Wade.

"Are you on the way home?" I didn't even bother to keep the eagerness out of my voice. Aiden had been away from Harvest working for Ohio's Bureau of Investigation for a full year. I was ready for him to come home.

"Not quite yet. That's why I'm calling. I just finished up everything in Columbus. I had to brief the agents taking over a few of my ongoing cases. Then, I have to go back to my apartment and load the car. From there, I will drive to Harvest."

"I can't wait to see you. You will be here in a few hours then?"

"No, I actually got a call for my first PI case in Holmes County. The owner of Linzer Petting Zoo wants me to come out there today to meet with him. He doesn't have any other time this weekend to meet. Saturday is his busiest day, and he's Amish."

Amish meant he wasn't available on Sunday. I knew that.

"Oh," I said.

"I know that you had big plans for what we were going to do when I got home, and there is still time for all of that, just not today. I'm really sorry."

I tried to push back my disappointment. Over the last year, I'd only seen Aiden every few months. Between his demanding work at BCI and my busy schedule, we were always missing each other. I'd hoped that when he moved back to Harvest, things would be different.

"Bailey, are you still there?" Aiden asked.

I cleared my throat. "Yes, I'm still here."

"The only reason I'm taking this case is because it's the first one. Hanging up my shingle as a private detective is a risk. In Holmes County, the only way I'm going to get any clients is through good word of mouth. The petting zoo case has the potential to give me some momentum."

I wanted to smack myself for being even the least bit upset. I was a small business owner too.

Momentum was everything. "I understand, Aiden. I really do. Maybe you can stop by after you meet about the case."

"I'll do that. It will probably be late, but I'll text you when I'm done to see if you're still up. I can't wait to hold you in my arms again."

"I can't wait either," I said just above a whisper.

We ended the call, and I crossed Church Street.

The square and the church were buzzing at that moment with harried preparations for the Friday opening of the Blueberry Bash. I had to say, it was one of the largest productions I'd ever witnessed on the square, and that included the Christmas parade and live nativity, which had even featured a disgruntled camel onsite.

Camel or not, the Blueberry Bash was on another level. It seemed that every booth, as well as the gazebo, and even the pine trees dotting the green were dripping in blueberries. Who knew the fruit could provide such a dramatic décor?

The square's head groundskeeper, Uriah Schrock, directed young Amish teens on where the tables and booths should go. Uriah had recently been reinstated in his position as groundskeeper. He'd left for a few months in order to be with his children in Indiana, but he was back now and had taken over his post again with the help of Leon Hersh, an Amish teen who'd stepped into the role while Uriah was gone. I was glad Margot had let Leon stay on when Uriah returned. Both Leon and Uriah were so passionate about the job—almost as passionate as Margot—but no one really had much of a chance to reach her level of Harvest enthusiasm.

Uriah waved at me as I walked by. I stopped and he came over while Jethro rubbed his snout in the bright green grass.

"*Gude Mariye,* Blueberry Princess." Uriah grinned from ear to ear.

I groaned. "Margot already told you?"

"Oh, yes!" Uriah said with a slight smile. "She shouted it while she dashed across the square. She said she had very important business to attend to since we now have a famous blueberry princess."

"I'm not famous," I muttered.

He cocked his head. "Do people come to Swissmen Sweets because they want to meet you?"

I didn't say anything.

"I will take your silence to mean it is true." He chuckled. "That makes you famous."

"Jethro is the famous one." I gestured to the pig on the leash. "More than half of the time people come to the shop looking for him, and he's not even on every episode of my candy-making show."

"I'm sure Juliet Brook would be happy to remedy that and make him a constant fixture on the network." Uriah looked down at the little pig.

Jethro looked up, and a blade of grass hung from his lips.

I shook my head. "She certainly would, but my show is on Gourmet Television not Animal Planet."

Uriah cocked his head. "Am I supposed to know what either of those things means?"

I shook my head. "Not if you're Amish."

He grinned. "Then I thank *Gott* yet again that I am."

I smiled and started to say goodbye to Uriah when he stopped me.

"Before you go, would you like to see the princess throne?" Uriah asked.

"There's a princess throne?" I squeaked.

"There most certainly is. I made it myself. At what other time would I, an Amish man, have the chance to make a throne? I quite enjoyed it, I have to say. Don't tell the bishop, please."

I promised I wouldn't. Although he and I both knew he should be more concerned about the bishop's wife, Ruth Yoder, than the bishop himself. Bishop Yoder was an understanding and lenient leader. Ruth was not.

"I really don't think I need a throne."

"Of course you do," Uriah said with a mischievous twinkle in his eye. "It might put your mind more at ease if you see it before you have to put on your princess dress."

I wrinkled my nose. "I don't know how anything in that sentence could make me feel better about taking over the role of the blueberry princess."

He barked a laugh. "Let me show you."

I agreed and followed Uriah across the square to the other side of the gazebo. While I'd been speaking with him, the princess booth hadn't been in my line of sight, but as I came around the side of the gazebo, I wondered if it could be seen from space.

The princess booth looked as if the Magic Kingdom had exploded on an unsuspecting armchair. There was tulle, sequins, and glitter everywhere. It was so gaudy that it was almost pretty. Almost. It certainly went against the grain of Amish plainness.

"Wow, Uriah, you really went for it."

"I got Lois's advice on what a throne should look like."

Now, that made sense. Lois Henry would be the one person in the village who would be an expert on making a gaudy throne. She was an English woman Uriah's age, who had spikey purple-red hair and loved costume jewelry. She would certainly advise a bedazzled blueberry princess throne. She also happened to be the best friend of Millie Fisher, whom Uriah had admired his whole life.

"I didn't think there would ever be another time I would make something so lavish. It was fun, but if anyone asks—meaning if the bishop's wife asks—this was Margot's idea."

"It's so blue," I said.

His grin widened.

I tried to imagine myself sitting on the throne. It wasn't a comfortable thought. However, Jethro didn't have the same qualms. He jumped up on the throne, turned around twice as if making sure it was to his liking, and then sat in the middle of it and smiled at us. It was as if he had finally found where he belonged.

I had to unclip his leash and take a few pictures with my phone. "That's your real blueberry princess."

"Be careful what you wish for. If Juliet Brook sees Jethro sitting there, you will definitely be holding him the entire time you're in that seat."

I grimaced. There had to be a way I could get out of this whole blueberry princess mess. "I appreciate your preparing me. It's never good to be surprised over a throne, in my opinion."

He chuckled. "It's what friends are for. And I must confess it's my fault there even is a Blueberry

Bash. Margot came up with the idea of having a princess, but the original idea for this weekend was all mine."

I smiled. "And why is that?" I asked even though I already knew the answer.

He blushed ever so slightly. "You know Millie Fisher is partial to blueberries."

It was my turn to chuckle. Though they were best friends, Millie could not be more different from the outlandish Lois Henry. Millie was a sweet Amish woman and cared deeply for her community. She was also known to be a matchmaker of young Amish couples. She had been widowed young and never remarried, but Uriah had been sweet on her for years. Many claimed that he'd moved back to Ohio because of Millie. He never said that was the reason, but considering the Blueberry Bash, I was thinking that those rumors just might be true.

"Blueberries just might be the way to Millie's heart."

"I hope so," he murmured.

I told Uriah goodbye. I had to return to Swissmen Sweets and make a plan as to how I was going to get everything done and deal with the fact I no longer had a general contractor.

Jethro and I walked across Main Street to my candy shop. Before stepping into the store, I peered through the front window at the front shelves lined with glass jars filled with every sort of candy, from peppermints to gumdrops to gummy bears.

In keeping with the blueberry theme of the weekend, blueberry-flavored candies were prominently displayed. There were blueberry candy sticks, blueberry gumdrops, and my newest addition to the Swissmen Sweet offerings, blueberry-and-cream fudge. The fudge on the display shelf had been sprayed with shellac, so that it looked fresh all the time. It was no longer safe to eat, but my cousin Charlotte and I had made plenty of fresh blueberry cream fudge to sell all weekend long.

Up until the moment Margot had marched into the factory and drafted me to be the blueberry princess, I had been looking forward to the bash. Events like this on the square were really big draws for tourists and locals, and the more people on the square, the better the candy shop did.

I opened the door, and Jethro went into the candy shop first. Before I could even cross the threshold, the little pig squealed, spun around, and ran back toward me. If I hadn't been right behind him to scoop him up, he would have bolted into the street.

With the pig secure, I saw what had startled him so badly, and it was terrifying indeed.

Chapter Four

When I stepped into Swissmen Sweets, my cousin Charlotte Weaver was waiting for me. "Bailey!" she cried from behind the glass-domed candy counter. "You're going to be the Blueberry Princess!" She held up the large dress bag and shook it. I guessed it was the dress bag that had spooked the pig. It was enormous.

Jethro relaxed in my arms when he saw it was Charlotte who held the bag.

I groaned. Apparently in the short time since Margot had left the candy factory, she'd told everyone she'd met that I would be berry royalty. I wasn't looking forward to seeing the press release on the topic.

Charlotte tugged on her long red braid and grinned. "You'll be a great princess."

I snorted. Charlotte shouldn't be a judge of who was or wasn't princess material. She was several years younger than I and had grown up in a very strict Amish home, which she had left in her early twenties over a dispute about music. Charlotte was a gifted musician and organist, but her home district didn't allow musical instruments. She'd come to live with my grandmother Clara because *Maami's* district didn't have that kind of rule. I did not meet Charlotte until after she left her district because her strict community would not allow it.

Many people unfamiliar with Amish culture were surprised there were so many rule differences between districts. It was because the district bishop—who oversaw as many as forty families—made the rules for the people who lived in his community. If a bishop liked musical instruments, he might allow them, if he didn't like them, he might not. The bishops that outlaw them believe they distract members from focusing on God and the community.

However, one universal rule held true across the Amish faith. An Amish woman was to marry an Amish man. Even though my grandmother's district was more progressive than Charlotte's home district, it wasn't so lenient as to allow Charlotte to marry the English man she'd fallen in love with and stay in the community.

Ultimately, Charlotte had chosen love over her upbringing and left the faith in order to become engaged to Deputy Luke Little. After over a year of engagement, the couple was set to wed in just nine days. I was Charlotte's maid of honor and the ceremony was to be in the village square with a reception immediately afterward in Juliet's church just across from Swissmen Sweets.

I took a deep breath. The wedding was another reason I didn't need to take on this blueberry princess role. Swissmen Sweets would be providing all the desserts for the wedding, and I refused to let Charlotte help prepare any of them because she was the bride. I was sort of regretting that decision at the moment as she was my right hand in the kitchen.

Charlotte's green eyes sparkled. "I looked at the dress. I probably shouldn't have peeked, but I couldn't resist. It's so beautiful. I've never seen anything like it."

I smiled. "I get the feeling I've never seen anything like it either."

"You need to try it on. I want to see you in it." She clapped her hands.

That made one of us, but I knew she was right. I was nervous over the fact that Margot had said the dress might be a little "snug" on me. I wasn't sure what I would do if it didn't fit, and the idea of being sewn into the dress wasn't appealing.

Charlotte popped her head into the kitchen and called, "Emily, Bailey and I are going upstairs for a bit."

I heard the other shop assistant, Emily Keim, agree. Charlotte came around the counter, grabbed my hand, and dragged me into the little hallway leading to the stairs.

Jethro followed behind us.

My grandmother's apartment over the candy shop consisted of five small rooms. Her bedroom, Charlotte's bedroom, a half kitchen with just a sink, a bathroom, and a small sitting room at the very end. Charlotte's bedroom was the first room in the apartment on the right. When my father was young, this had been the room where he lived until he was a teenager and left his community for good, then eventually married my mother. Charlotte wasn't much different from my father in that way.

Charlotte placed the dress in its clear plastic bag in the middle of her bed. The small orange shop cat, Nutmeg, was also on the bed, staring down at the dress as if he didn't know what he was looking at. I couldn't blame him, I wasn't sure I knew what I was looking at either.

"Ta-da!" Charlotte said.

I forced a smile as I studied the dress. It was a pile of sequin, tulle, and—were those feathers? Every last element was blue. It also looked impossibly small. Maybe I would get out of this blueberry princess thing after all.

Charlotte went to the door. "Try it on. I'll wait outside."

She closed the door after her, leaving me with the cat and pig as audience.

I pointed at them. "If either of you mocks me while I try to get this on, you will be sorry."

Nutmeg swished his tail across the bedspread. Jethro sat on his haunches and stared as if settling in for a show. I sighed.

I undressed quickly, removed the dress from the plastic, and tried to pull it over my head. No luck there. I yanked it off and tried to step into the dress. That was even worse. It caught on my thighs and toppled me over onto the floor.

The bedroom door opened, and Charlotte came in. "Bailey, are you okay? What are you doing on the floor like that?"

I lay in the middle of Charlotte's bedroom rug. Nutmeg and Jethro now stood over me as if they were in the middle of debating whether I was dead or alive. "I'd say it doesn't fit. Can you help me get it off?"

Together, Charlotte and I were able to remove the dress without tearing it.

When I was back in my own clothes, I said, "I'll have to tell Margot this isn't going to work. I don't know why she thought the dress would fit me. It's way too small."

"Maybe it will fit me," Charlotte said timidly.

I raised my brow. In all likelihood the dress would fit my cousin. She was smaller and shorter than I was, but I never for a moment would have thought my formerly Amish cousin would want to wear something so . . . so . . . un-Amish. Charlotte still dressed plainly, even though she'd left the faith. Right now she wore a long denim skirt and a blue T-shirt with sneakers.

I laid the dress on the bed. "If you want to give it a try, you are more than welcome."

This time, I left the room so she could get dressed, with Jethro and Nutmeg following me downstairs and into the main room of the candy shop.

Emily smiled when I came in. "Are you okay? I thought I heard someone fall down up there."

I raised my hand. "It was me trying on the blueberry princess dress. Let's just say it was a failure."

Her blue eyes went wide. "What are you going to tell Margot?"

"That I can't do it. Unless she wants a blueberry princess in jeans and a T-shirt."

Emily patted the blond Amish-style bun at the nape of her neck. "I have a feeling Margot is not going to like that. When she dropped the dress off, she was very excited that you were going to be the prin—oh—" She cut herself off.

I turned around to see what had caught her attention.

Charlotte stood in the middle of the candy shop in a blue sequined ball gown that looked like it came directly from Disney World via a fairy godmother.

Jethro squealed and ran across the room where he dove into Nutmeg's cat bed in the corner. The little orange cat watched his antics with a scowl on his face.

Charlotte's face turned the same red color as her hair. "Does it look so bad that I scared Jethro?"

"He'll be fine. I think he was a little taken aback by your appearance. The dress does take up a lot of space."

That was putting it mildly. There were enough hoops and crinoline on the dress for a nineteenth century ball.

Charlotte crossed her arms as if she was trying to cover herself. "I'm so sorry, but I couldn't resist trying it on. I know I shouldn't have, but it was just so beautiful. I've never seen anything like it."

In truth, I doubted anyone living in Harvest had seen anything like this dress. It looked amazing on Charlotte with her bright eyes and red hair. She was a real-life Cinderella.

"Charlotte, it's beautiful," Emily said. "You really look like a princess."

Charlotte blushed.

"The dress suits you," I agreed.

"I'll go take it off," she said reluctantly. "You'll have to call Margot and tell her it doesn't fit you.

She doesn't have much time to find someone else to wear it."

I voiced the obvious solution. "You could wear it."

She wrinkled her nose. "Me?"

"You should be the blueberry princess," I said.

"You would make the perfect princess, Charlotte," Emily agreed.

Her eyes went wide. "Margot didn't ask me to be the blueberry princess. She asked you. She didn't ask me."

"She asked me by default and because she thought I might fit into the dress, but I don't." I didn't add that I was also Margot's first call whenever there was a problem.

Charlotte's face was pinched. "But . . ."

"It would be a great help to me if you could do it," I said. "I fired Wade Farmer today at the candy factory, so I need to find a new contractor soon."

Emily gasped. "You fired him?"

I nodded. "This project needs to finish on time, and it was clear Wade wasn't the person to do that."

Charlotte's face fell. "Oh, Bailey, I'm so sorry. I know that was the last thing you wanted to do."

I looked from one to the other. "It was, but he left me with no other option."

"Do you think the factory will be finished on time?" Emily asked.

"It will be," I said with way more confidence than I felt.

"It's awful that it came to this, but I'm glad you finally fired him," Charlotte said. "He wasn't doing his job, Bailey. You are too nice and gave him too many chances."

"You would have done the same thing," I said with a smile.

"I probably would have. But Cass wouldn't have."

She had a point there. Cass Calbera was my best friend and a lifetime New Yorker. She was also the head chocolatier at my former employer JP Chocolates. Cass didn't take any sass from anyone. I should be more like her when it came to business. I would remember that when I hired the next general contractor . . . if I could find one.

"What do I do as the blueberry princess?" she asked with a small quaver in her voice.

"You smile and wave." I thought of the glitzy blueberry princess throne and decided to leave that part out for the time being.

"I don't know. I could get in a lot of trouble." She gave the dress a forlorn look.

"Trouble? Trouble from whom? You're not Amish any longer," Emily said.

"I know." Her face flushed the same red color as her hair. "I guess it's just out of habit that I feel that way. After following those rules my whole life, I sometimes find it hard to believe I don't have to anymore. There was comfort in following them. There was always a right way and a wrong way to act. The English world has so much gray, and that's confusing. At least, it's confusing for a former Amish girl like me."

"It's confusing for everyone," I said. "But you won't get in trouble. Ruth Yoder might not be thrilled, but she doesn't have a hold over you anymore."

She nodded and straightened her spine. "You're right. It's just one weekend, yes?"

"Right," I agreed. "And maybe not even that long if the original blueberry princess is on the mend tomorrow."

"Do you think we should tell Margot about our plan?" she asked.

I shook my head. "It's better to just go with it, and if she complains, I'll tell her the dress doesn't fit me. I have the bruises from landing on the floor to prove it."

She gave a little twirl. "Okay. I'll do my best. I just hope nothing goes wrong."

"What could go wrong at the Blueberry Bash?" Emily asked.

I didn't want to consider the possibilities.

Chapter Five

Charlotte twirled again while Emily and I clapped. She really was the perfect blueberry princess. Jethro and Nutmeg watched her spin with wide eyes. They also backed up into the corner of the shop as if they were afraid of any flying sequins. I took a step back myself. The cat and pig were usually right about these sorts of things.

The bell over the candy shop's front door rang, and I half expected Margot to march into the shop and ask Charlotte to remove her precious dress.

"Good heavens! Is that your wedding dress, Charlotte? You are a vision. I have to say I'm surprised at the volume! I never would have imagined you'd go for something so flamboyant." Juliet Brook held her hands over her heart as tears came to her eyes. "Weddings always make me weepy."

Only Juliet Brook would think this blue monstrosity was Charlotte's wedding dress. Juliet was a true Southern belle and Jethro's owner, even though lately it seemed that Jethro spent more time with me than with her. She and Aiden had moved to

Harvest over twenty years ago to get away from Aiden's abusive father.

After moving to Ohio, they'd never seen the man again. Aiden rarely spoke of his father. As far as I knew, he had no interest in looking for his dad.

Juliet desperately wished we were more than boyfriend and girlfriend. I had to admit—if only to myself—I'd recently begun to wish that too. However, I would never be dumb enough to say so to Juliet. My relationship with her son was already under enough pressure.

Considering what Juliet had been through with her first husband, it was a true fairy tale come true when she fell in love with and eventually married Reverend Brook. Since Juliet had taken over the helm as pastor's wife, the church had become more and more involved with community events. She and Margot Rawlings had become co-conspirators on plans to up Harvest's profile with tourists.

"But shouldn't you be wearing white?" Juliet asked with concern, dropping her hands from her chest. As usual she was wearing polka dots. Today, it was a polka-dot skirt with a silk blouse, and red heels. Juliet was committed to her look all the way down to her polka-dotted pig.

Charlotte blushed red again. "My wedding dress is white."

"That doesn't look white to me." Juliet wrinkled her smooth brow.

I took this as my cue to step in. "Juliet, Charlotte is going to be the blueberry princess at the Blueberry Bash this evening. She was just trying on the dress."

Juliet patted her silky blond hair. "But Margot

was telling me that you were going to be the blueberry princess. I was so very excited about it. It was my hope that if Aiden saw you in a gorgeous gown, he would be inspired to pop the question."

"The dress is too small for me to wear," I said, making a point to ignore her comment about Aiden proposing. She'd made so many statements like this over the years, I'd become a pro at ignoring them.

"Oh, honey, all you need is a corset and we will squeeze you right in there."

Over my dead body.

"Are you here to pick up Jethro?" I thought it was best to change the subject before we started talking again about why Aiden and I weren't engaged yet. Or about corsets and squeezing.

She placed a hand on her chest. "I am, but doesn't he look so precious curled up on that little cat bed like that. Doesn't it just bring a tear to your eye?"

I glanced over at the cat and pig. Nutmeg was curled up on the bed with the pig's rear end and tail smacking him in the face. The cat looked as if he was contemplating biting Jethro's tail.

"Adorable," I agreed.

"I just hate to move him. Maybe he should stay with you awhile longer because he's so content right now."

"No, no," I said quickly. "He misses you."

As much as I liked having Jethro around, taking the little pig everywhere I went could be taxing at times. It was a full-time job because I always had to keep one eye on him, given his penchant for trouble.

She nodded as if I'd made a good point. "I know he does. I have been so busy at the church this last week and with the Blueberry Bash, I haven't been able to spend much time with Jethro, or with Reverend Brook for that matter. We need a little family time." She tapped her right cheek with a perfectly manicured pink fingernail. "Now that Aiden is back in town, the two of you should come over for dinner tonight. I'll make a roast."

A heavy roast on a warm summer night didn't sound very appealing. Besides, the invitation sounded like a trap to me. I knew Juliet wanted to talk about Aiden and me getting married.

"Aiden called me an hour ago. He is finishing up his work with BCI and then he has to meet a new client this evening when he arrives in Holmes County," I said. "Maybe another time?"

Aiden had been away from Harvest for over year while working for Ohio's Bureau of Investigation. During that time, he'd lived in Columbus and worked as a field agent. It'd been a dream job for Aiden, especially after working under the thumb of the surly Holmes County Sheriff for over a decade. However, after a few months, he'd realized that he missed Harvest, Holmes County, and me.

The distance was a major strain on us as a couple. There was even a time when I thought it would be better if we broke up and cut our losses. I was close to telling him that when he'd decided to leave BCI. I'd been so relieved. It was what I wanted, but not something I would have ever asked him to do. I was thrilled he was coming home, but nervous too. What if he gave up this career he always wanted for me and we didn't work out?

"He has work already?" She smiled. "I knew that

my son was going to be successful no matter what he does."

"I think so too," I said.

She sighed. "I was hoping that the two of you might want to come to dinner. I heard that you fired Wade Farmer as your general contractor. I thought a nice dinner might cheer you up. I'm sure you're stressed about the whole thing. You have been working so hard on that factory. I do admire your gumption."

I smiled. As crazy as Juliet drove me, she really was very sweet and caring.

Juliet bit her lip. "I'm concerned for you too. Wade Farmer is a hard man. The rumor in the village is that he holds a grudge. I'd keep an eye on him."

That was the last thing I needed to hear.

Chapter Six

The kickoff for the Blueberry Bash was at six o'clock sharp, but Margot had said she wanted me in position as the blueberry princess at five. Swissmen Sweets was to stay open for the duration to sell sweets to the people walking up and around the square. We usually closed at five on Fridays. I went outside and put up a chalkboard sign about the extended hours. *Maami* would watch the shop while I helped Charlotte get settled on her blueberry throne. I hadn't told Charlotte about the throne yet. It was just better for her to see it for herself. I wasn't sure my verbal description would do it justice anyway.

Esther Esh stood outside of her family's pretzel shop with her arms folded, glaring at the square. "Margot has gone too far this time. Look at the square. It's a circus. What does any of that have to do with the Amish?"

After I made sure the sign was upright and secure, I turned and looked at the square to assess what she meant. She had a point. Usually, there was a strong emphasis on Amish culture at square events because it was the Amish who brought tourists to Holmes County in the first place. There was nothing Amish about the Blueberry Bash.

The square looked like a carnival with food trucks parked on the curb and a man walking around in a blueberry suit. He was blue from the top of his head to the soles of his shoes. I spotted Margot, who was wearing a blue T-shirt and her standard jeans. There was even a dunking booth. That definitely wasn't Amish.

The front door of Swissmen Sweets opened, and Charlotte came outside in head-to-toe blue sparkles.

"Hi, Esther," Charlotte said as she picked at her tulle skirt.

Esther's mouth fell open. "You're involved in this? I know you're not Amish any longer, but this is taking it too far. Do you know how embarrassing this display is for the community?"

Charlotte glanced at the square. "It looks like fun, and you're right—I'm not Amish any longer. There are no rules telling me what to wear or where I should go. I'm just helping out the village and Margot."

Esther shook her head. "Margot Rawlings doesn't need any help making a mockery of things, but it seems to me that Swissmen Sweets is always there to lend her a hand. Esh Family Pretzels will not succumb to this blatant disregard for the Amish in the village. I'm closing my shop. I won't take money from people who attend such a ridiculous event." She went inside her shop and slammed the door closed

A second later we heard the deadbolt slide home.

Charlotte bit her lower lip. The bravado she'd showed in front of Esther melted away.

"Maybe I shouldn't be doing this. Do you think I'm mocking the Amish in Harvest?"

"Of course not," I said. "You know Esther. If she's not annoyed by something, it must not be a day that ends in 'y.' "

Charlotte laughed.

"Besides, other members of the Amish community will be there. Don't make a decision based on what Esther says. The bash was Uriah Schrock's idea in the first place."

"It was?"

I nodded. "And look, there's Millie Fisher now!" I pointed to the square.

Millie and Lois were walking around the grounds.

"Millie is a friend of Ruth Yoder," she said. "If it is all right that Millie is there, I should be able to go too."

"Let's go talk to Millie. I think she will put your mind at ease."

Charlotte and I crossed Main Street and walked to the square.

"Isn't it so nice that Uriah suggested blueberries for the weekend on your behalf?" Lois was asking as we joined them.

Millie wore a plain navy-blue dress and white prayer cap on the top of her head. In cold weather she would be wearing a black bonnet too. Millie was as different from Lois as possible. Millie folded her arms. "Don't be silly. Blueberries are in season. That's the reason for the theme of the weekend."

"Uh-huh," Lois said.

I held my tongue to keep from repeating what I had heard from Uriah. I wasn't going to get involved in this debate between friends.

Lois glanced over her shoulder and gasped. "Charlotte Weaver, you are a vision! What a glorious gown."

Charlotte blushed again. "I'm not sure I should be wearing it. What would Ruth Yoder say?"

"I have an idea," Lois said with a cackle.

"Charlotte, you have no reason to be concerned with what the bishop's wife thinks of your dress," Millie said. "Besides, as I have said many times before, Ruth's bark is much worse than her bite."

I wasn't as sure of that. I had tangled with Ruth before, and it seemed to me that her bark and her bite were both bad.

"If Millie says that, it has to be true," Lois said. "This is Millie's Super Bowl, an entire weekend about blueberries." She gave a mischievous grin. "One made possible by Uriah. Did you know he was the one who suggested the Blueberry Bash to Margot in the first place? All to impress Millie!"

Millie rolled her eyes. It was a trait I was certain she had picked up from Lois, and every time she did it, I had to stifle a smile.

"You make me sound like a blueberry fiend," Millie said as she adjusted her thin black shawl on her shoulders.

"That's what you are, aren't you? I have never met anyone who loves blueberries as much as you do." Lois turned to me. "Bailey, I thought you were going to be the blueberry princess."

"I can't fit into the dress," I said with a shrug. "I'm really broken up about it."

"I'm sure you are," Lois said with a chuckle. She

smiled at Charlotte. "You make the perfect blueberry princess. Your red hair complements that deep blue perfectly."

Millie put a hand on my arm. "I heard you had a run-in with Wade Farmer."

I wrinkled my nose. It was good to know the Harvest gossip mill was on the job. How many people had heard about the incident with Wade? I supposed I shouldn't be so surprised. I'd had both a camera crew and Margot there at the time. Even if the producer and cameraman wouldn't say anything in order to protect their content, there was nothing holding Margot back.

I inwardly groaned. By the end of the Blueberry Bash, it would be all over the county.

"What happened?" Lois wanted to know.

"I had to let him go. He wasn't working out as general contractor. There were too many delays, and the candy factory is on a tight schedule."

Lois cocked her head. "You know, you're not the only one who's said that. I've heard from at least two other people who've had business dealings with Wade that they were suffering delays, and Wade even demanded more money to speed up the process."

My eyes went wide. "That's what he did with me too! Who are these other people?"

Lois tapped the side of her face with her long, teal-polished nail. Lois wasn't a woman who was afraid of color, any color. "Let me think. It would be a young couple building a house out on Bishop Road. I can't remember their names, but they were English. They came into the café this morning for breakfast and told me all about it.

"Oh yeah, they had just started breaking ground in May, and then construction came to a complete halt. They didn't even get the foundation poured, and with the spring rains, the dirt walls caved in. It's a real mess."

I felt sympathy for the couple. Their situation was worse than mine. At least the foundation and frame of the candy factory were up.

"And then there's the new candy shop in Charm," Lois said. "I think it's called Swiss German Candies or some such thing."

I blinked at her. "A *new* candy shop?"

Why hadn't I heard about this new candy shop before now? It would be in direct competition with Swissmen Sweets. I let out a breath and reminded myself there were enough tourists who came to Amish Country to sustain more than one candy shop.

"How is their job going?" I asked.

"From what I heard, it's not," Lois said. "Wade refused to do any work on the job until they gave him more money up front."

Millie wrinkled her brow. "How did you hear all that?"

Lois put her hands on her hips and the bangles on her wrists clacked together. "I wait on tables at the café. People talk." She smiled. "And I have a friendly face too. People like to tell me their secrets."

"There must be something going on," Millie said. "Why is he insisting on so much money upfront from so many people? It doesn't make sense. Do the work, and then get paid. That's how the world works."

It was a very good point. Why *was* Wade asking so many clients for more money before he did the work on these jobs, and why were there so many jobs at a standstill?

Lois glanced at the gold watch on her wrist. "I'd better get back to the Sunbeam. My granddaughter will be wondering what's become of me, and we're bound to be busy. She made at least forty of her famous blueberry pies to sell this weekend."

"I hope she saved one for me," Millie said.

"Darcy always saves a blueberry pie for you," Lois said.

"*Gut,*" Millie replied.

I waved goodbye to the two friends before I turned back to Charlotte. She stood frozen in the middle of the square with her hands clasped together so tightly that her knuckles turned white.

"What's wrong?"

She dropped her hands and shook them as if they were sore. "Oh, it's nothing. You said I had a throne. Where is it?" She gasped. "There it is. Wow."

Wow was really the only word that could be used to sum up the throne. She hurried over to it. The rhinestones on her skirt caught the light as she went. All the while she kept glancing over her shoulder as if she expected someone to be following her.

I looked around but didn't see anything unusual. At least, I didn't see anything unusual in terms of Margot's events on the square. The blueberry man was a little odd, but not unexpected when Margot was involved.

Even so, it was clear to me that Charlotte was spooked, and whatever had upset her so much was much more than the *nothing* she claimed.

Chapter Seven

I walked around the Blueberry Bash with a tray of blueberry-and-cream fudge samples in the hope I would entice revelers to cross the street and shop at Swissmen Sweets. Blueberry and cream was one of my favorite specialty flavors, and needless to say Millie Fisher was a huge fan. An elderly English man took a piece from my tray and said, "This is delicious."

"You can find more across the street at Swissmen Sweets. We have a whole host of fudge flavors!" I said with a bright smile.

He thanked me and grabbed another free sample before he moved on.

The Blueberry Bash was the first event like this where Swissmen Sweets didn't have a dedicated table. Considering everything going on with the factory, I'd opted out of the extra work of manning a table and just asked Margot if we could pass out free samples. To my surprise, she'd agreed.

However, now I could see why. The food trucks Margot had organized were the main dining options for visitors. There were long lines at the taco truck, sushi truck, and the sub truck. It wasn't exactly Amish fare—or blueberry fare for that matter—but it seemed to do the job and attract more people to the square.

I glanced back at Swissmen Sweets and saw there was a line out the door of customers waiting for candy. I needed to get back to the shop to help *Maami.* It seemed my free samples were working a little too well.

Since I'd started building Swissmen Sweets Candyworks, my relationship with my grandmother had been a bit strained. She wasn't pleased with the idea of the factory, but said she trusted I knew what I was doing. She didn't understand why I wasn't happy with what we already had. We were making money and could support ourselves. She didn't know why I wanted more.

My grandmother was Amish to her core and had the great trait of Amish contentment. However, I wasn't Amish and never have been. Contentment was something hard to come by for a former New Yorker like me.

As the evening went on, Charlotte sat on the blueberry princess throne, smiled, and had her picture taken with English children on her lap like a Santa at the mall. The nervousness she'd experienced earlier melted away with every child's giggle. Charlotte loved little ones, and the excitement of the children—both English and Amish—over seeing a "real" princess put her at ease.

I handed out my last few pieces of fudge and turned to go to Swissmen Sweets to lend *Maami* a hand.

"Bailey King! What do you think you're doing?" Margot called from behind me.

I spun around and found Margot clutching her beloved bullhorn at her side and scowling at me. If I didn't know it would make her even angrier, I might have laughed. "I'm so sorry. I'm out of fudge samples."

"I'm not asking you about the fudge samples, and you know it. Why are you here handing out fudge, while Charlotte is wearing the blueberry princess dress?"

"Charlotte is better suited for the royal duties, and the dress didn't fit me. Trust me, it wasn't pretty."

"The film crew was expecting *you* as the princess. Your involvement was going to raise Harvest's profile. We need you in that chair."

I looked around at the hundreds of people milling around Harvest's main square, taking pictures, and lining up at the food trucks. How high a profile did she want for the village? What was popular enough? This was just day one of the Blueberry Bash. It seemed to me that Harvest's profile was already up.

"Is the film crew not here because you aren't the princess? I—we—were counting on the free publicity."

I bit my tongue to stop myself from saying that through *Bailey's Amish Sweets* I had given Harvest oodles of free publicity over the years. But now that she mentioned it, where were Devon and Z? I thought Devon had said she planned to film the bash. It was odd that they weren't here considering how eager Devon was to make a name for herself with Gourmet Television.

"I'm sure that Devon and Z will be here as soon as they can. Maybe they decided to shoot some B roll before coming."

Margot sniffed. "Well, you had better be right. We need this, Bailey. We need Harvest to be put on the map."

A dark-blue van pulled up behind the taco truck on the square. "Oh look, there they are now."

Margot glanced behind her. "Good." She shook her finger at me. "And if they want a shot of you in that princess dress, you have to do it."

Not happening. I couldn't even get the dress on.

Devon hopped out of the van and left Z to deal with the equipment.

"Bailey, I thought you were the princess," Devon said with a pout.

"There was a wardrobe issue. Charlotte took over the job, and I, for one, think she's the perfect blueberry princess."

"This will never work." Devon shook her head. "I already told the studio I'd be getting footage of the Blueberry Bash with you as the princess. It would be priceless."

"You can still get all the shots of the Blueberry Bash."

She pushed her Mohawk out of her eyes. "It's not the same. You can't change plans like that without consulting with production."

I frowned. "I thought you were making a show about the building of the candy factory. The Blueberry Bash doesn't have anything to do with that."

She narrowed her eyes at me, and I saw the ambitious woman underneath the façade of excitable producer. "Have you ever watched reality television? People want to know you and see you in ridiculous situations. They don't care about how a building is made. They want the humor. They want the disaster. They want the scandal."

I knew she was right, but I was still glad I wasn't the blueberry princess.

Her face cleared, and her smile was back in place. "At least Z can get some B roll here, and you'll be around. We'll make it work."

"Did you get any B roll this afternoon?" I asked.

"We did." Her answer was more clipped than I expected it to be.

"How was the footage you got this afternoon?"

A strange look crossed her face. "It was good. Oh, I had better help Z with the equipment." She ran back to the van.

Devon's reaction was odd, but I put it to the back of my mind.

The line to Swissmen Sweets was even longer than before, and I knew it was time for me to return to the shop and lend *Maami* a hand.

I crossed the square and was surprised to see Wade Farmer speaking with an Amish man—or at least a man who I assumed was Amish due to his clothing. The Amish man's back was toward me, so I couldn't see his face, and a broad-brimmed black hat covered his hair.

Wade was facing me, and I didn't want him to see me, so I ducked behind the sub truck and peeked around the side of it. If I'd known what was good for me, I would have gone back to Swissmen Sweets right then and there, but there was just something off about the two men's stance. The Amish man's back was rigid and his fists were balled at his sides. Could this be another person who had a beef with Wade?

Also, I was simply nosy.

"I am asking you to release my son," I heard the man say. "It is not the right place for him. It is not what *Gott* wants for his life."

Wade's brows went up. "It's not what God wants or not what *you* want? I know all about your district and how you restrict your members. Maybe that's why so many young people are fleeing it. Yours has to be one of the few Amish districts in the county that is getting smaller instead of larger. That should tell you something."

"You have no right to speak of my church and district so. Your opinion is of no consequence. I am asking you to release my son."

"Release him? He is working for me of his own free will. What you're asking is for me to fire him so he'll crawl home to you. I won't do that."

"I do not like that you work for that woman. I don't want my son around her. She corrupts young Amish people and pulls them away from the faith. I will not have that happen to my son."

"What woman?" Wade asked, not even trying to keep the exasperation from his voice.

"The *Englisch* woman from the candy store." With a long narrow finger, he pointed at Swissmen Sweets.

I stood up a little straighter. Not for a second had I imagined this conversation would involve me.

"I don't work for her anymore, and trust me, it's something that she will regret. She will regret it as soon as tonight." Wade spoke with so much venom in his voice, I shivered.

Chapter Eight

I spent the rest of the Blueberry Bash at Swissmen Sweets, selling candy and worrying about the conversation I'd heard between Wade Farmer and the Amish man. When the line of shoppers slowed, I shooed my grandmother upstairs to her apartment for the night. It took me a few minutes to convince her to go, but she had been working the counter alone for so long, she more than deserved a break.

Maami loved to work and she loved chatting with tourists, but I knew she was tired. And no matter what time she went to bed that night, she would be up at four the next morning to make more candy.

After *Maami* went upstairs, I organized the candy trays in the display cases and wondered what Wade had meant when he'd said I would regret his not working for me anymore. Was he planning on doing something to harm the candy factory? To harm me? I tried to shake off the feeling of dread and tell myself it was an empty threat.

My thoughts were probably going down a dark road because of what I had seen and heard over the last few years in Holmes County. I'd been caught up in a startling number of crimes. Wade's talk didn't mean anything was going to happen. But even though one side of my brain was telling me not to worry, I couldn't shake the nervous feeling.

My stomach was in a knot.

Swissmen Candyworks was my dream. It was something I'd wanted even when I'd worked for world-famous Jean Pierre in New York City, but I'd never voiced my ambition because I'd thought it wasn't possible.

As long as I worked for Jean Pierre, any candy I made was in his name, and until my grandfather died and I moved to Ohio to help my grandmother with Swissmen Sweets, there was no reason for me to leave Jean Pierre. I had been his protégé, and it would have been a very comfortable spot for the rest of my life if I'd wanted to remain. My grandfather's death had changed all that. And in an odd twist of fate, his passing was now giving me a chance to make my dream a reality. Even so, I would give it all back to have my *grossdaadi* here on earth, laughing and joking with me while we dipped buckeyes or pulled taffy.

When the Blueberry Bash ended later that night, I helped Charlotte out of her dress. As we put the dress into the dress bag and hung it on the back of the bedroom door she prattled on about the evening.

"Bailey, you will not believe how many blueberries Millie Fisher ate in the blueberry eating contest. I have never seen anything like it. She really loves blueberries. And the kids that came to sit on my lap were so cute. One of them asked if I knew the tooth fairy. I said that I did even though I have no idea what he was talking about! Amish kids don't have tooth fairies; that's for sure!"

I smiled and stopped myself from telling her about the conversation I'd overheard. She was so happy at the moment, I couldn't see any reason to ruin her mood.

I walked to my small rented house two blocks away from the candy shop and went to sleep. Or at least I tried to. I tossed and turned for hours, worrying about what Wade had said, then gave up trying to sleep a little after midnight. I quickly dressed and went downstairs. My large white rabbit, Puff, was sleeping on her dog bed in the living room.

Recently, I'd had to upgrade Puff from a cat bed to a dog bed because, to put it frankly, she was huge, and there were no signs that her growth spurt was slowing up. The rabbit was twenty-five pounds. If she got much bigger, I wouldn't be able to carry her to the shop each day to see Nutmeg the cat.

Nutmeg and Puff had no idea that cats and rabbits weren't supposed to like each other. They were the best of friends.

Puff stood up and hopped off her bed toward the kitchen.

I shook my head. "It's not breakfast time yet," I said. "I have to run out on an errand."

She twitched her nose and took a second hop to the kitchen.

I put my hands on my hips. "Puff, if I feed you

now, you'll still want breakfast in a few hours. This is exactly why you've grown so much."

She hopped again and stared at me with her blue eyes. I stared back.

Who was I kidding? I was never going to win a staring contest with Puff.

I sighed. "Fine."

I went into the kitchen, opened the refrigerator door, grabbed a crown of broccoli, and placed it into her bowl. I then refilled her water dish.

She hopped quickly over to the broccoli and began munching away.

"What am I going to do with you?" I asked.

She didn't even lift her head to acknowledge the question.

With Puff distracted, I slipped out the front door. It was a warm summer night, and I didn't need a jacket. I inhaled the scent of the flowers growing in my neighbor's yard. Penny was a wonderful gardener, and her yard was always pristine. However, sometimes I wondered if she loved gardening so much because it made it easier to spy on her neighbors. It seemed to me Penny always knew what was happening in the neighborhood—and in my own home—and she liked to talk about it to almost anyone.

I wouldn't be the least bit surprised if she saw me leave my house that very night. After several years living next door to Penny, I questioned her sleep habits and whether she slept at all.

"I'll just run to the factory to make sure everything is okay," I whispered to myself as I hurried down the sidewalk. "It will only take a few minutes."

If Aiden knew what I was up to in the middle of the night, he would have insisted on coming with me. Or actually, he would have insisted *he* check the candy factory by himself and I stay home. I didn't want that. I wanted to put my own eyes on the factory and prove to myself it was okay. I was probably being ridiculous to think Wade might actually sabotage the construction site. But at the same time, I knew that if I didn't check to make sure everything was okay, I'd never be able to sleep.

I reached the corner of Apple Street and Main Street on the square, and instead of continuing down Apple toward the factory, I turned on Main Street and made a beeline for Swissmen Sweets. There was a large flashlight in the shop that I thought I might need since there was no electricity in the factory.

I slipped down the small alley between the candy shop and Esther's pretzel shop next door. I was hyper aware of my surroundings because I half-expected Abel Esh to pop out from behind the pretzel shop. Abel was Esther's older brother and was notorious in the village. He was a surly Amish man in his thirties who had gone to jail for gambling and theft but had been released early because of overcrowding in the prison system. He hadn't liked me from the day I'd moved to Harvest, and I have to say the feeling was mutual.

Happily, though, as I came around the side of the building, there was no sign of Abel. I let out a breath. I hadn't seen him in a few weeks. I was hoping he'd left Harvest for good, but like a bad penny, he always seemed to turn up.

I didn't want to wake *Maami* or Charlotte, who

were sleeping in the apartment upstairs, so I quietly used my key and let myself into the back of the candy shop so I could go directly into the industrial kitchen.

As I stepped into the kitchen, the only light in the room was the ambient glow coming in around the edges of the swinging door leading to the rest of the shop. The illumination was from the large display windows out front. I didn't bother to flip on the light switch. I knew Swissmen Sweets' kitchen so well that I could have walked around it blindfolded and still have been able to make a full tray of fudge.

After a decade working in a busy kitchen in New York City, I stressed the importance of putting everything back in its place at night so we weren't scrambling in the morning looking for something. Not a spoon would be out of place in this kitchen. That meant the flashlight would be hanging on the back of the pantry door by the industrial mixer.

I walked over to the mixer, opened the pantry door and was about to grab the flashlight when the overhead lights came on. Startled, I dropped the flashlight on my foot and cried out.

"Bailey, you nearly gave me a heart attack. What are you doing in here?" Charlotte asked.

I scooped the flashlight off the floor. "I just came in for a second. I didn't want to wake you and *Maami*."

"So sneaking in the back door like a bandit seemed like a good idea."

"A bandit? Where in your Amish upbringing did you learn that word?"

"Luke is really into old Westerns and watches

them on TV. I might have picked up a phrase or two."

For some reason, it didn't surprise me that Charlotte's fiancé liked old television shows. Deputy Little had an old soul, and many times I'd thought he should have been born a hundred years ago.

"What are you doing up so late?" I asked.

"I came down to plug in my phone for the night." She waved her cell phone at me. Since Charlotte had left the Amish faith, Deputy Little had bought her a phone so the two of them could stay in touch, especially when he was out late on a case.

The apartment above the candy shop had no electricity, so Charlotte's only option was to charge the phone in the shop, which had electricity to comply with building codes and FDA food safety rules. Charlotte unplugged the industrial mixer and put her phone into its socket.

When she was done, she said, "I thought you went home earlier."

"I did," I said. "And then I came back."

"Don't tell me. You want to perfect the blueberry-and-cream fudge."

I wrinkled my nose. "Do you think the recipe needs to be changed? I thought it was pretty good as is."

She waved her hands. "No, no, the recipe is great. Don't change a thing! We have ten trays of it in the freezer for the Blueberry Bash tomorrow. I just know how you like to fiddle with recipes until you think they are perfect."

I rubbed the back of my head. "You make it sound like I'm never happy with any of my recipes."

"You have to admit, you do like to fuss with them."

I arched an eyebrow at her. "What's wrong with wanting to make something better?"

"What's wrong with being content with what you have?"

I smiled. "You sound like my *maami*. You're still Amish in your heart."

"Maybe I am." She pointed at the flashlight in my hand. "What's that for?"

When I didn't say anything, she folded her arms. "Are you going sleuthing? Has there been a murder that you didn't tell me about? You can't keep me in the dark about these things."

I sighed. When had Charlotte begun to think that if I was out at night, I must be investigating a murder? What had I become to make that a forgone conclusion?

"There's been no murder," I said. "I just want to check on the factory build site. I left in such a rush earlier in the day that I didn't check everything over as closely as I normally would."

"You're going to go there now? In the middle of the night?" She glanced down at her phone, which was still plugged into the wall. "It's almost one in the morning."

"I have to or I won't be able to sleep."

She cocked her head. "Does this have anything to do with Wade?"

"Why do you ask that?"

"Because he's the only person I can think of who would make you nervous about the condition of the build site."

"He might not be the only person. There are many Amish who aren't happy about the factory."

"That may be true, but they wouldn't do anything to harm it; Wade Farmer might."

She wasn't wrong.

"It'll just take me a few minutes to check the building site and then I'll go right home, I promise."

She sighed. "I'm going with you."

Chapter Nine

I didn't bother to argue with her. It wasn't often Charlotte made up her mind like that. But when she did, there was no changing it.

"Let's go out the front door," I said. "It's better lit that way." I looked up at the ceiling. "I hope we didn't wake *Maami.*"

We stepped into the front of the shop and stopped to listen for any sound from upstairs. It was silent. At least the second floor was silent. Nutmeg was not. The little orange tabby meowed at us to make sure we understood how put out he was by our nighttime interruption of his beauty rest.

"Shhh, Nutmeg, you don't want to wake Cousin Clara," Charlotte said.

He yowled at her in return. Apparently, the tabby did not care who he woke up.

Charlotte and I went out the front while Nutmeg continued to voice his complaints behind the closed and locked door.

"That cat has a set of lungs on him, doesn't he?" Charlotte mused.

There was enough light around the square with the gas-powered lampposts that I didn't need to turn on my flashlight. I was happy about that because I knew walking through the village by flashlight beam was sure to attract some attention from neighbors who lived near the square.

"What's the plan?" Charlotte asked, matching her stride to mine.

I glanced at her. "We'll just walk around the building and make sure it's secure. Then, we can go home."

"That doesn't sound too exciting."

"Nothing was stopping you from staying at Swissmen Sweets."

The factory came into view. At least there was enough light to see the structure because it was close to the village market and its well-lit parking lot. I had been in talks with the market owner about expanding his parking lot in conjunction with the factory construction to provide extra parking for both of our needs. As of yet, he hadn't agreed to anything. The market owner was one of the Amish citizens of Harvest who was unsure about the candy factory. I could understand his feeling that way since the factory was on his doorstep, but I was determined to be a good neighbor.

Expanding the parking lot seemed like a far-fetched idea at the moment since I didn't even have a contractor to spearhead the construction of the building. And it wouldn't be until Monday that I would be able to start looking for a new contractor. Tomorrow would be a busy Saturday at Swissmen Sweets, and Sunday, the entire county shut down out of respect for the Amish tradition of not working on the Sabbath. The thought of searching for a new contractor gave me a headache. It had seemed to me that Wade had been the only one who was willing to take on my giant project at a reasonable cost.

Charlotte and I walked past the closed market and up to my building. From the outside, it was impressive. I was determined to have the structure blend into the atmosphere of Harvest. So it was a four thousand square foot building being built in the style of a horse barn. It might have looked like a barn from the outside, but on the inside, it would be a state-of-the-art candy factory. Someday . . . I hoped.

"Watch your step," I told Charlotte. Around the building there were dips and deep tire treads in the ground that could cause us to trip.

The building shell looked forlorn in the light of the half-moon in the sky and the lampposts by the market.

"This is kind of creepy," Charlotte said.

I had to agree with her. "We'll make it quick, and then we can get back to bed. Tomorrow will be another long day, especially if you have to play the blueberry princess again."

Under the streetlight, she wrinkled her nose. "It was nice to do it once, but I'm hoping the real princess can take over tomorrow. Luke's parents are coming into town Saturday night."

"I didn't know that."

"I didn't either until Luke texted me tonight. I'm more than a little nervous. I've never met them before. They plan to stay through the wedding. As if I needed added stress to this coming week, you know?"

"You've never met them?" I asked. "You two have been together a long time."

"They live in Washington, DC. Luke and I always meant to go there for a visit, but he couldn't get away once he was promoted in the sheriff's department. His responsibilities tripled, and he was always afraid to be too far away from the county."

My brow went up. "Then you do need your rest so you are ready for their arrival. Let's go in and get this over with." I stepped through the open threshold onto the concrete foundation.

At this point in the construction, the factory was framed out, some of the windows were in, and the roof was in place. But that was it.

I was still waiting for the siding, the electrical wiring, the plumbing, and the list went on and on. I took a breath. Baby steps. This project was going to be much more manageable if I broke it up into bite-sized pieces. The only light in the building came from the parking lot outside. I turned on the flashlight.

The strong beam lit the entire front room of the factory. The room we were in was to be the sales room and gift shop where guests waited before taking a tour of the factory. At the moment, it just looked like a wide-open cavern of exposed lumber with sawdust and muddy boot prints on the concrete floor.

There was a scratching sound to our right.

Charlotte grabbed my arm. "What's that?" she whispered.

I turned the flashlight in that direction and the shining eyes of a raccoon looked back at me. The creature scurried across the floor to the main part of the factory.

Charlotte's fingers dug even deeper into my arm. "You might want to think about getting this building closed up. Raccoons can do a lot of damage. We once had a raccoon family in our attic and they chewed a hole in the ceiling."

Great. Something else to worry about.

I pried her hand off me. "He probably came in looking for something to eat, but there's nothing here. He'll move along and find a better place to be."

She dropped her hands to her sides. "Just keep in mind, raccoons hate cayenne pepper, and that's how my father finally got rid of them. My father sprinkled it everywhere. You could smell it just coming up the driveway. My eyes watered for months after that."

I could imagine. "I'll keep the pepper tip in mind, but when the building is sealed up, it won't be a problem."

"When will that be?"

It was a good question but not one I had an answer to.

"Let's make a quick loop and go home. This room is empty."

"Isn't every room going to be empty? There's nothing here."

I didn't answer. Instead, I went through the doorway to the next room, although I could have gone through the walls themselves since they were only framed out. We came into the main factory room. There was still some framing to be done to divide different areas of the factory and cordon off the visitor viewing area. The plan was to have a wall of glass between the guests and the factory workers. That was so that the guests could see everything going on in the factory while keeping the candy safe and free of contamination. The frame for that wall wasn't in place yet.

In its place was scaffolding that rose all the way up to the twenty-five-foot high ceiling. Wade's crew had been in the process of framing that wall when they'd stopped coming.

The room looked just as I'd left it that morning, and the open loading dock—because there was no garage door yet—gave a view of the parking lot and the village market just beyond. A shadow moved across the parking lot just out of reach of the lights. It was probably another raccoon, but it was an awfully big one. I shivered.

I was just about to say it was time to leave when Charlotte screamed.

I jumped and dropped the flashlight on the concrete floor. It clattered onto the floor, and the light went out.

"Charlotte, you really need to get over your fear of raccoons," I said in the dark.

"It's not a raccoon." Her voice trembled.

I found the flashlight and turned it on. The lens was cracked, but it still shone. "What is it?"

"A dead guy," she said barely above a whisper. She pointed above our heads. "Up there."

She stood under the scaffolding just inches from a brownish stain on the floor. I knew it hadn't been there when I'd met with Wade that morning.

I moved the flashlight's beam from my cousin to the scaffolding. Sure enough, I could see the shape of a person lying on the scaffolding. The way he was angled and the stillness of his form made my blood run cold. I could tell there was something very wrong here.

"Hello! Hello! Are you okay up there?" I called.

There was no answer. I handed Charlotte the flashlight. "Keep this pointed at the scaffolding, so I can see what I'm doing."

"What are you doing?" she asked with a shaky voice.

"I'm climbing up there to see if I can help him. Call 911. It looks like he's lost a lot of blood."

"I don't think you should go up there. What if you fall?"

"I'll be fine. The monkey bars were my favorite when I was a kid. I'm sure it's like riding a bike—you never forget how to do it," I said with much more confidence than I felt.

I started to climb up the side of the scaffolding. The trick, I told myself, was not looking down. The structure creaked and groaned with every move I made. As I climbed, I heard Charlotte on the phone speaking to the dispatcher, but I blocked out her words. I only concentrated on putting my hands and feet in the right places. I finally climbed high enough to peer over the edge of the platform where the man lay. I gasped.

"Bailey, are you okay?" Charlotte called from the floor below. "The police and ambulance are on the way."

"That's good. We might not need the ambulance after all, but we definitely need a hearse."

At my eye level on the landing lay a dead man, and not just any dead man but Wade Farmer, his bloody hand covering his chest.

Chapter Ten

"Tell me again what you were doing here in the middle of the night," Deputy Little said.

I frowned at him. Because of his relationship with Charlotte, I considered Deputy Little a friend. And since he would soon be married to my favorite cousin, he would be family in a matter of a week. I didn't appreciate being asked to repeat my story over and over again.

I took a deep breath and reminded myself he was only doing his job. I knew, too, that since I was involved in the case, he had to be extra careful to do everything right. The last thing he wanted was for the churlish Sheriff Jackson Marshall to call him out for favoritism. It had happened before where I was concerned.

I repeated my story about wanting to come to the factory to make sure it was secure and Charlotte offering to keep me company.

"I wish you hadn't brought Charlotte with you," he said with a sigh.

I could understand why he wouldn't want his future wife tied up in an investigation so close to the day of their wedding . . . or ever for that matter.

"She insisted on coming," I said, glancing around. Charlotte was nowhere to be seen. That struck me as odd, but I decided not to mention it to Deputy Little. I didn't want to worry him.

"I'm sure she did. She doesn't take no for an answer very often, and she wouldn't let you go out on this fool's errand in the middle of the night all by yourself. If you were concerned about security at the factory, you should have called me. I could have searched the build site and spared the two of you seeing all this."

He sounded just like Aiden, which wasn't all that surprising since Aiden had been his mentor for so many years.

I wanted to respond but was interrupted by someone nosily clearing his throat behind me. I turned to see Sheriff Jackson Marshall standing in the opening for the loading bay door. He was a large, heavy-set man, and seemed to fill the entire space. "Bailey King, when I heard you were here, I knew this was going to be just the kind of headache I don't need."

I frowned. For the record, his presence gave me a headache too.

Deputy Little stepped forward. "I was just having Ms. King go over her story again, sir."

The sheriff flared his nostrils like a bull, and actually the bull comparison wasn't very far off. "What kind of yarn is she trying to spin this time? We all know Miss King likes to tell a tale."

I felt my cheeks turn red hot. I hadn't made anything up any of the times I had been a witness for the police, and Sheriff Marshall knew that. I balled my fists at my sides. The sheriff was just trying to get under my skin. Maybe he was hoping I'd say something that would make me look guilty; he'd love to throw me in jail and put an end to this case. Sheriff Marshall hated to have an open case on his docket. He would rather tie up everything quickly and put an end to it. He would rather do that than arrest the right person for the crime.

Deputy Little nodded to me, and even though I would have preferred not to speak with the sheriff, I repeated my story as quickly as possible.

"Uh-huh," Sheriff Marshall said as he rocked back on his heels. "What she hasn't told you was she and Wade Farmer had a falling out just yesterday morning. Isn't that right, Miss King?"

My eyes went wide. "Yes, we had a conversation."

"I heard you fired him," Sheriff Marshall said in a challenging way. It was almost as if he expected me to deny it.

"Did you speak to him, Sheriff?" Deputy Little asked.

Sheriff Marshall's head snapped in his direction. "Of course not. I don't need to speak to a source to know what is going on." The sheriff hiked up his duty belt, which was sliding down his hips. "You know how this village is. People talk, and when people talk, I hear things." He looked back at me. "So it would seem to me you have a motive."

"What would my motive be?" I asked. "I already fired him as my contractor. Why would I want to hurt him now? He doesn't work for me any longer."

"Because he was angry with you for firing him.

He might even hold a grudge toward you over it. You wanted to hurt him first."

My heart sank. I had not killed Wade, but had the sheriff guessed my train of thought? I wouldn't have hurt Wade, but I'd been concerned that he wanted to hurt me. How would Sheriff Marshall know that?

However, rather than let him know that he was closer to the mark than I was comfortable admitting, I pointed to the scaffolding. "How would I get him up there?"

"Maybe you had help. I heard your boyfriend is back in the county."

Now, I was mad. The sheriff had never been a fan of Aiden's, even when Aiden was his second-in-command at the sheriff's department.

"I heard Aiden came back to Harvest with his tail between his legs. He couldn't take the heat working for the state. I told him when he left that he wouldn't be able to cut it, and he proved me right."

I bit the inside of my cheek to keep myself from saying something I might regret later.

Sheriff Marshall cared very little for his community. He would never understand Aiden's reasons for coming back. Since Aiden had left the sheriff's department and there were no openings in the Millersburg Police Department at his level, he'd decided to open his own private detective office. It wasn't easy to go from working within the system of law enforcement to outside of it. I would be lying if I said Aiden was completely happy with where he'd ended up. However, it was still early days.

"You might not have needed help at all. Perhaps you tricked Farmer into climbing up the scaffolding and then you killed him."

My mouth fell open.

"Sir," Deputy Little said. "It's difficult to believe Bailey would be able to overpower Farmer in order to kill him, especially in such a confined space at the top of this scaffolding."

"A gunshot does not take any strength."

Deputy Little closed his eyes for a moment. I had a feeling that he had wanted to keep the manner of death a secret for a little while longer. However, this was something I already knew. A gunshot was the only reasonable explanation for the blood on Wade's chest.

Deputy Little cleared his throat. "Sheriff, I think we should let Bailey go home now. There are no more questions to ask her now. We know where she lives and works. We can certainly follow up if we have further questions or concerns."

The sheriff's head swiveled toward the young deputy. "I hope you're not going to be soft on her, Little, because of your upcoming wedding to her cousin, who I noted was also here. I would hate to learn that your new bride was somehow involved in this crime," Sheriff Marshall said in a challenging voice. "Do not misplace your loyalty, Deputy. You are an officer of the law first and foremost."

Deputy Little clenched his jaw but made no other reaction to the sheriff's words.

What else could I know? Was it possible the sheriff really thought I'd killed Wade? How on earth would I have gotten his dead body on top of the scaffolding even with help? Or—as the sheriff had suggested—if I had tricked him into climbing up the scaffolding, how would I have done so? After firing him, there was nothing I could have asked him to do that he would have agreed to.

I couldn't even convince him to do anything when he'd worked for me.

"We can always follow up with her later if something else comes to light," Deputy Little repeated calmly. "It's going to be difficult to get the body down from the scaffolding, and I don't think that's something Bailey or Charlotte needs to see."

I swallowed. He was right. I didn't need to see that at all.

"Very well." The sheriff glared at me. "But I'll be taking the lead on this case now."

I bit the inside of my cheek to hold back the words on the tip of my tongue. I was well aware the sheriff was baiting me. Probably hoping I'd incriminate myself.

"I understand, sir," Deputy Little said. "Bailey, you're free to go."

I frowned at Deputy Little. Surely, I deserved the benefit of the doubt? As I walked away, I let out a sigh. I needed to cut Deputy Little a break. The sheriff was a difficult—no, impossible—man to work for. Deputy Little had to do everything by the book to avoid a reprimand. Or worse, being taken off the case.

This train of thought brought a larger question to my mind: Why was the sheriff even here? He was a hands-off kind of guy. When terrible accidents or crimes happened in the county, he was happy to send his young deputies out to do the work.

I really meant it when I said *young* deputies too. Everyone other than the sheriff was in their late twenties like Deputy Little or younger. It seemed to me the Holmes County Sheriff's Department was a revolving door of green deputies who started there for experience in law enforcement and quickly moved on because the sheriff was so difficult.

When Aiden had been second in command, the department retention had been better because he'd been a buffer between the sheriff and the other deputies. I knew Deputy Little was doing the best he could, but he didn't have as much experience in administration as Aiden. It also seemed the sheriff had increased his hold on the department since Aiden's departure. Maybe that was why he was at the crime scene, because he had even more control now?

Against my better judgment, I glanced up at the scaffolding one more time before I walked out of the factory. An EMT was trying to get Wade's body in a body bag on the platform. Wade's head rolled to the side and I saw his pale face and unseeing eyes. That was when I noticed the blood on the beams above his body. Why was there blood above him? I should have asked what kind of gun was used. Not that the sheriff would have told me or let Deputy Little tell me either.

I couldn't look at the murder scene anymore. My stomach turned and I bolted out of the factory.

When I was outside, I wrapped my arms around myself. During the time I had been in the factory, the temperature had dropped. It was close to sixty degrees, and I regretted not bringing a jacket. It was time to find Charlotte and leave. I should also call Aiden, but I was afraid if I did, he would come straight to the factory. It would not serve him well show up while Sheriff Marshall was on the grounds.

A person approached from around the side of the building, whispering to themselves or someone else. It didn't look like a deputy or EMT to me. Sadly, the flashlight had broken when I'd dropped it the second time, so my only light source was my cell phone.

I turned on the flashlight app and shone it in the direction of the approaching figure. I caught the glint of neon-yellow hair. "Devon, what are you doing here?"

The young producer froze and then turned to me. "Bailey, you nearly scared me to death. Don't you know a man died here tonight?"

"I know that," I said, trying and failing to keep the irritation from my voice. "I was the one who . . ." I trailed off. I wasn't sure telling Devon that I had found the body was the best idea.

"You were what?" she asked, leaning in.

"Nothing," I said. "What are you doing here?"

"I was up late, editing some footage we shot at the Blueberry Bash, and I heard the commotion outside the inn. When I looked out the window, I saw all the emergency vehicles outside the factory. I knew I had to get out here and catch whatever it was on film. I never guessed it would be a murder," she added excitedly.

Devon and Z were staying at Maribel's B&B. It was a new bed and breakfast that'd opened across the parking lot from the market. While the network would have put the pair of them up in one of the larger hotels in the county, Devon had said she wanted to be closer to the factory so she could gather footage at a moment's notice, which was obviously what she'd done tonight.

"Z didn't come with you?" I looked around.

She snorted. "No. I tried to rouse him. I texted, called, and even banged on his door, but the man sleeps like the dead."

I winced at her choice of words.

"Trust me." Devon tucked a lock of yellow hair behind her ear. "I plan to give him an earful about being more accessible. While we're on this assignment, we have to be reachable at all times. We never know when something will come up that we have might have to film." She frowned. "If Z doesn't up his game, I'm calling the network and telling them to send someone else. This show has to go off without a hitch. I need it to. Now, tell me everything." She put her cell phone in my face.

"Are you recording this?" I asked as I shuffled back from her phone.

"Duh!" she said as if it was no issue at all. "But we might have to reenact what happened when Z drags his sorry self out of bed. They do that on reality television when a pivotal scene is missed."

I wrinkled my brow. That didn't sound like reality to me.

"It's completely fine," Devon said as if she could sense my doubt. "Why do you think they wear the same clothes all the time? It's so they can repeat scenes that were interrupted.

"Now, is it true that Wade Farmer is the victim? What do you know about his background?"

I realized I knew very little, but that wasn't something I was going to share with Devon either.

I frowned at her. "I need to find Charlotte and go home."

"Wade *was* the victim then!" Her eyes gleamed in the light from my phone. "This project just got a lot more interesting. If we can tie the production together with Wade's death, we'll really have a winner. Candy and true crime wrapped up in a delicious confection. The viewers will gobble it up, and it might be just what I need to . . ."

What she needed for what?

Before I could ask, she held up her phone. "I'm going to see what I can catch on this since Z is MIA. That man is going to drive me to an early grave with his incompetence." She winced. "Oh sorry. Poor choice of words."

I grimaced. "You're filming this with your phone?"

"Z has all the camera equipment in his room at the B&B," she said, not bothering to hide the frustration in her voice. "We really should both have access to it. Because it's not like I don't know how to use it. I went to film school. I know how to press a button or two. Z is just a diva when it comes to his equipment. He won't let anyone touch it."

"He uses his own equipment?" I asked.

"No, he definitely uses the studio's equipment, but any time we're out on assignment, he acts like it is his own and he's the only person on the planet who knows how to use it properly. It's infuriating, and it might have cost me this scoop."

Scoop? Wasn't that a term reporters used when they were on a story? I'd never heard a producer from the Gourmet Network say that before. I suppose finding the next great food celebrity wasn't a scoop. In any case, the term she used struck me as odd, and I tucked the thought into the back of my brain along with her comment that this story was what she needed.

"I'm going to want to talk to you later about this. You have to tell me everything you know. Don't leave anything out. This is going to make our show a must-watch."

Just as she was about to go into the factory with her phone up and filming, Sheriff Marshall stepped out of the building with an unlit cigar in his hand.

I didn't know much about protocol, but I guessed smoking at the crime scene was a no-no.

"What do you think you're doing?" Sheriff Marshall bellowed at Devon.

Devon pointed the phone at the chief. "Sheriff Marshall, I presume. What can you tell me about Wade Farmer's death? Was it of natural causes?" She took on an ominous tone. "Or was it murder?"

Presume? Who said that outside of an Agatha Christie novel?

"Who are you?" the sheriff snarled back.

She held out her right hand to shake his. Her left hand still had the back of her phone pointed at his face.

He didn't move to shake her hand. "Put that phone down."

"I can't. I'm working. I'm a producer from Gourmet Television, and we're doing a documentary on Bailey King, Swissmen Sweets, and the candy factory. Obviously, if someone died in the factory during construction, we have to tell that story to be authentic. It adds depth to the documentary."

Depth? If Wade's dead body in the middle of my unfinished building was depth, I didn't want it.

"This was your idea, then," he turned to me.

Drat. I should have left when I had the chance. The last thing I wanted was to be tangled up in an argument between the sheriff and Devon.

Before I could answer, he said, "You won't be happy until Holmes County is turned into a laughingstock. What right do you have to put us on television?" He turned back to Devon. "Put your phone down. Now."

"You can't make me stop." Devon lifted her chin.

He glowered at her. "Yes, I can. This is my county. My rules are law. Put the phone down or spend the night in jail."

"You can't do that if I have permission from the owner to film here. And I do. *In writing.*"

"Whatever permission you have from Miss King is now irrelevant." He glared. "I'll be making the rules as to what can happen in this factory indefinitely."

Terrific.

Chapter Eleven

Seething and muttering about small-town cops, Devon stomped off in the direction of the B&B, and against my better judgment, I followed her.

"That country sheriff has a lot of nerve to treat me in this way," Devon huffed with each stomp. Her bright-yellow hair gleamed like a beacon in the parking lot lights. "Doesn't he know that I have the power of Gourmet Television behind me? He's just a country sheriff. I have a network."

Despite the seriousness of the situation, I held back a chuckle. Gourmet Television didn't have any power outside of making celebrity chefs from everyday cooks. They certainly couldn't take on any form of law enforcement, not even a "country sheriff."

"I'm calling the network's attorney just as soon as the office opens." She shoved the phone in her sweatshirt pocket. "He will not shut me out."

"It's Saturday," I said, trying to be helpful. "The admin offices at Gourmet Television aren't open today."

She put her hands on her hips. "Then I'm calling Linc Baggins directly. I have his cell number. Someone has to tell this sheriff person I'm within my rights to film. I have a show to make. I can't let his ego get in the way."

I had a few guesses as to how that conversation would go, and it wasn't in her favor. Linc would not want to bring any bad press to the network and causing an uproar in a murder investigation would certainly do that. It could get messy, and Linc hated mess.

She stomped up the steps of the B&B, which was a large, white Victorian, a bit of an oddity among the plain homes of Harvest. Needless to say, the original owner had been English, as an Amish person would not have ornate gingerbread added to their home when its purpose was only cosmetic.

"I'm going to wake up Z right now and regroup. That Sheriff Marshall will be sorry he messed with me." She folded her arms and looked down at me where I stood on the bottom step. "What are you doing? We have to talk about the future of the shoot."

I rubbed my forehead. "I'm going back to bed. And to be honest, the shoot is the last thing on my list of concerns."

"It shouldn't be. You signed a contract to work with Gourmet Television. You have to take this seriously."

I stared at her as if she had grown a third eye. Maybe she was taking this a little *too* seriously. "Of course, I care about the show, but a man died in my building tonight. Whatever is going to happen with this reality show is not at the top of my mind."

She opened her mouth as if she was going to say

something, but I interrupted her. "I have to find my cousin. Come to the candy shop in the morning, and we will talk it out."

"Fine. Don't think for a minute you're getting out of your contract."

I had never thought about that, but her comment made me wonder if I should have.

I walked back toward the factory and soon spotted Charlotte, who waved at me.

Weariness washed over me. Before the sun came up I knew that both the Amish and English community would hear that a dead body had been found in Bailey King's newfangled factory. Those who were against the idea of the factory—and there were many—would nod their heads smugly, knowing they were right about the factory hurting the village.

"Charlotte, where have you been?"

She didn't look me in the eye. "I was just standing outside the factory while you were being interviewed. I didn't want to be in there with Wade like that . . ."

I understood, but there was something about the way Charlotte avoided looking at me that I found unsettling.

"I did pop back inside to look for you just now. Luke said you left. Where did you go?" Charlotte asked.

It had been a long night, so I chalked up Charlotte's odd behavior to exhaustion. It was certainly what I was suffering from. "Sorry, I was talking to Devon."

"Devon? What is she doing here?"

"She saw the commotion and hurried over to get the scoop."

"Huh?" Charlotte asked.

Even though my cousin wasn't Amish anymore, there were a lot of English phrases and slang she didn't know. I guessed "scoop" was one of those words.

Behind Charlotte, Deputy Little and an EMT walked into the factory, but that didn't stop the deputy from looking back at Charlotte as if to make sure she was okay.

"What do we do now?" Charlotte asked.

I sighed. My factory—my dream—was lit up with floodlights that the deputies had brought in. It was an impressive sight. It was what I'd wanted. I had wanted it to be lit with bright lights when it opened, but not like this.

"Let's go home and think about it tomorrow."

Charlotte looked at the screen on her phone. "It is tomorrow. It's two in the morning."

I grimaced. That wasn't good news for Charlotte or me since we typically got up at four to make candy.

Charlotte must have realized this too because she said, "It's going to be a long day."

I nodded. As we walked back to the candy shop, I had a feeling it would seem lengthy for more than one reason.

"Why don't you sleep here tonight?" she asked. "You have to be back at the shop in a few hours."

"I don't think Puff would like it. There's too high a chance I'll get caught up in making fudge and not go home to feed her breakfast. That would never fly with my rabbit."

She laughed. "Probably not. She expects a full breakfast."

"Every morning or she's extra grouchy. No one

wants to deal with a twenty-five-pound grouchy rabbit."

Charlotte yawned and stumbled into the shop alone.

As I walked back to my little house two blocks away, I went over everything that had happened in the last twenty-four hours. There was my meeting with Wade, the Blueberry Bash, and now Wade's death, which the sheriff believed was murder, as did I.

I needed to tell Aiden what was going on. He was going to be upset that I hadn't called him from the crime scene, but it was for his own good. If he had shown up, it would have made an already difficult situation worse.

The sheriff hated Aiden. Sheriff Marshall had already insinuated that Aiden had helped me kill Wade. He wasn't above saying that right to Aiden's face.

Again, I wished I'd worn a jacket as a cool breeze ran down the back of my neck. I wrapped my arms around myself and turned onto the walk that led to my front door. There was movement on the porch, and I froze. I couldn't see what was there. The porchlight had been out for several weeks, and I'd been meaning to change the lightbulb. It was one of those things I never seemed to get around to doing.

I stepped back and prepared to run all the way back to Swissmen Sweets if I needed to.

"Bailey, it's me," a deep voice said.

I instantly relaxed when I recognized Aiden's voice. However, my relief morphed into annoyance. "Are you trying to scare me to death?" I whispered, overly aware of what a light sleeper my nosy neighbor Penny was. "What are you doing here in the middle of the night?"

"I came as soon as I heard about what happened at the factory. I wanted to go straight there and find you, but Little said you'd already left."

"How'd you find out about it?" I asked.

"Little called me to give me a heads-up. He was surprised I hadn't already heard from you."

I was close enough to him now to see the crease in his forehead, a sure sign he was frustrated with the situation and with me.

"Why didn't I hear from you?" He didn't even try to keep the disappointment from his voice.

I reached around him with my key and unlocked the door. "Let's talk about it inside. You know Penny's always listening."

He looked this way and that as if Penny was going to jump out of the bushes at a moment's notice. It wouldn't be out of the ordinary for her.

Aiden and I made it inside the little rental house with no contact with my neighbor, but I sensed she was watching. I'd know for sure when she asked me about my nighttime visitor later. She always did.

Puff hopped out of the kitchen with a piece of broccoli hanging from her lip.

"Looks like Puff is saving a snack for later," Aiden said.

As if she understood what he was saying and took issue with it, she chewed up the piece of broccoli. Her little rabbit nose twitched the entire time.

"Why didn't you text me?" I asked as I perched on the edge of my couch. It was a real couch too. The sofa was seven feet long and big enough for a solid Sunday nap, not that I ever had time for such an extravagance. The piece of furniture felt like an extravagance too. Every penny I'd made in my business and on my cooking show, I had put back into Swissmen Sweets. Now that I was building the factory, I was dipping into my savings too.

I hoped it would be worth it in the long run, and prayed everything would go as planned. Considering the way the night had gone, I was starting to have my doubts.

"I did, and I called too." He sat next to me on the couch. Puff hopped over and snuggled onto the top of his feet as she always did. If she was a cat she would have started purring. Aiden looked down at the large, white pile of fluff on his feet. "Looks like I'm stuck."

I turned to face him and sat cross-legged on the cushion. "You definitely are." I removed my phone from my pocket and saw the missed text messages and a call. "Sorry, I put it on silent during the Blueberry Bash and must have forgotten to turn the sound back on."

"Why did you silence it at the bash?"

My face flushed a little. "I was trying to avoid Margot so I wouldn't be volunteered for another duty. If I can't hear her text message, I'm not to blame for missing it."

He smiled. "I heard you were the blueberry princess. My mother called and told me in a rather lengthy voicemail. She wanted to remind me that blueberry princesses are very sought after, and if I wanted to marry you, I should propose immediately."

He shifted in his seat and my heart stopped.

For a moment, I thought he was going to pull a ring out of his pocket right then and there. Instead, he moved the throw pillow from behind his back and set it on the arm of the couch.

I could breathe again and said, "As it turns out, I wasn't the blueberry princess. I couldn't fit into the dress, so Charlotte took over. I have to say it was a great relief."

He raised his brow. "That's about as far from Amish as you can get."

I nodded. "Ruth Yoder made a point of saying that. She wasn't too happy with Charlotte for taking the role either."

He frowned. "Why does Ruth care what Charlotte does now that she's left the district?"

I shrugged. "Ruth cares about everything, and if she had her way, church members wouldn't even have the option to leave. Sometimes I think she believes that unhappiness is just part of life."

Aiden frowned. "It can be."

What did he mean by that?

"So why did I have to hear about the death at *your* candy factory from Little? Don't use the excuse that the sound was off on your phone."

It was my turn to shift in my seat. I grabbed the throw pillow behind my back and held it to my chest. "I was planning to text you in the morning. It was late, and I know that you're working on a case and just got into the village last night."

"I did, and I wanted to stop and see you." He ran his hand through his blond hair. "But I had a few things to finish up on my last case for BCI before I could hand it over to the next investigator; that put me behind. It's a long and complicated case. Making all the notes took time. More time than I expected. I had to cancel the interview with my new client, and I didn't leave the office in Columbus until almost midnight. I came straight here because I got the call from Little on my drive to Harvest."

"You haven't been to your new apartment yet?"

He shook his head. "I came straight here. You were the first face I wanted to see when I came back to Harvest."

I felt a smile form on my lips.

After a beat, he said, "Tell me what happened."

I took a breath and quickly repeated my story. By this time, I had repeated it so many times for Deputy Little and then for Sheriff Marshall, I practically had it memorized.

He took my hand. "That must have been awful. Are you okay?"

I gave him a small smile. "I'm a lot better than Wade Farmer."

He leaned back in the couch, and Puff huffed at his feet because he dared move an inch. "You didn't call me because Sheriff Marshall was there. That was your real reason, wasn't it?"

My face turned red. "I didn't want to make things more complicated than they already were. If you'd shown up, Sheriff Marshall would've been even more irritated."

Aiden rubbed the back of his neck. "I understand your reason, but now that I'm back in Harvest and working as a PI, I'm going to run into the sheriff sooner or later."

"I hope it's later," I muttered.

He sighed. "I know you're nervous about how

the sheriff is going to impact my business, but don't be. I can handle him."

I folded my hands in my lap and told myself not to say another word about it . . . for now.

"It's very possible I'll have to deal with him as I investigate my first case as a PI," Aiden said.

I sat up. "Tell me more about the case."

"There's some missing money at the Linzer Petting Zoo. The owner, Emmaus Linzer, wants me to be very quiet about looking into it, but I can set the case aside if necessary."

"Set it aside? Why?"

He took my hand again. "Why do you think? We have a much more serious situation involving you. We need to take care of that first."

"You should concentrate on the case you're being paid for." I took a breath. "It's your first case as a PI. You need to build your business. You can't set it aside. You only have so long to build a reputation."

He pulled his hand from mine. "You're more important than my new business."

"I appreciate that, and I know it's how you feel. I'm just concerned about how helping me could hurt you."

"Hurt me how?"

"I told you Sheriff Marshall came to the factory tonight, but there was something I left out. He said he'd be personally overseeing this case."

His frown deepened. "He hasn't worked a case in years. At least he hasn't to my knowledge. I wonder why Little didn't tell me. I would've expected him to if Marshall showed up at the crime scene like that."

"It depends on when he called you. When the sheriff showed up, Deputy Little was clearly surprised."

"Was Little taken off the case?"

"I don't think so, but the sheriff said he'd be taking it over."

He pressed his lips together. "All I can think is Marshall wants in on this case because it involves you and, by extension, me."

"But you've been away from the department for over a year and I've been involved in other cases in Harvest since you left. Why the sudden interest now?"

"Because I came back."

"And he feels threatened," I concluded.

Aiden stared at me. "Bailey, do you have a motive?"

My eyes went wide.

He waved his hands. "That came out the wrong way. I know you didn't do this. You couldn't have done this. But is there any reason why Wade's death might benefit you?"

"Well, I don't consider it a motive . . . but the sheriff might."

Aiden grimaced as he rubbed the back of his neck again.

"I fired Wade yesterday, and he said he would make sure I never found another contractor and that I'd be sorry. The sheriff might think that's motive, even though I was the one who was threatened, not the other way around."

"Why didn't you tell me about this yesterday?"

"It was your last day at BCI. I didn't want to bother you. It was an empty threat, really. What could he do to me?" I asked this with more confidence than I'd felt.

He pressed his lips together as if he didn't like my answer, but instead of arguing with me about it, he asked, "Did anyone overhear this conversation?"

"Charlotte—" I paused. "And it was filmed."

His eyes went wide. "You let the documentary people film it?"

"The show is about building a candy factory, all the highs and lows. They were there when I fired Wade."

"You know people on reality TV produce their own lives, don't you? It's not really reality. You don't have to show everything."

"I wanted my show to be truthful."

"I can appreciate your desire for authenticity, but it might come back to haunt you."

I shivered.

CHAPTER TWELVE

The next morning, I texted Devon. **Can you meet me at Swissmen Sweets at 7am?**

I needed to see her sooner rather than later. I had to talk to her before Sheriff Marshall had the chance to see the video of my argument with Wade.

A text came back right away. **I'll be there in twenty.**

"Bailey, what are you doing on your phone so much this morning?" *Maami* asked as she stirred caramel. Making caramel was one of the trickiest things we did in the candy shop. If you didn't pay attention, it would crystalize or even burn. *Maami* was a pro at it and hadn't burned a batch of caramel in decades.

"I know you have to use it for business and such, but it is quite distracting." She poured the caramel into a pan and placed it into the industrial refrigerator to cool. She then removed a cool tray of blueberry-and-cream fudge from the refrigerator and set it on the metal island in the middle of the kitchen.

"I'm sorry, *Maami*. I just needed to take care of a few things for the documentary."

My grandmother wrinkled her nose. As a devout Amish woman, she didn't believe she should be on camera because it would be creating a graven image of herself, which was forbidden in the Bible. Or at least, that was the traditional interpretation of the scripture by the Amish.

Maami changed the subject, just as I expected her to.

"I wonder if Charlotte is ill. It's not like her to sleep this late. Do you think I should go up and check on her? I'm quite concerned. It's almost seven. She's usually the first one in the kitchen each morning."

This was true. Charlotte woke up every morning ready to work and with a smile on her face. If I wasn't a morning person too, it would be annoying.

"I told her to sleep in as much as she could. We both were up late last night. I don't have time to sleep, but that doesn't mean she can't."

"At the Blueberry Bash?" *Maami* asked. "Did it go very late?"

"The bash was over at nine." I frowned. "That reminds me. I need to ask Margot if she still needs Charlotte to be the blueberry princess for the second day."

"I would hope not. I know Charlotte is not Amish any longer, and I'm not saying she should be. I like Luke Little very much and am happy about their upcoming wedding. But it just doesn't seem like something she should be doing with her close ties to the Amish community.

"If it wasn't the Blueberry Bash that kept the two of you up, what was it?" she asked as she began cutting the fudge into one-inch squares.

"I went to the candy factory late last night. Charlotte came with me."

"Why?" Her clear blue eyes widened. "Is anything wrong at the factory?"

The fact that I'd fired my contractor was something I had hoped not to share with *Maami* until I found a new one. She was apprehensive about the candy factory in the first place. She worried it was too ambitious, and like many Amish people, being more and more successful was not an end goal for her.

"Were you worried about the factory after you fired Wade Farmer?" Her face softened.

I raised my eyebrows. "How did you know about that?"

She shook her fudge knife at me. "Bailey King, when will you learn that there are no secrets in Harvest?"

I groaned.

She went back to cutting. "Ruth stopped by the candy shop while you and Charlotte were at the Blueberry Bash. She told me you let him go. She was quite concerned and felt I should know because Wade is the type to hold a grudge. Were you worried about that too?"

I nodded. "I just wanted to check on the factory since Wade was so upset when I let him go. I thought that he—he might do something rash."

"And was anything missing or harmed?"

"The building was fine." I sighed and went on to tell her what Charlotte and I had discovered.

Maami dropped the knife on the table and put a hand to her chest. "Oh my. The poor man. Do you think he was working on the factory when he died? Was it some sort of accident?"

I shook my head. "I doubt he was working on the building after I fired him. Lately, he's hardly worked on it even when he was being paid to."

"Won't the police wonder why you thought to go there last night?" *Maami* sat on a stool at the worktable.

"They will," I said. "They are already asking questions." I picked up a basket of Jethro chocolate bars, white and milk chocolate pigs created in the likeness of Jethro that were our top seller. I carried them through the swinging door to the front of the shop.

I slid the tray into the display case and closed the door behind it. When I looked up, I found Devon Cruz staring through the window. Her nose was pressed up against the glass, and she cupped her hands around her eyes to see better. And here I thought Jethro's snout prints on the glass were an issue.

I had to admit Devon was punctual. It was seven on the dot. I opened the door and let her inside. This time she had a large camera bag with her.

"You got a camera from Z, I take it."

She looked down at the case. "No. I had this overnighted to me. It might not be as high quality as what Z has from the network, but it will do the job. I can't risk missing any more footage because Z wants to sleep."

I flipped over the maple paddle-back chairs that had been placed seat down on the three small round tables in the front of the shop.

When I finished flipping over the chairs, I invited Devon to sit.

She did and set her camera bag on the table. I sat across from her.

"Where's Z now?" I asked.

"Who knows? I suppose he's still sleeping. I wasn't going to wait for him to get his act together. There's a crime happening, and I need to be on it!"

I wrinkled my brow. Her mention of the crime didn't sit right with me. Wasn't she supposed to be in Harvest to produce a show about the candy factory?

"We don't know that it's a crime," I said. "The sheriff hasn't made any announcement to that effect."

"Did you see the dead guy? It was definitely murder. No one can shoot himself in the chest like that. He would not have died immediately. He would have bled out. It's a painful way to go. There are easier ways to take yourself out."

I winced. "How do you know where he was shot?"

"I have my ways."

The manner in which she said that made me uncomfortable. I cleared my throat, preparing to reveal why I'd called her over here. She wasn't going to like it. That much I was sure of.

"You were filming yesterday when Wade came into the factory. Where is the recording?"

"I don't have it."

"You mean Z has it. Can we get it from him? I know we'll have to give it to the sheriff's department, but if I could see it first, it'd be a big help."

She eyed me. "You want to see how bad you looked when you fired Wade."

I swallowed. "I just want to know everything the authorities do."

"To cover yourself. I get that. You need to watch your back. Everyone I've talked to has said there's bad blood between you and the sheriff going years back." She leaned over the table. "Do you want to talk to me about it?"

I narrowed my eyes. "Who have you talked to?"

"The citizens of Harvest. Getting the community's reaction to the factory is important to the overall story and gives it some local color."

"What is the general reaction?" I asked even though I was afraid to hear the answer.

"Mixed. Mostly apprehensive from both the Amish and the non-Amish in Harvest. They are afraid of how this new factory will impact the town. Traffic. Noise. That sort of thing. These people aren't big on change."

No, they were not.

But it was what I'd expected to hear. It'd been a hard-fought battle to get the factory through the village council, and all the members of the council were English. It had been one of those times it was good to have Margot in the mix. As the community planner, she was able to convince the rest of the members of how beneficial it would be for Harvest to have a major attraction like this.

To be honest, I wasn't sure my candy factory was going to be a major attraction. I was no Hershey, and I certainly didn't plan to build a theme park around the candies. I had let Margot speak on this point at the meeting because I had been at my wits' end. The council had already said I couldn't build the factory once. It had been my second and last shot.

As I thought about it, I wondered when Margot was going to call in that favor, because I knew she would. I didn't believe the blueberry princess would count because I'd passed the duty on to Charlotte. Margot always got what was due to her. It was her special talent.

"If you're worrying about the sheriff seeing the footage, he already has."

My stomach dropped. I'd at least wanted to see it before Sheriff Marshall did so I knew what I was dealing with. Instinctively, I looked out the window. I half-expected to find him outside with handcuffs in hand. He wasn't there. Maybe he planned to wait until we opened at ten to make an arrest, so that I suffered maximum embarrassment.

"Did he take the film?" I asked.

"He took the file, yes, straight from Z's camera."

"All of it? Why?"

"Looking for more evidence." She shrugged.

"So he has the recording." My face fell. "But you are surprisingly calm about it."

"He has one copy. I didn't say there weren't others. There are duplicates of it already with the network, uploaded to the cloud. I have backups to my backups."

That was good to hear as far as the documentary went. It didn't help me out though.

"Can I watch what happened when Wade was there?"

"Sure." She pulled her phone out of her jeans pocket. "We can watch it on the cloud right now."

While Devon worked on bringing up the video, I tapped my foot. There was no doubt in my mind that Sheriff Marshall would go out of his way to blame me for the murder. He'd wanted to throw me in jail for years. He resented the close relationship I had with the Amish community even though I wasn't Amish. He'd never had that kind of closeness with them, but he couldn't fault anyone except himself. Since he'd become sheriff over twenty years ago, he'd tried to blame the Amish for everything that went wrong in Holmes County. It was baffling to me how he got elected over and over again, and also how he raised so much money and support to run his elaborate campaigns for reelection.

As the sheriff, he certainly was pulling the biggest salary in the department, but I knew what Aiden had made as his second in command. Holmes County was still small and rural and could only pay so much to its county employees.

Devon and I sat side by side, staring at her small phone screen. The scene in the factory from the morning before played out just as I expected it to. Jethro zoomed around the scaffolding, Wade stormed into the room, we argued, I fired him, and Margot appeared with yet another village-related emergency for me to fix.

There was nothing there that I didn't remember or didn't expect to see. It might be enough evidence—circumstantial or not—to convince the sheriff I was behind Wade's death. I had to admit, Z was a great cinematographer. He'd captured Wade's and my reactions perfectly, as well as Jethro's antics.

I imagined Z was probably frustrated working this job in reality TV. By the looks of what he could do, he was destined for something bigger. I didn't say that to Devon though. Any compliment to Z would be taken the wrong way.

"That's all I have from the factory that morning," Devon said.

The scene ended and the recording flipped over to the Blueberry Bash. I could see Charlotte in her glitzy gown sitting on her throne. She was lovely even when dressed like a blue-sequined puffball. In that dress, I would have looked like the unfortunate girl from *Willy Wonka & the Chocolate Factory*.

Z had caught me walking around the square handing out pieces of fudge, as well as what looked like an argument between Margot Rawlins and Ruth Yoder. I'm sure it was about the Blueberry Bash and how Ruth thought it inappropriate in an Amish town. However, to be fair, Ruth thought most English events were inappropriate for Harvest.

Devon made a motion as if she was about to turn off the recording, and I grabbed her hand. "Wait, wait, go back. That's Wade."

The film showed Charlotte talking to some children, but behind Charlotte, Wade could be seen walking with a gray-haired Amish man.

They walked in the direction of the pine trees on the edge of the square and disappeared.

"Can you play that back again and zoom in?"

Devon did as I asked. The image was grainy because the two men were in the background of the recording, but it was clear enough for me to make out who Wade was with. My breath caught. It was Charlotte's father, Sol Weaver. He must have been the man I'd overheard Wade talking with behind the food truck. Wade had told Sol he was going to make me pay for what I'd done.

Chapter Thirteen

"What is it?" Devon leaned closer to the screen. "Do you recognize the man walking with Wade in this footage?"

"I . . ."

"Do you?" she asked a little more forcefully this time. "Tell me if you do."

"I'm just surprised it's an older Amish man, that's all. All the men who worked construction with Wade were young. I've never seen him with this man before. I don't believe it's a member of his crew."

She sat back in her seat and folded her arms. "Tell me what's going on. You're bothered by something. I did you a favor by showing you this footage. You might have executive producer rights, but the final say remains with the show."

I didn't know how to respond. She was right. She had done me a favor by showing me the footage. It was a huge favor actually, especially now that I'd discovered Sol might be involved. I would be surprised if he was the killer because he was a strict Amish man. He would not go against the church and the district laws on violence. He wouldn't kill anyone.

I bit the inside of my cheek as I recalled the many times I'd discovered violence in the Amish community. Even murder. Just because I didn't want Charlotte's father to be involved, I couldn't take him off my possible people-of-interest list.

Hadn't Sol said something to Wade about his son? I thought back to the conversation. Yes, he had said he wanted Wade to release his son, Charlotte's brother. What did that mean?

A sinking feeling came over me.

Charlotte had never mentioned a connection between Wade and her father, but that didn't mean anything. It wasn't unusual for children in a strict Amish home not to be aware of their father's business. This was especially true for a daughter.

I had more questions than answers, but I knew for certain I would have to ask Charlotte about it. I wasn't looking forward to that conversation.

Over the last several months, my cousin had tried to make amends with her family, and she'd invited them to her wedding. She knew it was unlikely they would even respond let alone come, but every day I watched her check the mail coming into Swissmen Sweets with hope in her eyes. Every day her face fell when there was no response from her mom and dad.

Despite everything her parents had done, I wasn't surprised she had invited them to the wedding. Charlotte had a forgiving heart. I didn't know if I would have been able do the same if my parents had turned their backs on me the way hers had. I liked to think I would, but I knew it'd be a lot harder for me than it was for my cousin.

There was something else that disturbed me about seeing Sol with Wade. It had to do with what I'd heard Sol say about me.

The Weavers had not been happy when my grandmother and I took Charlotte in after she'd left her home district. I'd heard a rumor from Ruth Yoder that the Weaver family was angry with my grandmother's district for welcoming Charlotte. I believe they thought Charlotte should have been sent back to her district in shame.

I supposed now they blamed Bishop Yoder and the rest of the community for the fact that Charlotte had left the faith entirely. They would think Charlotte had too much freedom. Clearly they'd forgotten that the basis of the Amish faith was the freedom to join the church or not. Each and every individual had to make a choice. It was the one time everyone was on an even playing field in Amish culture.

Because faith—and choosing to believe in God—was the foundation of their entire community.

I knew very little about Sol Weaver other than the fact that he was from a more conservative district than my grandmother's. That community was also my grandmother's home district. *Maami* grew up there and left when she married my *grossdaadi*, Jebidiah King.

Charlotte's father was a severe man. Even though Charlotte wasn't officially shunned by her home district because she had never been baptized into the church after she entered *rumspringa*, her family treated her as if she were shunned. They never forgave her for leaving. They didn't, or couldn't, understand why her love of music was so important to her, so important that she would leave the only life she had ever known.

"You have to tell me who that Amish man is," Devon said again.

There was the sound of footsteps on the stairs. I turned to see Charlotte coming down. She wore her long red hair in a braid, a long denim skirt, and a plain yellow T-shirt. She could pass for any of the Mennonite girls living in the county.

Charlotte might have adopted technology and a more modern lifestyle when she'd left the Amish church, but she still struggled with her outward appearance being too English.

A month ago, I'd bought her a pair of jeans, which I had seen her wear just one time. It was almost as if she was embarrassed to dress English. This made me wonder what she would wear to her wedding. I'd offered to take her wedding dress shopping and even offered to pay for the dress. It was the least I could do. Charlotte was an essential part of Swissmen Sweets, and I hoped she'd prove herself even more invaluable at Swissmen Candyworks . . . if it ever opened. However, Charlotte said she already had the dress covered.

"Good morning, Devon!" Charlotte said with a smile. "I didn't expect to see you here this early." She gave me a questioning look. "Is there taping scheduled in the shop today? Did you tell Cousin Clara?" She looked concerned.

Charlotte knew how *Maami* felt about the documentary. At times my grandmother was present in a scene, but I asked Devon to be very conscious of not filming her face out of respect for my grandmother's beliefs.

"Devon and I are going over some of the footage from the last several days . . ." I trailed off.

Charlotte's eyes brightened. "Because of the murder! You're looking for clues in the film. That's genius."

Devon and Charlotte smiled at each other, and I had a sneaking suspicion I'd be in serious trouble if the two of them teamed up. Also, I noted that Charlotte might not want to dress like an Englisher, but she didn't mind acting like one when it came to criminal investigations.

Of course, I had only myself to blame for that.

"We might have found something too. Wade was speaking to an Amish man at the Blueberry Bash. Since you were Amish, you might know who it is." Devon turned the screen in Charlotte's direction.

Before I could stop her, she leaned over the phone.

All the blood drained from Charlotte face. "I know who that man is."

"Who?" Devon sat up straight.

"My father."

Devon's eyes lit up as if she'd just won the jackpot. "Your father?"

Charlotte nodded and fell into the empty chair at the table as if she didn't think her legs could hold her up any longer.

Devon's gaze turned to me. "Were you planning on telling me that?"

"I wanted to talk to Charlotte first."

She pointed at me. "So you did know who the man was."

I didn't respond.

I patted Charlotte's back because she appeared to be in shock.

"What would my father be doing talking to Wade?" Charlotte asked. "It doesn't make any sense. Dad doesn't like Englishers or English events. He wouldn't speak to a man like Wade. He wouldn't be at the Blueberry Bash at all unless he had a very good reason."

"There lies the mystery," Devon said with sparkling eyes.

Charlotte looked at her. "Why are you so interested in this? Aren't you making a show about candy?"

It was a very good question, and one that I had wanted to ask more than once.

"It's all part of the candy factory's story, isn't it? Wade died in the factory. It's not my fault if something like this lands in my lap."

"You're going to include a man's death in the documentary?" Charlotte gasped. "I don't know much about television, but that doesn't sound like a show about food anymore."

Devon pressed her lips together and looked as if she was considering what to say when her phone vibrated on the table. The name *Linc Baggins* appeared on the screen.

"I have to take this." She picked up her phone and camera bag and hurried out of the candy shop without another word.

Charlotte watched her go. "Something weird is going on with her. She seems a little too happy that Wade is dead."

I couldn't have agreed more.

Chapter Fourteen

The shop opened and we were immediately inundated with two tour buses of seniors on a day trip from Cleveland. There was little time for Charlotte and I to talk about her father or what we should do about his involvement in the case, but when lunchtime came around there was a break in the customers.

This wasn't unusual. Lunchtime was typically a slow period for us because visitors were eating in the many restaurants in the county instead of shopping. I finally got a chance to speak to Charlotte alone as my grandmother went up to her apartment for a break.

She grabbed a handful of black licorice from a jar and then sat at one of the café tables. I knew this was bad news. Charlotte only ate black licorice when she was down. She claimed the taste made her realize there were worse things in life than whatever her current problem might be. She hated black licorice.

She popped a piece in her mouth and grimaced.

I sat across from her at the table. "Black licorice, huh?"

She nodded. "It might not be enough. Is there a candy worse than this?"

"Not that I can think of, but I like all candy, even licorice."

She put another piece in her mouth.

"I got some good news," I said. "While you were with a customer, Margot called. The original blueberry princess is on the mend and will be taking over the throne tonight."

She nodded.

I frowned. I had hoped that would cheer her up, but I had to remind myself she was grappling with the possibility her estranged father might know something about Wade Farmer's murder.

She held a third piece of licorice in her hand but didn't put it in her mouth. "I need to talk to my *daed*," she said, using the Amish word for dad for the first time. Since leaving the church, Charlotte tried to speak only English, but every so often, the Pennsylvania Dutch came out. It happened more often when she was upset, sort of like the black licorice eating.

"And I have to talk to him soon." She swallowed. "Devon said the sheriff's department already has a copy of the recording. Luke will be able to identify my father just as quickly as I did. He'll have no choice but to question my father. That's not really how I want *Daed* to meet my future husband for the first time."

"Have you heard from Deputy Little yet today?"

She shook her head. "No, but he doesn't text or

call when he's at work. He's very focused on his job."

I knew what that was like from dating Aiden.

"How do you want to handle this? Go to your family's farm? Where's the best place to find him?"

She shook her head. "No. I can't go back there without causing a huge scene. It's Saturday. Every Saturday, my father and some of my siblings sell kettle corn outside the Linzer Petting Zoo."

I raised my brow. That was the same petting zoo Aiden was investigating. Could there be a connection?

"Do you think he still does that?" I asked. "You've been away from home for several years. Your father could have changed his habits."

"He doesn't change ever. I think—no, I know—that was part of the reason why I had to leave my home district. Nothing changes there. They have been following the same rules for the last hundred years and will be following the same rules for a hundred years more no matter what the English world does. At least Cousin Clara's district makes some adjustments so that its members can function and make a proper living in the English world. Change can be good."

I knew that there were several Amish people in my grandmother's district—including the bishop's wife—who would not agree with Charlotte's sentiment on change.

"He should be at the petting zoo until five," Charlotte said. "Can I leave for a couple of hours?"

"I need to drive you. You don't have your license yet, and it will take you forever to get there by horse and buggy. Emily comes in at two this afternoon. She and *Maami* should be able to handle the shop until closing time at five."

"What about the Blueberry Bash? Will we be back in time? I know I'm not the princess any longer, but aren't we handing out samples of blueberry-and-cream fudge again?"

I slapped myself on the forehead. She was right. How could I have forgotten about the Blueberry Bash that evening? There was to be a blues concert in the gazebo as the big event that night.

Handing out samples wasn't something I could ask Emily or my grandmother to do. They were both devout Amish women and would be uncomfortable. Besides, Emily had two small children at home that needed tending. I always hated to keep her over her shift for any reason because I knew she only worked at the candy shop as a favor to me. Her husband—a kind but very traditional Christmas tree farmer—would prefer that his wife didn't work outside of the home.

"Let me make a phone call."

I removed my cell phone from my pocket.

"Sunbeam Café. We have the best pie in the county! What will you have?" Lois Henry said in my ear.

"Hi Lois, it's Bailey."

"Hey girl! Do you and the ladies need lunch delivered? My granddaughter made chicken salad and it's to die for. Way better than anything you can get in an Amish restaurant. Don't spread that around to the Amish though. You know they get prickly when I say that Darcy is the better cook."

"The chicken salad sounds wonderful, but I'm actually calling to ask a favor."

"Fire away!"

"Tonight, Charlotte and I have to talk to a few people, and Swissmen Sweets is supposed to hand out candy samples at the Blueberry Bash and during the concert. I hope to be back by then, but I can't be sure how long we'll be gone."

"And you want to know if I can do that for you?"

I relaxed. "Yes, I don't want to ask my grandmother or Emily. They wouldn't be comfortable."

"The event is a little too English I take it."

"Yes."

"It's no trouble at all. Millie and I will both help."

"Won't Millie be uncomfortable at the Blueberry Bash?

"Are you kidding? This is what she lives for! Her love of blueberries is legendary. It will be hard for me to tear her away tonight. Her motto is no blueberry left behind."

"I can't thank you and Millie enough for this. It's a huge help."

"It's no problem at all. Now before I go, I just have one question for you. Does this have anything to do with Wade Farmer's death in your candy factory last night?"

I bit my lower lip and didn't say anything.

"Your silence speaks volumes," she said knowingly. "You have a bit of sleuthing to do, is that it? Millie and I know all about that! We always support a little meddling here and there. The café is closed tonight because Darcy is selling her pies at the Blueberry Bash, so it will be a perfect time for Millie and me to help you out. What should we look out for in regards to the case?"

I sighed. There was no point in keeping this a

secret from Lois. She had already guessed correctly what Charlotte and I were up to. "If you can ask around about Wade, that would help. Did he have any enemies? Was anyone upset with him?"

"We know the drill. Don't you worry about it; we'll get right to the point."

I hoped I wasn't making a mistake by asking Lois for help. She wasn't the subtlest person in the village.

When Emily arrived for her afternoon shift, I told *Maami* that Charlotte and I had an errand to run, and that Lois had volunteered to hand out fudge samples at the bash if we didn't make it back in time. The two of them shared a look as if they knew it was something more than an errand. Rather than answer their questions, I went outside to wait for Charlotte, who said she needed to run upstairs to the apartment to grab something.

Across the street, the square was starting to fill up with Blueberry Bash revelers. The bash was starting at three that day since it was Saturday, but Margot expected it to run until nine again. It was the last day of the celebration as there were no festivities in Harvest on Sundays out of respect to the Amish living in the village. However, I knew that Margot would change that rule if she could, so she could have three-day celebrations on the square.

I spotted Margot walking around the grass with her bullhorn in hand. She nodded at passersby and had a very pleased expression on her face. She was in her element. Another roaring success on the square. I had to admit, she was good at what she did. No one else had been able to organize as many events in the village. That being said, I wished that she asked me for help a lot less or that I had more backbone about saying "no."

"Bailey! Bailey!" Juliet hurried across the square in yellow high heels that were a perfect contrast to her blue-and-white polka-dotted dress. Under her arm she held Jethro. His head bobbed up and down at her haste.

I steeled myself. Here was my chance to put my backbone into practice. I was going to say no and just tell Juliet straight out, I couldn't take her pig every time she needed to do something. I had things to do too.

"Can you take Jethro?" she asked in a breathless voice. "I just can't keep an eye on him at the bash. There is too much going on. The church is sponsoring the concert, so everything needs to be perfect."

I took a breath. *Be strong, Bailey. Grow a backbone! Just say no!*

"Juliet, you know that I would love to, but—"

"Oh good! I know how close you and Jethro are and that you love spending time with him. If I didn't know that Jethro loved me with his whole heart, I might even be jealous of your closeness." She set Jethro on the sidewalk, pulled his leash from her dress pocket, and clasped her hands together. "Oh, Bailey, I feel like we have been a family forever. I truly can't wait until it's official. Have you and Aiden had any of those important conversations?"

"You know that I care about Jethro, but Charlotte and I have some errands to run this afternoon. Can he stay in the church with Reverend Brook?"

It wasn't much of a backbone, but at least I'd made a second attempt to get out of the situation. I called that progress.

She clipped the leash onto Jethro's collar. "With the reverend? Goodness, no. Jethro can't stay there because my beloved husband is playing with the band tonight at the bash," she said with a great deal of pride. "That's one reason the church is a sponsor. The biggest reason, of course, is outreach to the community. We can't get more members if we aren't out among the people."

"I didn't know Reverend Brook plays an instrument."

"My girl, you should come to church more often. The reverend is a gifted saxophone player. He is just tickled at the opportunity to play with the Dahlia Brothers. This is like a dream come true for him, to be able to play real blues and not just hymns on Sundays. I'm so happy for him. Reverend Brook is not as excitable as I am, you know."

I knew. Everyone knew.

"To see him looking forward to something like this has me over the moon. Since the reverend will be busy, I will be handing out church flyers and talking to people about all we have to offer. I can't be worried about Jethro when I am trying to reach out to others for the Lord!" She said this as if the very idea was preposterous. She put the end of the leash in my hand.

I looked down at the toaster-sized polka-dotted pig. It seemed I had no choice.

She flounced away. How she walked so gracefully across the grass-covered square in her high heels, I would never know.

Charlotte came out of the candy shop. To my surprise, she was wearing the jeans I had bought her and a checkered blouse. Her long hair was freshly brushed and tied back with a pink ribbon. She looked like a fresh-faced farm girl circa the 1960s. She blushed. "I just thought I would give the jeans a try again. They are very comfortable."

"You look adorable," I said with a smile.

It wasn't lost on me that Charlotte had decided to dress "more English" when she was about to talk to her father for the first time in years. I had to believe this was some kind of statement on her part, but I made no comment on it. I was going to let Charlotte cope with this situation however she chose.

I tugged on Jethro's leash. "Ready to go?"

She looked down at the pig. "Jethro's coming?"

"It was unavoidable."

She laughed because she knew I could never say no to Juliet.

It didn't bode well for my marriage to her only son.

On the drive to the Linzer Petting Zoo, Charlotte didn't speak a word. She stared out the window and watched the green rolling hills and large white barns of Holmes County pass by. I didn't press her to speak. She'd confide in me when she was ready; there had to be a lot on her mind.

I wasn't particularly close to my own parents, but there had never been a time when they'd stopped speaking to me. I knew I could call them any time and they would pick up the phone and talk to me no matter where they were in the world—they traveled a lot.

Charlotte didn't have that. When she'd left her

district, she'd left all contact with her family behind. *Maami* and I had become her closest family. I loved my cousin and cherished the closeness we had, but I knew she missed her parents, brothers, and sisters. She'd given up so much to live the life she wanted.

It was a summer Saturday afternoon, and the petting zoo was bustling. People came from all over to see the animals, and from the car we could hear cows mooing and children laughing. I'd lived in Holmes County for several years, but this was the first time I'd been to Linzer Petting Zoo, even though it was one of the top destinations in the county. That wasn't something I planned to tell Margot because if I did, no doubt she'd want to open a petting zoo on the square in Harvest.

I shifted the car into park and opened my door. Charlotte didn't move. The humidity of summer filled the car as what was left of the cool, conditioned air escaped.

"Are you okay?" I asked.

"I think so. I just never thought I would speak to my father again. And I definitely didn't think it would involve murder. That's if he's even willing to speak to me. I'm just trying to prepare myself for the possibility that he'll ignore me completely. It will hurt if that happens."

"Do you want to stay here and let me talk to him?"

She looked at me for the first time since we'd left Swissmen Sweets. There was determination in her eyes. "No. This is something I need to do. Something I've needed to do for a long time. He might not want to speak to me, but there are things I need to say to him. I think when I do say those things, I'll finally be free of my old life so I can move forward with Luke.

"When I left all those years ago, I knew it would be forever. I never expected to speak to my parents again. They made it very clear how they viewed my decision. I'm sure by now word has gotten back to them that I have left the Amish faith. But now that I'm engaged to Luke, I want them back in my life. Getting married is a huge life event, and it doesn't feel right that they won't be there. I wouldn't be who I am without them."

"You sent them a wedding invitation. Have you heard back?"

"In a way, yes. It returned unopened." She looked out the window again. "It wasn't because I had the wrong address. My family has lived on the same plot of land for generations."

"Do you think they knew it was a wedding invitation?"

"Maybe. Or they just knew it was mail from me, and they refused to open it. I know they've heard rumors about me. They must know I'm marrying an Englisher. Not just any Englisher either, a sheriff's deputy. Someone who is in law enforcement and carries a gun. That can't sit well with them." She folded her hands in her lap. "I know it's silly, but I wanted them to come to the wedding to see that I was okay. That I turned out all right and am happy. I wasn't asking them to be fully back in my life."

"You are happy, aren't you?" I asked nervously because she certainly didn't sound happy at the moment. It was disconcerting to hear Charlotte sounding so down. She was the most positive person I'd ever met, and it wasn't because her life had been easy either.

She scratched Jethro between the ears. "I'm happy. I love working at the candy shop, and I'm excited about the factory. I know it will be a great opportunity for both of us. Above all, I love Luke. He is a good man. True, he may not be Amish, but that doesn't make him any less good. I can't think of anyone else, Amish or English, who can measure up to him in my eyes."

I held onto the steering wheel. "Then I think when you speak to your father, you need to go in there with these thoughts in mind. You're happy and you don't need his approval to be happy. Don't let his displeasure rob you of your joy."

She smiled. "Bailey, you always give the best encouragement. This will be hard, but I've done much harder things in my life. Also, we need to speak to my father before the sheriff does. That conversation won't go well at all." She unbuckled her seatbelt and opened her door.

When we were within a few feet of the main barn, my stomach grumbled. Outside the barn, and just before a visitor paid admission to go in to see the animals, there was an old shed converted into an outdoor kitchen. The scent of popcorn and barbeque filled the air.

I had Jethro tucked tightly under my arm, and he wiggled. He smelled the food too and was ready to eat. Then again, Jethro was a pig and therefore always ready to eat.

A young Amish girl came up to us holding out a sample-sized bag of kettle corn. "Would you like to try a sample?"

"Thank you." I took the kettle corn. The bag was still warm. I put a piece of corn in my mouth, and sweet and salty flavors melded together in a perfect bite. "This is delicious."

The young girl smiled, and deep dimples appeared in either cheek. She turned to Charlotte and offered her kettle corn as well.

Charlotte stared at her. "Miriam Lee?"

Chapter Fifteen

The girl blinked at her. "*Ya.*" Her face flushed red and she whispered, "Charlotte?"

Charlotte nodded and tears came to her eyes. "The last time I saw you, you were still in braids. Look at you now with your hair up and wearing a prayer cap."

Miriam Lee blushed. "It is your old cap that I wear. It's a little piece of you that you left behind." She glanced over her shoulder as if she was afraid she might be caught doing something wrong.

Charlotte's eyes filled with tears. "I can't think of anyone I would want to wear it more."

Miriam Lee looked at Charlotte in her jeans and blouse. "You're not dressed in the Amish way. What has happened?"

Before Charlotte could answer, a man's sharp voice called, "Miriam Lee!" followed by a string of Amish sentences I didn't understand.

Charlotte sucked in a gasp. It was her father, Sol Weaver.

Miriam Lee hurried over to her father, who continued to chastise her as she went back to the giant cast-iron kettle, which hung over a roaring fire. Beads of sweat gathered on her forehead as she stirred the popping kernels. The heat coming from the kettle must have been close to unbearable on the warm summer afternoon.

Sol glared at Charlotte. They had the same fiery red hair, although Sol's was fading to gray, and they had the same pale skin and intelligent green eyes. Even so, he didn't acknowledge or make eye contact with Charlotte. He went back to the kettle corn shed.

"*Daed*!" Charlotte said and then added something in their language.

I wished I had spent more time learning Pennsylvania Dutch when my grandmother offered to teach me. Jethro fought to get down, so I clipped on his leash and set him on the ground. In the process, half of my bag of kettle corn fell into the dirt. Jethro took it upon himself to clean up the mess.

Sol's back stiffened. He'd heard Charlotte but didn't stop. Instead, he went into the booth and snapped at Miriam Lee, snatching the corn paddle from her hands.

Miriam Lee dropped her head, but not before tears gathered in her eyes.

"What did he say to her?" I asked in a whisper.

"He told her not to speak to strangers." Charlotte's voice cracked.

Jethro had his snout on the ground and was living his best life. It seemed I wasn't the only one who'd dropped a few kernels of kettle corn in the dirt. At least one of us was having a good time.

"I don't know what to do," Charlotte whispered.

"He's not going to speak to me. He won't even look at me."

I was at a loss myself. If Sol wasn't going to speak to Charlotte, how were we to find out what he knew about Wade Farmer's death?

"Maybe—"

But I was interrupted by a booming voice. "That's quite an eater you have there. Maybe we should hire him to clean up the grounds at the end of the day. I'd have the goats do it, but they have far less discretion on what is food and what is not. They would eat the wood siding right off of my barn if I let them" He chuckled. "How do you like the petting zoo?"

The middle-aged man had a blond beard and shining hazel eyes. His nose, which was a little too small for his broad face, reminded me of a button.

I smiled. "We haven't gone into the barn yet. We got a little sidetracked with the kettle corn."

He rocked back on his heels. "Oh my, *ya,* that can happen. Sol Weaver has been the one making kettle corn here for decades. I wouldn't think of asking anyone else to do it. His is the very best. I've had folks come to the zoo for the corn and never see the inside of the barn. I hope you won't be one of those people. We just got a parakeet display that is my pride and joy. I have always wanted to include those little birds in the zoo and am so glad I could finally add them. Children in particular love them. There is nothing I enjoy more than hearing the sound of children laughing. If I don't hear laughter and squeals coming from the barn, I haven't done my job." He glanced down at Jethro again. "Is that Juliet Brook's pig?"

I smiled. "It is. Do you know the Brooks?"

"*Ya,* I do. They have brought children from their church here many times and their youth group helped close up the zoo for the winter last year. They are good people even if they are *Englischers.* Personally, I don't care if a man is *Englisch* or Amish as long he is honest." A strange look crossed his face, and I remembered that Aiden was working a case involving missing money at the Linzer Petting Zoo.

"I'm Bailey King," I said, but I didn't hold out my hand for a handshake. Most Amish men do not shake hands with women outside of their family.

"It's nice to meet you. Emmaus Linzer here. How did you end up with old Jethro?"

I was dying to ask him about the case that Aiden was working on for him, but I refrained from saying anything because I didn't want to compromise Aiden's position with the petting zoo owner.

"Juliet asked me to watch him while she and Reverend Brook were at the Blueberry Bash this afternoon."

He nodded. "I thought it was him. He is a very distinctive pig."

That was certainly true.

"Well if Juliet ever wants to outsource his skills as a pig vacuum, have her give me a call."

A pig vacuum? I'd heard Jethro called many things over the years, but this was the first time I'd heard him called a vacuum, not that it wasn't fitting.

"I'll let Juliet Brook know he might have a job lined up if the acting thing falls through."

He laughed so hard he placed a hand to his chest. "You do that. I don't think I can pay as well as Hollywood." He smiled at Charlotte. "Well, I'll be, Charlotte Weaver, I haven't seen you in years." Even though it was clear she was no longer Amish, he made no comment on her leaving the faith. "Are you here visiting your family?"

Charlotte glanced in the direction of her father and Miriam Lee. Sol had his back to us, but Miriam Lee seemed to be watching us out of the corner of her eye. "I was trying to, but my *daed* won't speak to me."

He nodded. "Sol is a strict man. He would not be happy with the choices you have made in your life." He spoke without judgment. "Would you like me to talk to him?"

"Do you think it will do any good?" Charlotte asked.

He shrugged. "You never know with Sol. He's a prickly sort, but it doesn't look to me like you are getting much of anywhere on your own."

Charlotte gave a slight nod, and Emmaus walked over to the kettle corn. Emmaus and Sol spoke to each other in hushed voices. Sol gestured angrily with his hands and shook his head.

"They are speaking too quietly for me to hear what they are saying," Charlotte said. "But by the looks of it, *Daed* doesn't want to speak to me."

I agreed. Sol appeared to be very much against the idea of talking with his daughter.

Emmaus patted his shoulder and said something else, which seemed to calm Sol. He gave a slight nod. Miriam Lee watched all of it with eyes as wide as dinner plates. I was certain she could hear every word they said.

Emmaus clapped Sol on the back and walked over to Charlotte and me. "I have *gut* news. Sol will talk to Charlotte, but only Charlotte." He glanced at me. "He doesn't want you there. He knows who you are and thinks you're a bad influence on the community." He said the last part in an apologetic tone.

This wasn't news to me. I already knew that from the conversation I'd overheard between him and Wade at the Blueberry Bash.

"I have to talk to him alone?" Charlotte squeaked.

"You'll do fine," I said. "Jethro and I will be right here waiting for you." I gave her a hug. "This is your chance, maybe your only chance to get out everything you have been waiting to say to your father all these years. You have to take it. I'm rooting for you."

"*Danki*, Bailey," she said, using the Amish word for thank you. She straightened her shoulders and walked toward the kettle corn as if she was going off to war, which wasn't a great comparison because the Amish were pacifists.

"I've known Sol for over fifty years," Emmaus said. "She has a tough road ahead of her to make amends with her *daed*. When Sol makes up his mind about a person, it is made up. It's safe to say that he will never like you."

That was a cheerful thought. "Jethro and I will just wait here until she's done."

"Where is the little guy?" Emmaus pointed at my feet.

I looked down, and Jethro was gone. I was holding onto his leash, but there was no polka-dotted pig at the end of it.

Chapter Sixteen

"Looks like he slipped the noose," Emmaus said cheerfully.

I lifted up the leash and found the collar still attached. I guessed that it hadn't been properly tightened around his neck, and he'd shaken it loose. I realized I hadn't checked the collar when Juliet handed over the pig.

I looked around. The petting zoo grounds were crowded with tourists. I had zero hope of seeing the small pig in the crowd. I prayed that he wouldn't get stepped on. My stomach twisted. If something happened to Jethro, Juliet would never forgive me and I would never forgive myself. As much trouble as he was, I loved that little pig. I had to find him.

A middle-aged Amish woman marched toward us carrying a chicken that had a crown of dangling white feathers springing from the top of its head. The hem of her plain blue dress was encrusted with mud or worse, and she wore muddy work boots on her feet. "Emmaus, there was a pig loose in the barn. I told you the pigs need to stay in their pens. They can't be wandering about. They're too smart and get into too much trouble. I have too much to do here to deal with a bunch of pigs running around."

"Kelli Anne, dear, I have kept the pigs in their pen as you have requested time and again. I would never do anything to make your life more difficult, my love."

I took Kelli Anne to be Emmaus's wife.

She scowled in response to his comments. "You and I both know it's I who keeps this place running. You may be the face of Linzer Petting Zoo, but I am most certainly the muscle."

Emmaus laughed, but his humor didn't reach his eyes.

I clapped my hands together. "The loose pig must be Jethro. Can I run in and grab him?"

Kelli Anne scowled at me. "You brought Juliet Brook's pig to the petting zoo?"

"I—I . . ." She had a very stern stare that left me tongue-tied. Ruth Yoder could take some scowling lessons from Kelli Anne Linzer, and considering Ruth's epic scowl, that was saying something.

Emmaus chuckled. "Of course. You'd better hurry or someone might think that little pig is for sale. We wouldn't want him to end up in a roasting dish."

I gasped at the very idea, and my heart sank. I glanced back at Charlotte, who was standing in front of her father with slumped shoulders. That conversation wasn't going well, but I had to save Jethro.

I left Emmaus and his wife and ran toward the barn. As I wove around people who were coming out of the building, I kept an eye out for any pigs in their arms. I hoped that Emmaus had been joking about someone wanting to take Jethro.

I slipped by the ticket booth, and the Amish teen working at the desk called after me, "It's three dollars to get in."

Rather than stand there and argue with him. I reached in my pocket and came up with a ten. "That should cover it." I ran into the barn.

As I went through the gate, I heard him mutter something about crazy *Englischers.* I can't say that I blamed him.

The barn's smell hit me like a brick wall of hay, manure, and dust, and it took a moment for my eyes to adjust to the dim light. When they did, my mouth fell open. There were animals all around me, literally everywhere. A llama walked by me with a pygmy goat and a goose in tow. There was a pen that was full of baby rabbits and another with ducklings. To my right, there were sheep and to my left there was a donkey holding his head over the door of his pen, waiting for the carrot that a young boy held out to him.

Children and adults wandered through the middle of the barn holding carrots they'd bought from the farm to feed the animals.

Two young goats stood on either side of me, trying to get their noses in my jeans pockets.

"Hey, there's nothing in there for you," I protested.

One glared at me with his slanted pupil, and I had the distinct feeling he was judging me. It seemed you were not welcome in the barn without snacks.

"I'm not here to feed you," I muttered. "I'm looking for my pig."

He walked away as if he had heard it all before from visitors without carrots.

"Mommy! There is a piggy in with the birdies!" a child called in a high-pitched voice. "Come see!"

The child's mom was speaking to another adult in a conversation that looked like it might take a while and involved someone named Jennifer in the PTA. This woman was not a fan of Jennifer.

The little girl pulled on her mother's sleeve again. "Mommy!"

The woman looked down at her daughter. "Can't you see that I'm talking? Whatever it is will have to wait."

The girl dropped her hand from her mother's sleeve and lowered her head.

I stepped closer to her. "Where did you see the piggy?" I asked.

She looked up at me with bright eyes. Perhaps it was because I was an adult who cared about her pig story. She glanced at her mom, who was still deep in conversation, and then pointed across the barn.

In one corner of the barn there was a hand-painted sign that said, "Parakeets!" This must be the new enclosure Emmaus was so proud of.

"Thank you."

I hurried across the barn.

Outside the parakeet enclosure, there was an Amish teenager selling tiny paper cups of birdseed for one dollar.

"Would you like to buy some birdseed for the parakeets?" she asked.

I nodded and handed over my dollar bill. I took the birdseed and stepped through the first screen door. When it was completely closed, I stepped through another screen door and found myself in a small garden full of birds.

Parakeets flew in all directions. Some jumped onto the top of my sneakers and began pecking at my shoelaces. Ten other people were in the enclosure, and they were all surrounded by parakeets as they held out their tiny cups of seed.

I had forgotten I was even holding mine until a blue parakeet nipped at my hand trying to get to the seeds.

"Ow! Okay, you can have it." I held out the cup of seed to the little bird.

I didn't see Jethro. I would have thought that in a room filled with tiny colorful birds, he would stand out.

I walked around the room with the blue parakeet gripping the edge of the tiny cup with its tiny talons. Finally, I saw Jethro. He was in the very back corner, sitting on the barn floor with an expression of sheer confusion on his face.

Dozens of blue, yellow, and green parakeets were perched on Jethro. There was even one on his curly tail. His brown eyes bugged out of his head as he tried to decide what to do. It seemed he was frozen by indecision.

The parakeets on the little pig turned in my direction as one and looked at me. It was a tad disconcerting, and my little blue parakeet abandoned me to settle on the tip of Jethro's snout.

Jethro wiggled his snout and the blue parakeet pecked him just once. Jethro's eyes rolled around in their sockets, and I thought there was a good chance he might faint.

"Is that a statue or a real pig?" a teenage boy in a

Millersburg High School jacket asked. "The pig doesn't even blink. How can it be real?"

"He's real," I said. "Trust me."

I removed Jethro's leash from my pocket and held it out in front of me before slowly moving toward the pig.

"Hey, buddy! It's time to go home." I gripped the collar, ready to slip it over his head.

I didn't want to scare the little birds, but to be fair, they'd shown no fear when I'd approached. But I would have to disrupt them just a little bit to get Jethro out of the barn.

I leaned forward and slid the leash over his snout, bumping the blue parakeet in the process. Suddenly, I was enveloped in a cloud of yellow, green, and blue feathers, as the parakeets swirled around Jethro and me. There were so many birds that I lost track of what was up and what was down and fell onto my backside. Thank goodness there were no parakeets on the ground just below me.

Jethro squealed and jumped onto my lap as if I could save him, but truthfully, I was of no use when under parakeet attack.

By this time, a crowd had gathered around us, shouting and trying to shoo the birds away. Someone scooped Jethro off my lap, grabbed my arm and pulled me to my feet. All the while, I kept my eyes squeezed closed for fear the birds might peck them out.

"You can open your eyes now," a soothing and familiar voice said.

I opened them to find Aiden standing in front of me with Jethro in his arms, trying and failing not to smile.

I brushed what I hoped was dirt—but was more likely bird doo—off my bare arm. "You can go ahead and laugh. If I wasn't involved in the great parakeet attack, I would laugh too."

He smirked. "The great parakeet attack? Is that what we are calling it?"

"It was a traumatic event for Jethro and for me—it deserves a name."

He nodded as if that made complete sense.

Jethro's brown eyes rolled and his mouth hung open. It was almost as if he had tales to tell about his experience. I couldn't help but wonder how he'd gotten into this predicament in the first place.

While Aiden held him, I put Jethro's leash and collar back on, making sure they were secure but not too tight. Aiden then set him on the barn floor.

"Oh, he's so cute," a little boy said and gave Jethro a carrot meant for the zoo animals. Jethro, who had no qualms about eating someone else's food, scarfed it down.

"Let's get out of here before Jethro eats all the carrots," I said.

When we were outside the barn, Aiden touched my cheek and then showed me the blue feather that he had removed from my face. He let it float to the gravel-covered ground. "What are you doing here?"

I sighed. "I brought Charlotte to speak to her father. He sells kettle corn here every Saturday."

"She wanted to talk to him about her wedding?"

"Yes, and Sol Weaver might have been one of the last people to see Wade Farmer alive. We wanted to talk to him before the sheriff did."

"How do you know that?"

I quickly told him about the video Devon had.

"And the sheriff has this video."

I nodded. "He might not know who Sol is, but Deputy Little most certainly will when he sees it. Charlotte wanted to speak to her father first. You know her old district has no trust in the police."

"I do," Aiden said thoughtfully, most likely thinking about his own case in the same district, one likely made more difficult by the Amish residents' reluctance to help. "Why are you in the barn rather than with Charlotte?"

"Sol refused to talk to me. He would only speak to Charlotte alone. It's actually a surprise he'd even speak to Charlotte, considering the way her family has treated her since she left them."

"It is a surprise. Isn't her family shunning her?"

I swallowed. "Not officially. She was never baptized into the church, but they haven't spoken to her since she left."

"Poor Charlotte." He shook his head. "You would never know everything she's been through to see her. She's always so happy and smiling. You would think her family life is perfect."

I was about to agree when Charlotte came tearing through the crowd. She waved at me. "Bailey, come on."

I tried to grab her arm to stop her, but she kept going. "Charlotte, what's going on? Are you all right?"

She looked over her shoulder. "We have to go home." Her voice broke into a sob before she disappeared out of sight again.

Chapter Seventeen

Aiden wanted to go with me to check on Charlotte, but I asked him to stay back. Whatever had happened to make her so upset probably wasn't something she wanted to repeat in front of her fiancé's best friend. I couldn't blame her for that. I wouldn't want to share my sorrows with Deputy Little.

I also assumed Aiden was here interviewing Emmaus Linzer about the missing money at his zoo. I didn't want to get in the way of Aiden's work.

I found Charlotte standing outside my car with her face buried in her hands.

"Charlotte?" I asked as loudly as I dared.

She shoulders jerked up and down with each silent sob.

Jethro walked over to her, dragging me along with him at the other end of his leash. The little pig leaned against her right leg as if he was trying to offer a shoulder to cry on. While the pig was providing emotional support—I guessed he really was a comfort pig after all—I balled my fists at my sides. What had her father said to her to hurt her so much? I had half a mind to march over to the food trailer and tell Sol Weaver what I really thought of him.

Charlotte finally realized that Jethro was leaning against her leg, so she bent down and scratched him between the ears. It was his favorite spot for a scratch.

"Charlotte, what happened?" I asked.

She looked up at me with a red face and teary eyes. "The conversation didn't go well. *Daed* said I was no longer his daughter, and God had been testing him when I was his child. Since I am no longer his child, he passed the test."

"That's awful."

"It's what I expected him to say or close to it, but it doesn't hurt any less to actually hear it. The worst part was he wouldn't even let Miriam Lee look at me for fear my earthly ways would rub off on her."

Charlotte's "earthly ways"? That didn't make any sense at all. She was the most wholesome person I knew, and that included all the Amish people I had met. There was no one better than Charlotte.

"In some ways, I wish my sister hadn't even been there. It was even harder to be rejected by her than by my own father. I knew how *Daed* would be, but I thought if I ever ran into one of my siblings again . . ." She shook her head as if she couldn't complete the thought. She wiped her eyes. "Before he said all that, I did ask him about Wade. I thought it was best to discuss Wade before I got into the wedding talk. I had a feeling that as soon as the topic of the wedding came up, he would shut me down."

Who knew that murder would be the less awkward conversation between Charlotte and Sol?

"And what did he say about Wade?"

"My brother Jericho has been working for Wade for the last few months, and *Daed* wasn't happy about it. He wanted Jericho to quit. My brother kept saying he would, but never got around to actually doing it. *Daed* was tired of waiting and decided to take matters into his own hands as the man of the house. He would make Wade let Jericho go.

"He'd heard Wade would be at the Blueberry Bash and went to see him there. Don't tell Margot, but my dad wasn't impressed. In fact, he had even harsher words to say about the Blueberry Bash than Ruth Yoder did."

I raised my brow. "So your father asked Wade what exactly?"

"He asked Wade to fire Jericho, but *Daed* said Wade refused."

"I know this is a tough question to hear, and even more difficult to answer, but do you think your father would hurt Wade because he refused to fire Jericho?"

She looked me in the eye. "I know he would."

I swallowed. "How can you say that with so much certainty?"

"Because I know my father. The most important thing in the world to him is to keep his children on the straight and narrow. He wants them to find salvation, and it is his belief—but not the belief of all Amish, mind you—that the only way to do so is by following the rules of our Amish district. He doesn't even believe the Amish in other districts can be saved."

I raised my brow. That was a very rigid belief system, even for a conservative Amish man like Sol.

"But murder?" I asked.

"Salvation is more important than the lives of others." Her voice was blunt.

I shivered. It was little wonder to me now that Charlotte had felt so stifled in her home district. I knew she must worry about her brothers and sisters, like Miriam Lee, who were still part of that community.

"The only way to clear this up is to speak to my brother Jericho. He can tell us why he chose to work for Wade when my father was so adamantly against it. There is no lack of construction jobs in Holmes County. He could have easily found work somewhere else if he'd chosen to."

"If he'd chosen to" was the key statement. Why did he want to work for Wade Farmer? The man had been prickly in the best of moods. I couldn't imagine wanting to work for a boss like that. Then again, Wade's temperament wasn't that much different from Sol Weaver's, so maybe it was just what Jericho was used to.

"Where do we find your brother?" I asked.

"I doubt he's at home if he and my *daed* are fighting. I think I know where he might be. I'll show you the way."

Charlotte and I got into the car, and she gave me turn by turn directions out into the middle of nowhere. Or at least, that's what it felt like.

When she asked me to drive down a dirt road, I was beginning to lose faith in her navigation skills. I gripped the steering while my little SUV bounced up and down in the bumps along the road. They only thing that could have made it worse was if recent rain had turned the road muddy. Thankfully, we were into the driest part of the summer, so I was spared from getting stuck in the mud.

"Where are we going?" I asked Charlotte for what seemed like the hundredth time.

Just as before, she ignored my direct question and said, "It's just up ahead."

The trees on either side of the road gave way to a clearing at the edge of a large pond.

"Jericho likes to come here to get away and go fishing when he's upset. I figure with everything going on, he would need to escape."

My tires crunched on the gravel parking lot as the SUV came to a stop.

"There he is," Charlotte gasped.

Before I could even put the car in park, her seatbelt was unbuckled and she was out of the door. Jethro snuck his head between the two front seats for a better look.

"Come on, Jethro," I said. "We need to find out what's going on."

I got out of the car and went to the back seat, where I snapped on Jethro's leash and lifted him out of the car.

The grasses and weeds around the pond were up to my knees. I tried not to think about the ticks, snakes, and spiders that must live in the brush. Thankfully, I was wearing jeans and sneakers, but to be safe I carried Jethro to the water's edge.

Charlotte stood a few feet away from a lone Amish man standing at the water's edge with a fishing pole. A white five-gallon bucket and a tackle box sat at his feet. He was younger than I'd imagined, clean-shaven, and clearly a relative of Charlotte's because his hair was the same shade of red.

"What are you doing here?" Jericho asked.

"I wanted to talk to you," Charlotte said.

His eyes cut to Jethro and me. If he thought it strange I was carrying a polka-dotted pig under my arm, he didn't say so.

"I'm not supposed to be talking to you," he said in English. "You are shunned."

Charlotte gave a sharp intake of breath. "That is not true. I was never baptized into the church. I am not shunned by the church."

"Do you think that really matters to our father?" He glanced at me again. "And what is she doing here if you want to talk to me? I'm not going to talk to you in front of the *Englischer* who ripped you away from our family. Do you have any idea what it was like for the rest of us when you left?"

I pressed my lips together to hold back any words to defend myself. I had not ripped Charlotte away from her family. Leaving was her choice. Just as it was her family's choice not to have any relationship with her after she'd left.

"Was it difficult?" Charlotte asked.

Jericho set his fishing pole against a boulder along the water's edge. "Was it difficult? *Daed* was even harder on us than before. If one of the children so much as smiled at an *Englischer*, we were sent to our rooms without dinner."

"I'm sorry. I didn't think—"

"That's just it. You didn't think how leaving would affect the rest of us. You left five brothers and sisters at home, and never once thought about us when you made your choice."

Charlotte's shoulders slumped and tears came to her eyes. "I'm sorry. I should have been thinking of all of you and not myself. I was selfish."

I bit the inside of my lip. I wasn't of the belief that Charlotte was selfish for wanting a different kind of life. She'd left in self-preservation. I knew if she could, she would have taken her younger siblings with her. That hadn't been possible. At the same time, I understood the guilt she must feel having left them behind.

Charlotte appeared unable to speak as she digested everything her brother had said. I took my chance to step into the conversation. "How long have you worked for Wade Farmer?"

His mouth fell open. "How do you know anything about that?"

"We just stopped by Linzer Petting Zoo and spoke to your father."

Jericho looked to Charlotte. "He spoke to you?"

"*Ya,*" Charlotte said, and it seemed her ability to speak had returned.

"Why would be speak to you? He shunned you. It goes against everything that he believes."

It was a good question, and one that neither Charlotte nor I could answer. Why had Sol spoken to Charlotte when he could have ignored her altogether? When they wanted to, the Amish were experts at pretending someone wasn't there. I knew this from firsthand experience. When I'd first moved to Harvest, there were customers who would ignore me and only deal with my grandmother at the candy counter. Maybe they were like Ruth Yoder, who worried that if there were more Englishers and English businesses in Harvest, the town would lose its Amishness.

"You must know he was working on my candy factory," I said and adjusted Jethro in my arms. He was much smaller than Puff the rabbit, but he did become heavy if I had to hold him for a long time.

Jericho narrowed his eyes, and I was certain that he wasn't going to answer. However, he surprised me by saying, "I do—did—work for Wade. *Ya,* I know he was building your factory. I told him from the start I never wanted to be on that particular project because you took my sister from her family."

Again, I refrained from saying anything about his claim that I'd taken Charlotte from her family and community.

"It was the one request he granted me in all the time I worked for him."

"What did you do for him? Did you like working construction?"

He glanced in my direction. "I was one of his apprentices. The other was Naz Schlabach. Someday, I want to have a business much like Wade's. I want to be the boss. I don't want to be the fifty-year-old climbing on a roof or installing flooring. I wanted to hire people to do that for me. I have been working in construction since I was thirteen. Wade was the first person who was willing to show me how the business side of things worked. My *daed* wasn't going to do that. He didn't want to do anything that made any of his children more independent. I think he wanted us all to live on the farm together forever. I wasn't going to do that. Wade was as different from my *daed* as a person can be."

"You said 'was,'" Charlotte said. "So you know that he's dead."

"I heard." His voice was clipped.

"What do you know about his death?" I asked.

"That he died at your jobsite and you shot him," he snapped.

I gasped.

"How do you know he was shot?" Charlotte asked in a small voice.

It was a good question. As far as I knew, the sheriff's department hadn't released the details of Wade's death.

"A lucky guess," he snapped back.

Charlotte looked at me, and I knew we were both thinking the same thing.

He was lying.

Chapter Eighteen

Knowing Jericho would not correct the lie, I decided to pursue another avenue with my questions. "When was the last time you saw Wade?" I asked.

"Why does it matter? He's dead, and I no longer have a job with him. My *daed* got what he wanted in the end like always. The only time he ever lost was when Charlotte left."

Charlotte shifted back and forth on the bank of the pond. The mud under her feet made a squishing sound.

I wanted to say that was exactly why it mattered, but Charlotte spoke first.

"I know you're angry at our *daed* right now, and I don't blame you, *bruder*, but we need your help to find out what happened to Wade. Don't you care about that?"

"Wade was my employer, not my friend."

Was that Jericho's way of saying he didn't care?

"Have the police spoken to you?" I asked.

"Why would the police want to talk to me?"

"You were Wade's apprentice," I said. "You must have a lot of knowledge about him. They will want to speak to Naz too."

"I don't know anything about his life. We spoke about work; that was all."

"Okay, how was work going? I got the impression Wade was running out of money."

He scowled. "He was not *gut* at managing money. That was one thing I tried to help him with when I was his apprentice. I tried to account for all the work his builders and men did on every job."

"He asked you to help him with that?" I asked.

"*Nee*, I took it upon myself to do it. Wade told everyone who worked for him to take more responsibility and get clients of their own and start new ventures that would benefit the company. Being Wade's apprentice, I saw how disorganized the office was. He was sloppy about recording funds and incoming and outgoing shipments and workers to jobsites. Keeping in mind what he said to all staff about taking more responsibility, I started organizing the office and trying to make sense of the money side of the business."

"What did you learn?" Charlotte asked.

He looked at his sister. "Things weren't adding up, but I didn't know why. In fact, I never knew why because Wade found out what I was doing and was furious. I had seen Wade angry many times. He had a short temper, but I have never seen him as angry as he was when he found me organizing his papers in the office. I thought he would fire me on the spot or worse!"

"Why was he so mad?" Charlotte asked.

"He said I was invading his privacy and would not let me explain what I was really doing."

"Did he fire you?" I asked.

"I think he was going to, but he died before it happened. Either way, I am out of work."

"So this was recent?" I asked.

"It was Friday morning," Jericho said.

And by Friday night, Wade was dead. How could these two events not be connected?

Another thought struck me. If Wade had been planning to fire Jericho on Friday, why did he sound like he wanted to keep Jericho working for him during his conversation with Sol Weaver? Had he just wanted to get a rise out of Sol or had he decided to give Jericho another chance? It just didn't make sense to me.

I understood why Wade was upset over Jericho going through his papers. Even if Jericho's motives were innocent as he said, I wouldn't like it if Charlotte went through my business documents and bills without telling me. For me, it had more to do with how I organize things and fear something might be lost, rather than because I had anything to hide.

"Wade stopped working on my building weeks ago," I said. "And I heard there are other places where he halted work. Why?"

"He told me he stopped working for you because you would not pay him what he was owed."

"That's not true," I said. "He asked for more money than we originally agreed upon."

He glared at me. "That wasn't his version of the arrangement."

"I'm sure," I said. "Did he say the same thing about the other jobs he put on hold?"

"*Ya*, he said all of you owed him money, and he wasn't going to do any more work until he got paid."

I pressed my lips together. It seemed I would need to talk to those other business owners. I was especially interested in the new candy shop being built in the county.

Jericho picked up his fishing rod. "That is all I have to say about it."

"Do you know anyone who might have wanted to hurt Wade?" I asked.

"Other than you?" he challenged.

I folded my arms. "Yes, other than me."

"I don't know. Wade was an angry man. I learned much from him, but I can't pretend that I liked working for him. There were many people who got upset with him, but that is the nature of construction. Someone is always upset."

"What about his family? Was he married?" I was surprised I hadn't thought to ask this before. It was something I should have asked Deputy Little or even the sheriff.

"*Nee*, but he was engaged. At least that's what he told me when I first started working there. He said he would be gone for a few months in the spring for his wedding and to travel with his new wife."

I wrinkled my brow. That was just about the time he stopped working on Swissmen Candyworks. Had he been married and away on a long honeymoon without telling me? I supposed when it came to Wade, anything was possible. He wasn't the most communicative person I had ever met.

"Was he gone like he said he would be?" I asked.

He shook his head. "He never left, and I never heard him say a word about his fiancée again." He flipped over the bucket, lifted it up by the handle, and grabbed his tackle box as well. "I have to go."

"Where are you going?" Charlotte asked.

"Home. It's the only place I have to go. I'm out of options. I can't hide from our father by this fishing hole forever. I will tell him that I'm no longer working for Wade. I hope that will be enough for him to forgive me."

"Jericho, I am still your sister. If you ever need help, just find me at the candy shop. I'm there most of the time. We haven't spoken in a long while, but I will always be here for you when you need me."

He looked at her as if he was assessing whether she was telling the truth. I knew she was. Charlotte was the most sincere person I'd ever met. If she said she wanted to help, she really wanted to help.

But I didn't know if Jericho realized the truth about his sister as he walked away without a word.

Chapter Nineteen

When Charlotte and I got back to the village, the Blueberry Bash was in full swing. Charlotte didn't so much as glance at the festivities as she went into Swissmen Sweets, saying that she had a headache. I considered going after her, but I sensed that my young cousin needed some time alone. The day hadn't gone the way she'd wanted, but that was no surprise. Her father had rejected her just as he always had over the last several years. I hoped that she would find a bright spot in the fact that Jericho had been willing to talk to her. No, the conversation hadn't gone exactly well, but it went better than Charlotte's talk with her father.

This brought another thought to mind. What about Charlotte's mother? What did she think about all this? I had met her once when Charlotte left the district. She was a severe woman. I supposed that she would have to be to remain married to a man like Sol Weaver for so long. I was surprised that Charlotte never asked about her. Perhaps she'd been too overwhelmed with everything that was going on when she'd spoken to her father and brother.

I think in some ways, Charlotte had hoped that her conversation with her *daed* would lead to a new beginning with her parents and siblings. It was true that they would never live as a family again, but I knew that Charlotte really wanted them to come to her wedding. I had wanted that for her too. It was unlikely to happen. She hadn't even had an opportunity to bring it up with her father. And because he was the head of the household, it would be his decision whether the family attended. Neither Charlotte's mother, Jericho, Miriam Lee, nor any of the other children, had a vote in the matter.

I tugged on Jethro's leash. "Come on. Let's go find your mom."

I saw Lois moving around the square with a basket hanging from her arm, handing out samples of Swissmen Sweets fudge. Every time she gave a bash-goer a piece, she pointed at the candy shop, and said that they just had to stop by. Many of them started walking in the direction of the candy shop after chatting with Lois. If she kept this up, I would have to hire her as my PR woman for the shop and the factory.

"I just love candy," one woman was saying to Lois as I got closer. "I live on the other side of Millersburg and can't wait until the new candy shop in Charm opens. Then I won't have to drive all the way to Harvest for my Amish candy fix."

I stopped walking when I heard her comment. Should I be worried about this new candy shop in Millersburg? Healthy competition was a good thing, right? That was the saying, anyway.

Lois clicked her tongue. "That new store isn't going to be nearly as good as Swissmen Sweets. It will be worth the drive to come to Harvest."

"It's always worth the drive to Harvest," Margot said as she walked by with a piece of blueberry pie in one hand and her bullhorn in the other. "What's going on here?"

I wasn't surprised Margot had asked. Any time Margot heard someone say anything slightly negative about Harvest, she had to step in and point out the error of their ways.

"It's nothing to worry about, Margot. We were just speaking about the new candy shop opening in Charm," Lois said in a calming tone.

Her tone didn't make any difference as Margot's face turned an alarming shade of red. "A new candy shop? In Holmes County? Does Bailey know about this? Where is Bailey?"

Uh-oh, it was time for me to melt into the blueberry-loving crowd. I wasn't going to be made an example of again.

"Bailey needs to do something about this!"

I scooped up Jethro and ducked around the gazebo, but not before Lois gave me a small wave. She'd known I was there all along. I was grateful she hadn't pointed me out to the woman. Or worse yet, to Margot.

On the other side of the gazebo, I could see the original blueberry princess on her throne. She waved, smiled, and sat for photos with the children on her lap. Seeing how slim she was, I could understand why her dress hadn't fit me. The dress hung off her. It was actually too large for her.

"Are you sad that you couldn't be the princess?" a voice asked.

I turned around to find Devon followed by Z.

Z held a camera on his shoulder, and Devon held the mic.

"I'm not sad in the least."

"Well, I am," Devon said. "It would have been great television. I hate missed opportunities like this."

"Sorry to disappoint you," I said with no remorse in my voice.

She pressed her lips together. "Where have you been all this time? I thought you would be here passing out free samples of your candy again. Instead, the woman from the café is doing it. Not that I blame her. She is good at her task. I saw so many more people take samples from her than any of the other food vendors here. She is a force."

"She is that," I agreed. "Lois is a good friend to the shop and to me."

"Dev," Z put in. "Are we going to get any more shots? I'm hungry and ready for a break."

Devon scowled at her colleague. I would hazard a guess that Devon didn't believe in breaks. She was going to have a tough time with the talent at Gourmet Television if that was the case. I had met many of the celebrity chefs at network events, and most of them were very particular about how many hours they filmed. Now that I'd been doing my show for a few years, I could see why. If you let it, being on television could take over your life.

"Fine," Devon said. "Take five minutes."

"I'll be back in twenty." Z lowered the camera from his shoulder and stalked off.

Devon watched him go. "I really need to replace him. His heart is just not in this story." She turned back to me. "You never answered my question as to where you have been."

I frowned. "Something came up."

"And you didn't tell me about it. We're doing a documentary on you, and that's hard to pull off when you don't tell me where you are or what you're doing." She narrowed her eyes. "You are teetering close to breaching your contract."

I frowned at her. "You are doing a documentary on the construction of the candy factory. Where I was today didn't have to do with that."

At least it didn't directly have to do with that, I thought to myself.

She rolled the microphone back and forth in her hand. "You were investigating the murder, weren't you?"

I wrinkled my nose.

"I see that I guessed right. Were you looking for Charlotte's father? I can't help but notice she's not here. Maybe because she's still talking to her father?"

"Listen, I know I have to work with you as producer of this show, but you promised to leave my Amish family out of it as much as possible. That is in the contract."

"Charlotte's not Amish any longer, now, is she?"

"No, but her family is, and they—whether they like it or not—are my relatives too. Please leave them out of it. They have nothing to do with building the candy factory."

"But do they have anything to do with the murder?"

"No," I said even though I didn't know that for sure.

"Well, you can tell Sheriff Marshall about it

right now. He's just over there." She waved. "Sheriff Marshall! Sheriff Marshall! Bailey has something to tell you."

I clenched my jaw as I looked in the direction she pointed. Sheriff Marshall ambled across the square's bright green grass, grass that was pristine due to the care of Uriah Schrock and Leon Hersh.

The sheriff came over to us. "Miss King, nice to see you again. It seems we've been playing catch-up all day long."

"What are you talking about?" I knew the question sounded harsh and maybe a little disrespectful, but the sheriff was on my last nerve.

"Well, I just happened to be at Linzer Petting Zoo to interview a witness, and I was told by the owner, Emmaus, that you and that little red-headed cousin of yours were just there." He cocked his head. "Now, what would the two of you be doing at the petting zoo in the middle of the day? Shouldn't you be making candy?" He raised his bushy graying brow.

I pressed my lips together, and out of the corner of my eye, I noticed Devon had discreetly raised her cell phone and was likely recording this entire exchange. I thought about telling her to stop, but then decided it might be useful to have the sheriff's words on record.

Sheriff Marshall cocked his head to the other side. "You don't want to talk about it, I see. Maybe we should go to the station to discuss it."

Sitting at the sheriff's station in an interrogation room with Sheriff Marshall was the last thing I wanted to do. "We were visiting Charlotte's family. They have a kettle corn stand there on Saturdays."

"How funny," he said in mock amusement. "I

had a chat with Sol Weaver myself. Now, that is interesting."

I swallowed a smart remark, feeling grateful Charlotte wasn't hearing this. I was also tired of playing games with the sheriff. We could go around and around like this for hours and resolve nothing.

"You spoke to him because Devon caught footage of Sol talking to Wade at the Blueberry Fest just hours before he died."

He shifted his stance and his expression too. His brow furrowed as if he was annoyed that I'd ruined his fun talking around the matter at hand. That was just too bad. I was tired of playing the sheriff's games.

"Yes," was his reply.

"And did you learn anything interesting?" I asked, doubting he had any idea what Sol and Wade's argument had been about. Devon might have recorded them in the background, but she hadn't caught their words. Only I had heard what they'd said to each other. And I wasn't about to repeat it to the sheriff because it only made Sol Weaver look worse. It could get Charlotte's brother Jericho into trouble too.

"Sol wouldn't speak to me. I told him I'd come back with a warrant."

My chest tightened. "A warrant for what?"

"For his arrest, because from what I can tell, he wanted Wade Farmer deader than anyone." He smiled, making his words that much more distasteful.

Chapter Twenty

Charlotte would be heartbroken when she heard the news. Not that I wanted to take blame for the murder, but I had to build some doubt in the sheriff's mind that Sol Weaver was the killer. "I thought you were convinced that I killed Wade Farmer."

"Do you want me to arrest you?" His bushy gray eyebrows moved like two restless caterpillars.

I had to look away. "No, but I'm just making a point that there must still be other suspects in the case. It hasn't even been twenty-four hours since the murder. Is that really enough time to find the killer when there are no witnesses?"

"I'm good at my job. Why do you think I took over this case? It was because I wanted it solved quickly, which I have done. It's good for me to show the boys every now and again what an excellent investigator I am."

The boys? I bit my tongue to stop myself from reminding him that there were at least two female deputies who worked in the department.

"You have to have a better reason to arrest Sol. One conversation at the square with Wade is not enough to prove he's the killer. There were hundreds of people at the Blueberry Bash last night. Who knows how many of them Wade spoke to?"

He eyed me. "Perhaps their conversation is insufficient proof, but the fact that Mr. Farmer was shot with Sol Weaver's rifle is all I need."

I gasped, and then I collected myself. "But how can you know it was his rifle?" I asked. "Most Amish don't register their rifles. It's not required by state law." I didn't add that some Amish still wouldn't register them even if it was required by the state.

"True. His rifle wasn't registered. However, it was found in the dumpster behind the market the night of the murder. The bullet and the gun are a match. Sol Weaver shot Wade Farmer in cold blood through the heart."

My stomach churned. "That's awful, but how do you know the gun was Sol's rifle?"

"His name is on it," he said smugly.

I licked my lips. There was nothing I could say to dispute the facts. If Sol's name was on the gun, then it was likely his. However, I still couldn't believe Charlotte's father would kill a man just because that man would not fire his son. "Did Sol know the rifle was used?"

"Oh, I have already asked Sol where his rifle is."

"And what did he say?"

"He claimed it was stolen weeks ago, but there is no police report about the missing gun. It all hinges on his word, which I don't put much stock in."

"You can't go on the lack of a police report. Very

conservative Amish men like Sol don't file police reports for such things. They don't even file police reports for violent crimes," I argued. "They would want to find the stolen item and deal with the person who took it on their own."

He shrugged. "My hands are tied. I'm just waiting for the judge to sign the paperwork, and then I'm bringing him in. I thought you might be happy. You can go back to making candy and working on your factory. You'll need a new contractor though," he added as if I didn't already know that.

"Bailey! Bailey!" Juliet waved from across the square at me.

The sheriff made a face. It didn't surprise me that he wouldn't care for someone who was as cheerful as Juliet Brook.

"Go back to your life," the sheriff said. "This investigation is over. It would also serve you well to tell that boyfriend of yours to say away from my department. I will not have him meddling." He stalked away.

I frowned. What did he mean by that? Had Aiden been meddling as the sheriff claimed? Or was it just a warning for the future? I decided to worry about that later. Sol Weaver's predicament had to be my focus now. The sheriff's investigation might be over, but mine was just beginning.

"Oh, Bailey," Juliet said when she reached me. "Did you see Reverend Brook on the stage? I'm swooning." She fanned herself.

I turned in the direction of the stage in front of the gazebo. Reverend Brook and the jazz band were playing. Festivalgoers sat on blankets and lawn chairs in front of the concert. I blinked. The reverend—who was typically a reserved guy—swayed back and forth as he played his saxophone, and he was wearing a black sequined vest of all things.

"He seems to be really enjoying it," I managed to say.

She beamed. "He's never as happy as when he's playing music. He really should play his saxophone in church more often. It might bring more of the stodgy members to their feet."

I didn't comment on that. I knew nothing about the stodgy members of Juliet's church.

She bent down and picked up Jethro. "My little piggy wiggy. Did Bailey take good care of you?"

Jethro's eyes bugged out of his head as she squeezed the little pig close to her chest.

"Thank you so much for taking such good care of him. Jethro loves to be with you. You are like two pigs in a blanket."

I didn't know how I felt being called a pig in a blanket, but I smiled anyway. Since the comparison came from Juliet I should take it as a compliment. "It was no trouble," I said even though it kind of was.

"Oh, I will remember that when I ask again." She beamed.

Lying never pays off.

She looked in the direction the sheriff had gone. "Is everything all right? You seemed to be having a very intense conversation with the sheriff."

I forced a smile. "Everything is fine."

"Was he talking to you about Wade?" she asked in a low voice. "It's such a terrible shame. Wade was a longtime member of our church."

I stared at her. "Wade Farmer went to your church?"

That was the last thing I'd thought she was going to say. Though I knew it was an unfair assumption on my part, Wade didn't strike me as a God-fearing man.

"Oh yes, he has been a member for thirty years or so. His attendance tends to be sporadic. He comes and goes as he pleases, but he has done a few construction jobs on the church, which has been so helpful. His work is impeccable. That's why I gave you his name when you were looking for a contractor."

I had forgotten it was Juliet who had initially given me Wade's name in January. She had just been trying to help. Sadly, now, I wished she hadn't.

"Does his family go to your church too?" I asked.

She pressed her lips together. "He doesn't have any family that I know of. His parents have passed on and he's not married. He never spoke of any other relatives."

"I heard he was engaged."

She sighed. "Yes, well that was true. He was engaged, but the bride broke it off. Wade texted Reverend Brook when his bride-to-be canceled the engagement. Personally, I don't think that is appropriate information to share on text message. I can only assume he was so distraught that he could not bring himself to tell the reverend in person or on the phone. People nowadays say all sorts of things in texts, don't they?"

"What can you tell me about his former fiancée?"

"Nothing."

"Nothing?"

"I don't know anything about her, not her name

or where she was from. She was a complete mystery. Reverend Brook didn't know either, and it was a stressor for him. He likes to meet and get to know a couple before the wedding, but Wade said she wasn't coming here until a week before the ceremony. But instead of coming as they had planned, she canceled."

Poor Wade. I'd never thought I'd have much sympathy for the surly contractor, but I had to have some for the man who'd been left at altar, or close to it.

She shook her head. "I can't believe Reverend Brook will officiate over Wade's funeral when he was supposed to be officiating over his wedding. It's such a terrible shame."

It really was.

"Do you know any of Wade's friends? Was he close to anyone at the church?"

"Oh, I don't think so. Wade was one who always had his guard up, as if he was expecting everything to go wrong at a moment's notice."

I could understand after what had happened with his engagement. "If you think of anything else about Wade, can you let me know?"

Her clear forehead puckered. "Bailey, I hope you aren't putting yourself in any type of danger. You know that's not what Aiden would want."

"I'm not. I just would like to know what happened to Wade."

"You have a natural curiosity that cannot be stopped. I have always found it to be an endearing quality in you. I think many people do."

Not the sheriff, I thought.

CHAPTER TWENTY-ONE

I managed to sleep through the next night . . . sort of. I went to bed knowing that Sol Weaver had likely been arrested for Wade Farmer's murder. I had wanted to tell Charlotte what was happening, but she wasn't at Swissmen Sweets after the Blueberry Bash. *Maami* said she had gone with Deputy Little to pick up his parents at the airport.

Poor Charlotte, she was getting married soon, meeting her in-laws for the first time, and dealing with the murder. Deputy Little was second-in-command at the sheriff's department. He had to know if Sol Weaver had already been taken into custody. I couldn't imagine he would keep this a secret from his bride. Even so, I wished I'd gotten the chance to see Charlotte before she left, so I could tell her what was going on, and also tell her we would fight it. I would do whatever I had to in order to prove her father's innocence or possible guilt.

I just wanted to get to the truth . . . whatever the truth might be.

I didn't see Aiden that night; he texted to say he was working late going over the financial accounts of the Linzer Petting Zoo. It was just as well because I was so tired from lack of sleep the night before. He also told me that he had a contractor friend name Jonah Beachy, who was interested in talking to me about the candy factory job, and he could meet me at the factory at four in the afternoon on Sunday. I readily told Aiden to confirm the appointment.

I was up at four the next morning and out the door at four thirty. My idea was to arrive early and finish my paperwork at the candy shop, and then sleuth in the afternoon before my meeting with the new contractor. As it was Sunday, the shop was closed; so typically, I paid bills and placed orders on Sundays.

I chuckled at the very thought of sleuthing. If my mother could see me now, she would grab me by the ear and try to drag me back to Connecticut. Not that I would allow her to.

When I stepped into the candy shop just shy of five in the morning, I found Charlotte sitting on a wooden stool in front of the stainless-steel island, crying into a pot of fresh blueberry jam that she was stirring.

"Charlotte?" I asked.

She dropped the spoon into the pot.

"Bailey!" She jumped out of her seat and rushed toward me, enveloping me in a hug. She smelled of blueberry and the lemon dish soap we used. "Bailey." Her voice was muffled as she cried into my shoulder. "The sheriff arrested my father for Wade Farmer's murder, and it's all my fault."

I stepped back from her embrace and held onto her shoulders. "How can it be your fault?"

"If I'd never left home, Jericho never would have started working for that awful man, and my father would have had nothing to do with Wade Farmer." Her voice cracked.

"That's ridiculous. You can't blame yourself for putting all this in motion." I rubbed her back.

"I can't help it. Jericho was right. I put myself before my family when I left."

She had, but I didn't think that was necessarily wrong. Charlotte was responsible for doing what she needed to do to be happy.

"What does Deputy Little say?" I asked.

She grabbed a paper towel from the roll on the counter and wiped her face. "He says the same thing you do. That it's not my fault, but it is. I know it is."

"And what does he think of the arrest?"

"He says it's solid. My father's hunting rifle is a perfect match to the bullet casing they found in the candy factory." She took a breath. "They found it close to the murder scene."

"I heard."

She pressed the paper towel to the side of her face. "My *daed* didn't do this."

"But you said yesterday that he is capable of killing someone who led one of his children astray."

She wouldn't meet my eyes. "Yes. And I have learned over the last several years that anyone who is pushed far enough is capable of committing a crime, even you or me."

I didn't argue with her on that point, since I had come to the same conclusion.

"But my *daed*, he's frugal. Even if he killed Wade, he would not have thrown away his rifle. It is over eighty years old and belonged to his grandfather. I know the Amish aren't supposed to put too much value in possessions, but just like anyone, some things have sentimental value to us. Think of how Cousin Clara treats her mother's dishes in her apartment or the oil lamp that was her grandmother's."

"The sheriff said his name was carved into the hilt."

"Yes, my *grossdaadi* did that—he was also named Sol Weaver. My *daed* was named after him. Can't you see why he couldn't have done it? He would have been better off killing Wade and taking the rifle home with him. He would not throw it in a dumpster where it could so easily be found."

She had a point and confirmed what I had been thinking about the rifle myself. Finding the rifle in the dumpster just a few yards away from the crime scene seemed a little too convenient. Of course, it wasn't too convenient for the sheriff, who just wanted the case to be wrapped up as soon as possible. It didn't matter to him if he arrested the wrong man, just as long as he made an arrest and convinced the general public that Harvest was still the quiet, sleepy, rural community they had always known.

"Did Deputy Little tell you that's what happened?"

She nodded. "He told me on the way to the airport to pick up his parents. He knew it was bad timing for me, but he didn't want me find out later and wonder why he hadn't told me."

"Why didn't you call me? I would have come to be at your side."

"I didn't think of it. Everything happened so fast, and then Luke's parents were there." She wiped a tear from her eye. "I don't even want to know what they thought of me. I barely spoke on the ride from the airport to their hotel. I didn't know what to say. My mind was whirling over what I had just learned about my father."

I nodded. Deputy Little had picked the wrong time to tell Charlotte about her father's arrest. There wasn't a good time for such news, but it would have been better if he'd told her and then let her stay home so she could digest the information while he went to the airport to pick up his parents by himself. He could have made up an excuse as to why Charlotte couldn't come with him.

"What do we do now?" she asked.

"I had planned to go visit Wade's other clients who were having problems with him. One is English and one is Amish."

"You won't be able to speak to the Amish client on Sunday."

"Probably not, but we can take a look at the new candy shop in Charm. That's where the Amish family is. Maybe it will give us an idea of what they are planning for the new shop."

"You want to snoop on the new shop, don't you?"

"No . . . well . . . maybe a little."

She threw her paper towel in the trash. "Bailey, are you worried about competition from the new shop?"

"Why would I be?" I asked with a worried sounding voice.

"I want to go with you when you talk to the other clients."

"What about your lunch with your in-laws to be?"

"I can ask Luke where we are meeting. You can drop me off there. He can take me home."

I pressed my lips together. It wasn't that I didn't want Charlotte to go with me. It was always nice to have her company, but I didn't know if it was wise to involve her any more than she already was involved. Her family was a huge part of this case. I didn't want Sheriff Marshall to get the idea that she knew something and then charge her with obstruction of justice, or something similar.

However, I knew if I were in the same position, I would have insisted I go along too. Charlotte was very much like me in that way.

"All right," I agreed. "We'll leave at ten."

"I'll be ready," she said and then left the kitchen.

I watched her go with an ache in my heart. I had never seen Charlotte so upset. She hadn't even been this upset when she left her community. I wanted to solve this case before her wedding so she could enjoy her big day. I wanted my happy-go-lucky cousin back.

Chapter Twenty-two

When I came out of the kitchen just before ten, Charlotte was waiting for me on the other side of the counter, but she wasn't alone. Devon Cruz was also sitting there, texting on her phone. When I appeared, she shoved her phone into her pocket. "Bailey! Finally. Let's go. We have a murder to solve."

I looked at Charlotte. "When I came down into the candy shop from the apartment, she was already here."

"Your grandmother let me in on her way out to church," Devon said as if she'd anticipated my question as to how she'd gotten inside the locked building on a Sunday morning. Nothing in Harvest was open on Sunday morning, not even the one gas station in the village.

Letting Devon inside sounded like something that my grandmother would do. She was far too trusting. Devon could have easily said that I had a meeting planned with her that morning. My *grossmaami* would take her declaration as fact.

Devon folded her hands on the table. "I need to know what's going on with the factory construction. My bosses have heard the news about the murder and are calling me from New York. They want to pull the plug on this. We can't let that happen."

Under the circumstances, canceling the documentary didn't sound like a horrible idea.

"I can't tell you when work will start again. I have to find a new contractor."

"This is Amish Country. Everyone here knows how to build or is related to someone who does. You'll be able to start in no time. There's nothing to hold you back."

Charlotte shifted uncomfortably in her seat.

Devon covered her mouth. "Oh sorry, the killer is your dad." She made a face. "That's unlucky."

"My father didn't kill anyone," Charlotte said. "And Bailey and I are going to prove that."

"Oh!" A bright sparkle came into Devon's eyes. "I'm going with you then. We need this on camera."

I folded my arms. "You can't come with us."

Her eyes went wide. "I have to. It's my job right now to document your life and that's what I'm going to do."

"It's hard enough getting people to speak to us about a man's murder. They aren't going to do it with a camera in their faces," I said.

"I won't take the camera. I'll just use the information for backstory." She flattened her hands on the tabletop. "You want me there. I'm great at getting information out of people. How do you think I'm so young and successful?"

I shook my head. At least she was modest about it.

"If you don't let me go, I will follow you. I have the rental car just outside."

I rubbed my aching head. Arguing with Devon was only wasting precious time, and I didn't want to be part of a high-speed chase through Amish Country. "Fine, you can come."

Devon jumped out of her chair and clapped her hands. "Let's go!" She stopped. "Where are we going?"

"We'll tell you on the way."

During the drive to Charm, I told Devon that we were going to see clients who'd also experienced construction delays because Wade was asking for more money.

"Suspects, you mean," was her response.

Bringing Devon had been a lapse in judgment on my part. The only thing that would have made this trip worse would've been having Jethro with us. Thankfully, I hadn't yet heard from Juliet that day about pig sitting. I hoped that would be the case for the rest of the day. I loved Jethro like my own pet—for the most part—but having a pig in tow did make it a little bit more challenging when I was trying to find a killer.

The house that was under construction was way off the road. Tire tracks in the dirt were the only indication of the driveway. The earth was disturbed to the left of the driveway in a line that I guessed was the electrical connection to the house, which was buried underground. It was a helpful landmark to keep us on the driveway because at times I was driving directly on weeds.

"This is really rural," Devon said from the back seat.

Charlotte and I shared a look.

Finally, we came upon a giant hole in the ground. A backhoe loomed over the hole. The operator lowered the digger into the earth and came up with a bucketful of dirt. The machine made a grinding noise as it turned and dumped dirt and rock on a growing pile ten feet from the hole's edge.

The machine came to a stop and shut off as we parked. A man climbed out of the backhoe. He was covered from head to foot in mud. He even had mud in his goatee. His eyes were bloodshot and there was dust on his eyelashes as if he'd rubbed his eyes with his dirty gloves. He looked hot and miserable and I felt instant sympathy for him.

However, the sympathetic feeling didn't last long.

"What do you want?" we heard him call through the open windows in the car. "This is private property. You need to leave! I don't allow solicitors on my land. Whatever it is you're selling, I'm not buying."

"That's not the warmest welcome I've ever received," Devon muttered.

I was willing to bet it wasn't the worst welcome that Devon had received either.

"It looks like he's having a bad day," Charlotte said softly. As usual she was giving the stranger the benefit of the doubt. However, I agreed. From his appearance and the half-dug hole in the ground, it seemed the man was having a very bad day indeed.

I stepped out of the car, and the man bellowed at us again. "What do you want? I told you I'm not buying!"

"We aren't selling anything," I said.

Behind me the car doors opened and Devon and Charlotte both got out.

"Three women?" He looked over my shoulder at them. "Are the three of you lost or something? Is the GPS not working on your phones? That happens sometimes way out here. That's why I like it." His tone was a bit calmer and he relaxed his stance. I supposed he didn't take us as a threat or as sales people any longer.

I stepped forward. "We are looking for Russel Kite. We were told this was his property."

He removed his gloves. "That's me, and this is my property." His guarded tone was back. "What do you want?"

"I wanted to talk to you about Wade Farmer."

"Wade Farmer? Did that good-for-nothing send you here? I have a message for you to take back to him. No more money. He fleeced me enough. All I am trying to do is build a house, and he took advantage of that. I'm done with contractors. I'm doing it myself. He cost me my marriage. I owe him nothing."

I raised my brow. "Your marriage?"

"My wife left me over this land. I bought it years ago before I met her, and I always planned to build a house here. When I first met Wade, I thought he was the man to do it. He liked my plans and the creative details of the home that I wanted to include." He pointed at the hole in the ground. "He never got any further than this. He didn't even finish digging out the basement. Everything was taking so long, and I wasn't going to give him one more red cent if he didn't do what he'd already agreed to do. We came to a standstill. My wife lost her patience and left."

I grimaced. It sounded very similar to my own dealings with Wade, but at least I had a structure standing and hadn't lost a spouse over it.

"I'm doing it myself from here on out. Now, I can only work on the weekends because of my day job, so it's going to take a long while. However, I don't have my wife around anymore to nag me about hurrying up."

I stared at the raw hole in the ground. It didn't look as if the work was going very well.

As if he knew what I was thinking, he said. "I have to dig out the basement again. Wade's crew did it, and it caved in two days later. I told him that it would rain and this could happen. I asked him to shore the walls up before the rain hit, but as usual he didn't listen to me. He was so focused on his upcoming wedding, there was no time for anything else. He was acting like a woman if you ask me."

I let the last comment slide because I just wanted to get to the facts. "You knew he was getting married?"

His eyes slid in my direction. "I overheard him talking to his fiancée on the phone. Something about her needing more money to put a deposit down on her dress or some such thing. He said he would send the money as soon as he could. He saw me eavesdropping and when he got off the phone, he explained that it was his fiancée who was planning their wedding out of state. The destination wedding was making things more complicated. At that time, we were on good terms so I told him that I understood what a bridezilla was like. I had one of my own. Nothing was good enough for her. I should have known that wouldn't change when we were married."

I raised my brow. Was this man really half of the "nice young couple" that Lois chatted with at the Sunbeam Café? I wasn't seeing much nice about him. However, Lois had the ability to see the good in people just as Charlotte did. Maybe that was something I needed to work on.

"So if you want to talk about Wade Farmer, I suggest that you turn around and leave right now and find someone else to talk to about him. I have nothing kind to say about the man."

"Wade Farmer is dead," Devon blurted out, holding up her camera as if she was ready to record his reaction.

I stopped just short of slapping my forehead. I knew bringing Devon with us was a bad idea.

"Dead? How could he be dead? I just spoke to him this morning," Russell said.

Chapter Twenty-Three

"You spoke to Wade this morning?" I asked. "That's not possible."

"Why are the three of you looking at me like that is so unbelievable?" He pulled his phone out of his pocket. "Here's the call right there."

"Because he's dead," Devon said. "He's been dead for two days."

"I just spoke to him. He can't be dead. I'm telling you, I had a conversation with him."

Russell grew angrier by the second, and I knew we weren't going to get anywhere if Devon and Russell got into a dead/not dead argument.

"What did you talk about with him?" I asked.

"What is it every time he calls? Money. He was asking for more money. He said if I wanted my basement dug out again, it was going to cost me. I told him I would see him in court."

"You planned to sue?" Devon asked.

"Why not? Everything on this job has been behind. It's not to do with the supplies like he said earlier. I found out who all his suppliers were and called them. Every last one of them told me that my materials had shipped to Wade's workshop. He was holding them hostage, hoping for more money up front from me. No ma'am, that was not going to happen. Do I look like I was born yesterday?"

"No," Charlotte said quietly. The rhetorical question was lost on my formerly Amish cousin.

"The man you spoke to, how did you know it was Wade?" I asked.

He narrowed his eyes at me. "Do you doubt my story?"

Yeah, I did because Wade Farmer died two nights ago, but I wasn't going to say that to a man who could run a backhoe.

When I didn't say anything, Russell went on, "He called from Wade's number."

"His cell number or his landline?" I asked.

"Landline," he snapped. "I don't know why that would make a difference."

It made a difference because I knew the sheriff's department had found Wade's cell on him at the crime scene. If the call had been made by the cell, it would have been very significant. The landline still told me something though. It told me that someone had broken into his workshop to make that call or that person had a key. The fiancée maybe? She was the most likely person to have a key, right? But Russell would have known he was speaking to a woman. Wade had no other family to speak of, but he was supposed to have been married in the spring. Spring had come and gone, and the wedding never happened. Had the wedding been called off or delayed? As of yet, no one had been able to answer that question for me.

"You said that Wade was getting married. Do you know his fiancée's name?"

"No. Why would I know that? It's none of my business, nor do I care. All I wanted from him was to finish my house. He's not doing what he should, so I'm suing him for all he is worth."

It seemed the fact that Wade was dead was completely lost on him.

"Did it sound like Wade?" Charlotte asked.

I glanced at my cousin. It was a good question and one I should have asked from the start.

"More or less," Russell said.

He must have seen the incredulity on our faces because he said, "Wade said he had a cold, which was why his voice sounded a little off. I took him at his word."

I frowned. It sounded like this was the only time Russell had taken Wade—in this case a false Wade—at his word.

Russell put his gloves back on. "I have to get back to work. I don't know what your story is, but if you see Wade, tell him he's not going to pull the wool over my eyes again."

"One more question," I said.

"If I answer it, do you promise to leave?"

I nodded.

He brushed dirt off his arm, not that it helped much. "What is it?"

"Where were you Friday night?"

He scowled, and I didn't think he would answer. "I was at the Blueberry Bash. That's where my wife told me she wanted a divorce."

When we got back in the car, Devon spoke up. "He really thinks Wade Farmer is still alive. Even if I believed that, I would still pull out my phone and check the news to verify I was right. Why didn't he do that?"

"There's no service out here," I said, looking at my own phone. "He'd be lucky if his text messages were still coming through. He's also furious, and all he's conscious of right now is his anger at Wade."

"Sounds like it's understandable," Charlotte said. "Wade was doing the same thing to Russell as he was to you. Asking for more money before he would work." She paused. "And if he was asking for all that money for his wedding, why didn't he get married like he said he would?"

"I've been wondering the same thing," I said as the car bumped down the dirt driveway. "Let's go back to Swissmen Sweets."

"It's more than that too," Devon said. "Wade cost Russell his marriage, or at least that's how he sees it. His wife left him the evening of the Blueberry Bash, and hours later Wade is dead. Seems to me those two things are connected."

She had a point, and I would normally be in agreement with her, but the issue I was having was the way Wade was killed. It didn't seem to me that it was a murder of sudden rage or anger. If it had been, then Russell would be at the top of my list.

No, Wade had been shot through the heart with a rifle. It was as if he had been hunted. I shivered at the very idea. I still didn't know why Wade had been up on the scaffolding in the first place, and I don't think the sheriff knew either.

"I thought you said there were two stops that you needed to make," Devon chimed in, breaking me away from dark thoughts. "I want to be there when you do that. It will be great for the documentary to show you checking out the rival candy store."

"The owners are Amish, and it's Sunday. It would not be a good time for me to meet them," I said.

She fell back in her seat. "Oh right. The Amish and Sundays," she said as if the Amish purposely honored the Sabbath to make her life more difficult.

Truthfully, I was planning to check out the new candy shop later in the day, but I didn't want Devon with me. It was hard enough to talk to an English witness with her around. It would likely go much worse with an Amish one.

Twenty minutes later, we arrived back in the center of Harvest. It was a summer Sunday afternoon and there were people spilling out of Juliet's church, but very little else going on. Devon leaned over the seat. "Are you going to call the sheriff and tell him what Russell said?"

I parked the car in one of the spots just in front of Swissmen Sweets. Since it was Sunday, I didn't have to worry about taking a customer parking space.

I planned to report what I'd learned to Deputy Little, not the sheriff directly. I doubted Sheriff Marshall would be receptive to anything I had to say in relation to Wade's murder. To him, it was an open-and-shut case.

I was saved from answering the question by Charlotte, who gasped, "They're here."

"Who is . . ." I started to ask, but I trailed off when I saw Deputy Little walk across the square with a couple who appeared to be in their late fifties. The older man looked like Deputy Little in about twenty years. He was the same height and had the same wide shoulders. He even cut his hair like Deputy Little too.

Charlotte quickly finger-combed her hair and looked at her reflection in her visor's mirror. "I forgot Luke was bringing his parents to the candy shop after church. How could I have forgotten that? They wanted to meet you and Cousin Clara because I talked about you both so much during our phone conversations." She looked at me. "How horrible do I look?"

Devon leaned forward again. "Who's Luke?" She peered over Charlotte's shoulder. "Is that the sheriff's deputy? Looks like we have someone to tell about Russell's crank call!"

"Devon, wait!" I said, but it was too late.

"Deputy!" Devon called.

"Oh no," Charlotte whispered.

My sentiments exactly.

Chapter Twenty-Four

"Someone called him pretending to be a dead man, and you aren't taking me seriously!" Devon cried.

Deputy Little glanced at his parents.

"Lukey, are you going to introduce us to your friend?" his mother asked.

Lukey? Quiet Deputy Little didn't look like a Lukey to me. I didn't think that Deputy Little cared for the nickname either, based on the bright shade of red his cheeks turned.

Deputy Little's mom held out her hand to Devon. "You must be Bailey. It's nice to finally meet you. We've heard all about you from Charlotte. She really thinks you are the cat's meow. I'm Lukey's mother, Beth, and this is my husband, Hal." She paused. "I have to say that I didn't expect your hair to be so wild. Charlotte said that you have a program on cable television, and I would not think that yellow would look all that well under the harsh studio lights." She chuckled. "But what do I know? We don't have cable at our house. There is just garbage on television now, don't you think?" She slapped her cheek. "You wouldn't think that since you are on it." She tittered.

"Mom," Deputy Little said. "She's not Bailey." He pointed to me. "She is."

I waved.

"Oh." Beth dropped Devon's hand as if it was a hot plate. "Then who are you? Another cousin?"

"No," Devon said. "I'm the producer of Bailey's new show. However, right now, I am a concerned citizen who wants to report a crime to the deputy."

Beth placed a hand on her chest. "Oh my! Luke, can you ever get away from your work? I wish that you had become a mechanical engineer like your father. The hours are regular and you get all the holidays off."

Deputy Little didn't even react to her comment, which made me think it was something she'd said many times before.

Hal Little stuck his hands in his pockets and observed the entire scene. He didn't say a word. I guessed that Deputy Little got his quiet nature from his father, not from his talkative mother.

"Mr. and Mrs. Little." Charlotte tried to usher the couple toward Swissmen Sweets. "Bailey and I were just going into the shop to wait for your visit. We are so glad you're here. Cousin Clara is still at church and will be until late afternoon, but you can come in and see the shop." She looked at me.

I nodded and removed the shop key from my pocket.

"Hey," Devon said. "Did anyone hear me? I said that I have to report a crime."

"Charlotte," Deputy Little said. "Why don't you take my parents inside, so I can speak to Devon?"

I handed Charlotte the shop keys.

She unlocked the door and said, "You will have to try some of Bailey's blueberry-and-cream fudge. She came up with the recipe just for the Blueberry Bash. There's no bash today because it's Sunday. I'm sorry that you missed it."

"Oh, we are too," Beth said, following her husband and Charlotte into the shop.

I stayed where I was on the sidewalk in front of Swissmen Sweets.

"Bailey?" Deputy Little raised his brow at me.

"I want to be here for this. I was with Devon when she learned about the crime."

"Charlotte was with you too." It was a question but came out as a statement.

I gave a slight nod.

He sighed. I knew Deputy Little didn't want his bride-to-be involved in any criminal investigations, but it was out of his control.

"Tell me what happened," the deputy said.

Devon quickly recited how the visit to Russell's house site had gone, and I jumped in every so often to add details or offer a small correction. Devon made Russell seem a lot more hostile than he'd actually been. It was true he hadn't been happy we were there, but I'd never felt I was in danger. At least, not too much danger.

"The three of you shouldn't have gone out there alone," Deputy Little said when Devon finished her story. "You didn't know the man or what he was capable of, and you were in the middle of nowhere. You can't tell me the cell reception was good out there."

It hadn't been, but I saw no reason to say that.

Deputy Little folded his arms. "I'll speak to Russell. It's clear that someone was impersonating Wade. The question is why. We know it wasn't Charlotte's father who made the call. He's in the county jail." He cast a sympathetic look toward the candy shop, where his fiancée was showing his parents around.

"How is Sol doing?" I asked, looking over my shoulder as if I was afraid that Charlotte might come outside and hear.

"I checked on him this morning, and he's angry but okay." From the way Deputy Little winced when he said it, I guessed that a lot of Sol's anger had been directed at him.

"I think we should all go talk to Russell now. I'll just get my cameraman and we'll head out. It'll be a great scene for the show."

"The show?" Deputy Little asked. "You're not going to record this."

"Why do you think I'm helping you? It's not out of the kindness of my heart."

"I didn't think it was," I muttered.

Deputy Little shot me a look that said I wasn't helping the situation. He then glanced at the candy shop. "I hate to leave Charlotte alone with my parents, but I should be the one who speaks to Russell not . . ." He didn't finish his statement. We both knew that he was thinking about the sheriff.

"Charlotte and I can entertain your parents for a bit while you speak to Russell," I said.

"I'll go with you, Deputy," Devon volunteered.

He stared at her.

Devon's phone buzzed. She read the screen and her demeanor completely changed. "On second thought, you need to handle this one alone. I have to go." She took off across Main Street and the square in the direction of her B&B.

"What was all that about?" Deputy Little asked.

"If I knew I would tell you."

"I'd better go before she comes back and changes her mind. I'll run inside and say goodbye to my parents." He twisted his mouth. "It would be a big help to Charlotte if you could stay with her. My mom can be a tad overwhelming."

"Got it."

Deputy Little and I entered the candy shop, and he explained that he had to do a quick interview for the sheriff's department.

Beth shook her head. "Oh, Lukey, I wish you were in another sort of work. Don't you want to be with us? Our visit is so short."

"I won't be gone long," Deputy Little replied. "In the meantime, you can get to know Charlotte better."

My cousin's eyes went wide as if she thought that was a frightening idea.

"I can help Charlotte show you around too," I said.

"Well, it will be very exciting to have a village tour with a celebrity. Won't it, Hal? If we enjoy it, we might even consider getting cable again."

I smiled.

Deputy Little took that as his cue to bolt.

"Charlotte was such a dear and showed us around the candy shop. It's just darling. I'm so surprised you are able to do so much in such a small space. It really is remarkable. My own kitchen is twice the size of yours here, and I always feel like I'm running out of counter space."

"I'm disappointed so much is closed today," Hal Little said.

"It's out of respect for the Amish traditions," I said.

"I can see that, but they need to think about the non-Amish too. They should think about making money. They're losing revenue being closed on a Sunday."

I didn't bother to reply. It wasn't anything that the business owners in Harvest hadn't heard before.

"There is a lot of lovely scenery. We could go for a drive," Charlotte suggested.

"I get car sick," Beth said. "The rolling hills around here really do a number on my system. No. We want to see the candy factory!" Beth Little said. "It's so exciting that you are able to build something so grand."

I glanced at Charlotte, who shrugged. In the sheriff's mind the case was closed, so I was welcome to go back to my shell of a building when I was ready. I just hadn't expected the first time to be with Charlotte's in-laws-to-be.

"I'd like to see it too," Hal said. "Charlotte said she will be working there."

"Yes, some of the time at least. We have to finish the build before we make decisions about the staff."

"I want to see it especially if Charlotte is going to be working there. We need to know it will be safe for her."

I forced a smile. "We can go to the building. There was a small accident on the scaffold. We are in the process of dealing with . . ." I trailed off.

As far as I was aware the Littles knew nothing

about the murder, and I planned to keep it that way.

Beth waved her hand. "We don't mind a little mess. We know it's a construction site. You should have seen our property when we built our house. Drywall is the worst. The dust gets everywhere. It's enough to drive you crazy."

"We aren't at the drywall stage yet, so dust won't be a concern," I said.

"Oh good. Dust is terrible for my allergies. I just cannot tolerate it." She scrunched up her nose. "It tickles my nose just thinking about it."

Beth and Hal Little followed Charlotte and me across the square.

"I don't know if they like me," Charlotte whispered.

I glanced over my shoulder. As we walked, Beth and Hal appraised everything. It was as if they were giving everything they saw a grade in their heads. From the furrow of Hal's brow, I guessed Harvest was barely passing.

"Why do you say that?" I asked Charlotte.

"Because they keep asking questions and when I answer, they say, 'that's interesting.' But I think for them 'that's interesting' actually means the opposite."

I patted her arm. "You're overthinking it. Besides, even if they don't like you, they live hundreds of miles away. You won't really have to deal with them."

"Charlotte," Beth called from behind us. "Did Lukey tell you that we are planning to move to Harvest in a couple of years? By then, we assume that they two of you will have children, and we want to be part of our grandchildren's lives. So we will leave the house where we have spent the entirety of our marriage to move near you. Lukey doesn't seem interested in looking for work by us." She said this last part as if it were a bit of a sore spot for her.

Charlotte stared at me with terror in her eyes. So much for the hundreds of miles away promise.

Hal looked left and right. "It's really like a ghost town here. You would never know anyone lived in this place. It's creepy. I hope things pick up or living here will be a bore. I'm retired, not dead."

Creepy was the last word that I would use to describe Harvest, and I had to wonder what kind of excitement Hal Little was searching for.

"You will have to excuse my husband," Beth said. "We live on the outskirts of DC, and we are used to the hubbub of the city. This is so different. How did you manage to adapt after New York?"

"It was a change," I admitted. "But I found that I like it. It also helps that the shop is closed on Sunday. It forces me to take time off. That was something I would never have done in New York."

Charlotte gave me a look. She knew that I rarely took time off work even on Sunday, but managing the business without customers did feel a little bit like a vacation to me.

We turned the corner and the market's empty parking lot came into view. My heart skipped a beat. The last time I walked through this empty parking lot, I found a dead body. I bit the inside of my lip. I wasn't sure this was such a great idea. I hadn't been inside the building since the discovery, and I didn't know what condition the deputies and crime-scene techs had left it in.

"Charlotte, I'm going to run ahead and make

sure everything at the factory is okey dokey," I said in a fake cheery voice.

Her eyes went wide as if she immediately understood what I was getting at. I needed to make sure there were no signs of murder.

I took off at a jog toward the candy factory.

"Where is she going?" Beth called behind me.

I was out of breath when I reached the side door of the factory. Running wasn't a normal activity of mine. Taste-testing candy recipes was much more my speed.

I stepped into the building and was grateful for the afternoon sunlight pouring through the windows and the openings where windows should be. In the first room, there was nothing out of order. A cinder block and a few dusty boards sat in one corner. They had been there ever since Wade stopped working on the job.

I went through the framing into the largest room, where the factory space and the scaffolding were and where Charlotte and I had found the body. There were no signs that a murder had taken place there. There was no visible blood on the concrete or bullet holes in the two-by-fours. Deputy Little had arranged for the stains to be cleaned for us, and by the looks of it, it had been done recently because the floor under the scaffolding was still wet.

I let my shoulders sag as relief washed over me. I looked up at the scaffolding. Now, I just had to figure out how to hire a new general contractor, get this scaffolding out of here, and make my deadline for the grand opening. It was going to be no small feat to accomplish any one of those things, let alone all three. In fact, I was starting to believe that making the August deadline for the grand opening was an impossible task.

I turned to go back into the first room in order to greet the Littles and Charlotte. I was almost across the threshold when I heard a creak above me.

I looked up and saw nothing. Shaking my head, I was about to turn and leave, when I heard the creaking sound again and the scaffolding swayed slightly.

Had a squirrel or a raccoon gotten into the factory and climbed that scaffolding? It was certainly possible. There were so many wide-open entry points into the building.

I walked back into the room. "Hey! Hey, squirrel! Get out of here."

Above my head I head the distinctive sound of a footstep—and one a lot heavier than a squirrel's.

CHAPTER TWENTY-FIVE

My mouth felt dry, but I wasn't going to run away from whatever or whoever had made that sound. "Hey! Who is up there?"

There was the sound of running feet moving across the scaffolding, and the structure shook as someone shimmied down the back. Could it be the killer coming back to the scene of the crime? This worry cost me precious seconds of indecision. In that time, a person dressed in dark clothing ran through the loading dock.

I snapped out of my daze and ran after them. By the time I got outside, the intruder was gone. Whoever they were, they could run fast. By the brief look I'd gotten of the clothing and build, it'd likely been a man. I couldn't know that for sure though.

Just to be certain the intruder wasn't still nearby, I ran around the back of the building. I didn't see anyone there. There was a noise behind me and I turned fast. Only to run face-first into a man's chest.

I rubbed my nose. "Aiden, what are you doing back here?"

"I was wondering the same thing about you when I saw you racing around the building. What's going on?"

"There was someone in the factory just a moment ago. I asked who it was and they ran." I tried to slow down my breath.

"Was it a man or a woman?" he asked. "Did you see the person's face?"

"I would guess a man, but I don't know for sure. I didn't see their face."

He put his hands on my shoulders. "Are you okay? You look a little spooked."

"For good reason. Whoever it was had climbed up on the scaffolding where Wade Farmer died. I can only guess that the person was up there because of the murder. I can't think of any other reason anyone would climb up there after what happened to Wade. They weren't there to finish my ceiling, I know that."

He frowned. "Let me go in the building and make sure that it's clear. Are you here alone?"

I shook my head. "No. Charlotte and Deputy Little's parents are walking toward the building. They might be here right now. I ran ahead to . . ."

"Make sure there weren't signs of a murder," he finished for me.

I grimaced. "Yes. I don't want Charlotte to have to explain what happened here to her new in-laws."

"At least my mother is more understanding of you in that regard," he said, trying to make me smile.

Aiden walked back around the building, and I followed him. We entered the factory through the loading dock and found Charlotte and the Littles in the main room with the scaffolding.

"That's where the fudge making area will be," Charlotte said, pointing to one corner of the room. "It's on the north side of the building, so it will be the coolest spot even in the summer. Of course we'll have central air too, but fudge does better in cool temperatures and we took that into consideration in the plans."

I raised my brow. I was impressed by Charlotte's speech. She had been listening when I rambled on for hours and hours about how I wanted the building to be and why. Maybe I should've made her my general contractor.

"Oh, Bailey," Charlotte said. "I hope it was okay that we came in." She glanced at Beth and Hal. "They couldn't wait to see it."

"We were surprised that you weren't here," Beth said.

I smiled. "I ran into my boyfriend outside. He came here to surprise me."

I didn't know if that really was the reason Aiden had come to the factory, but I didn't want to say he was here because of the murder.

"Aiden, these are Luke's parents," I said.

"It's nice to meet you. Luke is a good friend of mine, and he's always spoken highly of his family."

Hal held out to his hand to Aiden, who shook it. "You must be Aiden Brody. Luke spoke very highly of you too. It's a shame you left the department. He admired you quite a bit. However, I understand the need to try something new. I guess working for the state was a big step up for you. Where are you working out of?"

Aiden shifted his feet. "I'm working here in Harvest. I left Ohio's BCI to come back home."

"Are you back at the sheriff's department?" Hal asked.

"No. I'm working as a private detective."

Hal dropped both hands to his sides. "A private detective? Is that a wise decision? There is not a lot of stability with that work." He shook his head. "I would not be drawn to such a position with so much uncertainty."

I winced. Aiden didn't need any more discouragement about his business.

However, Aiden smiled and took the comments in stride. "I like a challenge." He changed the subject. "And I have to congratulate you on the upcoming wedding. Charlotte is a great person. She will be a wonderful addition to your family."

Aiden's change of the subject wasn't lost on me.

Beth glanced in Charlotte's direction as if to assess whether this was true.

My cousin's cheeks turned bright red at Aiden's praise, but everything he said was true. The Littles were lucky to have Charlotte join their family.

I squeezed Charlotte's arm. "Why don't you walk them around the building and keep explaining the vision. You were doing such a good job when I came in, I was sorry to interrupt."

"Really?" Her eyes brightened under the praise. Her response reminded me that I needed to tell Charlotte more often what a great job she was doing. I didn't believe it was something she'd heard much of growing up.

"Why don't you start in the front room where the tasting and retail space will be?" I suggested.

"Sure . . ." Charlotte said, looking from Aiden to me as if she knew we wanted a private moment.

However, there was nothing romantic about our conversation when it pertained to murder.

Charlotte led Deputy Little's parents back into the first room. When they were out of earshot, Aiden said, "Tell me everything you heard and saw when you entered the building."

I swallowed my annoyance that he was asking me to repeat my story. I knew it was just to help him understand the scene better. Once a cop, always a cop.

When I finished, Aiden walked over to the scaffolding. "I'm going to climb to the top and take a look. Maybe there is something that I can learn from a bird's-eye view."

The scaffolding didn't look like it was that safe. Some of the connections were rusted and the paint was crumbling off. I didn't like the idea of Aiden climbing it, but I knew that it was a waste of time to tell him to stop.

He shimmied up the side of the structure as if it were the monkey bars on the playground. He didn't look down once. When he was at the top, I could hear him walking back and forth on the platform. It was the same footstep sound that I'd heard when the intruder was up there. The sound of boots on the wooden boards echoed through the building.

"There's nothing up here." He leaned over the side and looked down at me. "I didn't expect there to be. The sheriff wouldn't leave any evidence behind. I wonder why the person bothered to climb up here." He leaned farther over the railing. "Wait. I think I notice something."

"Be careful," I warned.

"I am. This is pretty sturdily built." He shook the railing. "It isn't going anywhere." He stood on his tiptoes and tried to reach up and touch the rafters.

"Please don't do that," I said. "What are you looking at?"

The railing wobbled, and to my horror, I saw it break loose from the scaffold. Aiden cried out.

I screamed.

CHAPTER TWENTY-SIX

I had my hands over my face. I didn't want to move them and find Aiden crumpled at my feet.

"Bailey," Aiden said.

I slowly opened my fingers to peek through them at the concrete slab.

"I'm still up here." Aiden waved.

All the breath whooshed out of me in a sigh of relief as I looked up. "You scared me to death."

He smiled. "I'm sorry about that, but I really did find something up here. I think we need to call Little."

I cranked my neck back. "What is it?"

"A bullet hole through the roof."

I remembered the blood I had seen on the beams. Deputy Little's cleaning crew had washed that away too.

"How did the deputies miss that?" I asked.

He pointed up. "My guess is the tar paper from the roof covered up the hole, but it was pretty windy last night. The wind moved the paper enough that I could see a prick of sunlight coming through." He pointed up.

I bent my neck back as far as it would go and saw the faintest dot of light. I shook my head. Aiden really was a good investigator to notice that, especially with all the light coming into the building from the many windows.

"What is going on in here?" Hal Little said as he came into the room. "We heard a scream."

Aiden climbed down the scaffolding. "I'm sorry. That was my fault. I climbed up there for a better view, and Baily got nervous."

Beth pressed a hand to her chest. "I would get nervous too. If you fell from that height, you'd surely die. There is no soft surface to land on."

I glanced at Aiden. He gave me a sheepish shrug.

"I admit it was stupid." He wrapped his arm around my shoulders. "I'm sorry, sweetheart."

"Don't do it again," I said with a smile.

He nodded and dropped his arm. "I have to make a phone call, so I'm going to step out for a minute." He disappeared through the loading door.

"These young men today," Beth said with the click of her tongue. "They are always running off."

"Where does our tour go now?" Hal asked. "We've seen this building. Is anything else in this town open? I'm not one to sit around and twiddle my thumbs."

"Charlotte, I'm sure Juliet and Reverend Brook are still at the church. Why don't you take Beth and Hal to meet them?"

"That's a good idea," Charlotte said. "Reverend Brook will be officiating at our wedding."

"I would like to meet him," Beth said. "I'd like to know how the ceremony is going to go. I have some suggestions. There are certain Little family traditions that must be included. Since Lukey is an only child, and last in our line, we must uphold tradition."

Charlotte swayed a bit as if she might faint. Between Wade's murder, her father being arrested, and a bossy set of in-laws, she wasn't having the best weekend.

"You will love the reverend and his wife Juliet," I said. "They are two of the kindest and most understanding people you will ever meet. I'm sure Reverend Brook would take any suggestion that you might have into consideration."

After Charlotte and the Littles left, I stepped out of the factory to look for Aiden. I found him pacing in the market parking lot, talking on the phone. I could tell he was upset by the way he moved his hands as he spoke.

"I think it's something worth looking into." There was a pause. "Yes, I understand that I'm not working for the department any longer, but I'm telling you this as a concerned citizen." There was another pause. "I understand." Aiden ended the call and clenched his phone in his hand as if he was afraid that he would slam it on the pavement if he didn't have a good hold on it.

"Is everything okay?"

He turned to me and took a deep breath. "It will be okay eventually."

"Who were you talking to?"

"The sheriff. I couldn't get hold of Little. Probably because he's at Russell's jobsite and out of cell range." He sighed. "I don't work for the department any longer so I can't radio him or call dispatch to do so. Because I couldn't reach him, I decided that I would do the right thing and report the bullet hole in the roof to the sheriff."

"How'd that go?" I asked even though I had a pretty good guess.

"As well as I expected."

"Is he coming out or sending a deputy?"

"He said no. As far as he's concerned, it's an open-and-shut case now that he has Sol Weaver in custody. He said it would have been worth his trouble if I found the bullet, which I didn't. He said that he had a bullet casing that was a match to Sol's rifle. He claimed that was all he needed."

"But won't it help his case against Sol to consider this evidence? It's more proof the rifle was fired inside the factory, and proof that whoever shot Wade most likely did it from below while he was on the scaffolding. I have to believe he climbed up there of his own free will. I don't know how anyone could have convinced him to go up there."

"The sheriff doesn't care about more evidence at this stage. He says that he is close to getting a confession out of Sol, and that's all he needs. I can imagine the tactics that he used."

My eyes went wide. "He wouldn't hurt Sol while he's in custody, would he?"

"Not physically, no. But I'm sure he's saying all sorts of things to Sol about what will happen to his family and his community if he doesn't confess. It might get to the point that Sol will be so confused he confesses because he's convinced that is the best way to protect his family and his Amish district. It won't matter that what Sheriff Marshall is saying is simply a laundry list of empty threats. I have seen the sheriff do it before. There are a few times that I thought an innocent Amish man was punished for a crime he didn't commit. I tried to stop those bullying tactics whenever I could. I can't say that I was able to stop him every time."

"Then we have to find the real killer before the sheriff is able to break Sol's spirit," I said. "As awful as Sol has been to Charlotte, he's still her father, and I can't let him go to prison for a crime he didn't commit. Charlotte is getting married. I don't want this black cloud over her head."

"I agree," Aiden said. "However, we have to also keep an open mind to the possibility that Sol might have done it. The sheriff is right that he has a good motive, and he certainly has a history of holding onto a grudge. The situation with Charlotte is a perfect example of that."

I knew that Aiden was right; I had to keep an open mind about Sol. However, it was still difficult for me to believe that he would be dumb enough to use his own gun with his name on it and dump it so close to the crime scene. Sol might not be the nicest guy in the world, but he wasn't stupid.

"I'm surprised Devon isn't with you," Aiden said. "She seems to always be around."

"She was with Charlotte and me earlier when we spoke to Russell. She took off when we got back into the village."

He nodded, but his comment made me wonder again what Devon had been up to. Why did she want to tag along on the investigation when it had very little to do with the construction of the candy factory?

Aiden looked at his phone. "I just got a text from Little. He's heading back to town after talking to Russell. He got my message about the bullet hole. He's coming straight here."

"Can he really do anything about it if the sheriff doesn't want to?"

"He can try," Aiden said. "Little is a good cop, and I know he will do his very best. At least the hole will be documented as evidence. The sheriff can ignore that piece of evidence if he chooses to though."

As much as I wanted to stay with Aiden when he spoke to Deputy Little about what he'd found, I knew I should go to the church to back up Charlotte. She wasn't having the easiest time juggling her future in-laws.

After asking Aiden to call me if he learned anything new, I left the factory and walked back through the market's empty parking lot. I spotted the dumpsters behind the building. On a whim, I went back in that direction. It was a warm summer day, and the smell of the garbage in the massive containers hit my nose when I was within a few feet of them.

I had thought about peeking inside to look for more clues but gave up that idea. The smell in the summer heat was too overpowering. I gave massive kudos to the crime-scene tech who had climbed inside and found the rifle. He was a very brave soul.

A pebble bounced off the side of the dumpster as if someone had hit it with the tip of their shoe and sent it flying. I spun around to see a young

Amish man standing at the end of the alley. He stared at me for a second and then ran down the alley.

He was fast. I was never going to catch him. "Hey! Hey!" I called.

He glanced over his shoulder, and this time I got a good look at the person. It was Jericho Weaver, Charlotte's brother.

Chapter Twenty-seven

What was Jericho doing in Harvest on a Sunday? Had he been the same person I had seen running from the factory? I debated hurrying back to the factory to tell Aiden about this latest development, but I received a text message SOS from Charlotte. It seemed that Beth and Hal were becoming restless, and Beth didn't believe her wedding ceremony suggestions were being taken seriously enough by Reverend Brook. Charlotte was in need of a rescue.

I left the alley and headed for the church. It was just an hour after the last service in the morning, and the parking lot was all but abandoned except for the sensible sedan parked in Reverend Brook's reserved spot.

A small shadow waddled out from behind the car and wiggled his curly tail when he saw me, just like a dog. Sometimes I believed Jethro thought he was a dog. He walked on a leash. It would not be surprising if he was a tad confused.

"Jethro, what are you doing out here by yourself?" This was unusual. Ever since Jethro had disappeared a few years ago and had been missing for days, Juliet always needed to know where he was.

I scooped up the little pig and tucked him under my arm. I felt his body relax. Just as Juliet didn't like Jethro lost, Jethro didn't want to be lost. I walked up the steps to the church's front door, which had been painted a striking shade of purple. The purple stood out against the simple white siding and made the main entrance easy to find.

There was no one in the entryway, but I heard the sound of voices floating toward me from the sanctuary. I entered the large room through the double doors. Juliet, Charlotte, and the Littles stood in the middle aisle of the church discussing what I assumed were the wedding plans.

Charlotte wanted a very simple wedding on the square. There would be cake and cookies in the basement of the church for an hour after the ceremony, and that was it. By the sound of the talk, both Beth and Juliet were on board for something much bigger. I could see now why Charlotte had sent the SOS. If Juliet and Beth teamed up against her, she was doomed.

"Oh, Jethro, there is my little boy. Were you being good playing in the church nursery?" Juliet cooed.

I handed Jethro over to his mistress and didn't bother to tell her that I'd found him outside. There was no reason to cause Juliet worry.

"Bailey, thank you for bringing him up to me. You always seem to know where to find him." She nodded to Beth and Hal. "Bailey is Jethro's best friend. I let Jethro play in the nursery when no one is here. He enjoys it and is very careful with all the toys. Aren't you, sweetie?" She bumped the tip of her nose against his snout.

Jethro wriggled in her arms.

She looked back at me. "What did you think about the nursery renovations? We want everything to be perfect for the little ones that are on the way. We are having a bit of a baby boom at the church, which is a glorious problem to have."

Before I could make up an answer, as I hadn't seen the new nursery, she said, "I look forward to the time when I will have grandchildren in that room."

I grimaced.

Beth clapped her hands. "I do too. I hope that you and Lukey won't wait too long before you have children. You don't want to be one of those older mothers, and Hal and I would not want to move to Harvest with no grandchild to visit."

"That's true," Hal said. "You and Lukey can come and visit us in DC. I'm not moving up here until we have grandkids."

Charlotte paled.

I didn't know if I should be concerned that both Charlotte and I were more comfortable talking about murder than babies.

"*Maami* should be home from church by now," I said. "This would be a great time for you to meet her. Deputy—I mean—Luke—is going to meet us at the candy shop."

Charlotte gave me a grateful smile.

As I hoped, *Maami* was at the candy shop. She had just come into the front room of the shop through the kitchen. She removed her bonnet and smiled as we trooped in through the front door.

"*Gude Mariye!*" she said with a smile. "It's so nice to see all of you. You must be Deputy Little's parents. We are just so fond of him."

What my grandmother said was certainly sincere. *Maami* would never say anything that she didn't wholeheartedly mean, and it was the perfect comment to soothe Beth, who still appeared a tad ruffled after the visit to the church.

Beth placed a manicured hand to her chest. "We are just so pleased to hear that. Aren't we, Hal?"

"Yes." Hal Little was a man of very few words.

"Your shop is so charming. I can't believe that you do all of this without modern conveniences."

"We do have electricity in the shop as you can see," *Maami* said as she nodded to the lights overhead. "We are allowed it for business, not personal use. Charlotte and I live in the apartment above the shop, and we have no electricity there."

"How quaint," Beth murmured. "When Lukey told me that he was moving to Amish Country to take his job as a deputy, I was shocked. He grew up in DC of all places. I would think that my son would have a case of culture shock, but he has seemed happy." She said this last part as if the jury was still out on Deputy Little's happiness.

There was a knock on the shop door. I closed my eyes for a moment. Who could it possibly be now? Charlotte went to the window and peeked outside. "It's Ruth Yoder."

Even *Maami* appeared to be surprised by this announcement. "What could Ruth want? I just saw her at church, and she didn't say a word to me about coming here."

"It's Millie Fisher too," Charlotte added.

"Now, that is an odd pair," *Maami* murmured. "Let them in, Charlotte."

Charlotte did as she was asked, and Ruth and Millie stepped into the shop. Millie nodded and greeted everyone pleasantly when she came inside. Ruth scrunched up her nose as if she smelled something bad.

"I didn't think that there would be so many people in the candy shop on a Sunday," Ruth said. Her voice dripped with disapproval.

"Ruth, this is Beth and Hal Little. They are Deputy Little's parents," *Maami* explained. "They are in town for the wedding."

"I see," Ruth said.

"It's very nice to meet you," Millie said, jumping in. "We just stopped by in hopes of chatting with Charlotte for just a moment. We didn't realize that she had guests." She glanced at Ruth. "Perhaps we will come back in an hour or two when everyone is settled?"

Ruth folded her arms over her apron. "I can't come back in an hour or two. This is Sunday. I am supposed to be spending it in worship and then with my family, not on some fool's errand."

Millie pressed her lips together. "Ruth Yoder, you know as well as I do this is not a fool's errand, and I do believe it would be best to come back later when everyone is settled and we can speak privately."

"Privately with whom?" Beth asked.

Millie folded her hands at her waist and looked very much like the perfect Amish grandmother. "Oh, it is village business. Nothing to concern you and your husband."

"It might," Ruth argued.

Millie shot her a critical glance. If anyone else looked at Ruth like that, she would have put them in their place, but I had learned that Millie Fisher was one of a handful of people in Harvest who weren't afraid to tell Ruth exactly what they thought. I hoped someday I would be just as brave.

"What is it?" Charlotte asked.

"Why don't the three of us go outside and chat," Millie suggested.

Ruth snorted. "If these people are marrying into this family, they should know the truth. I wouldn't want any surprises if I were in their shoes."

"The truth? The truth about what?" Beth asked with a pinched voice. She gripped Hal's hand.

"Charlotte's father is in jail for murder, and her mother wants her to come home," Ruth said as if she were reciting the weather.

The blunt delivery didn't make any difference to Beth Little. She crumpled into her husband's arms and began to bawl her eyes out.

"Ruth Yoder," Millie said. "Now, look what you did. You drove that *Englischer* to tears."

"I didn't know *Englischers* were so fragile," Ruth shot back. "I would think that going to prison was a common thing in the *Englisch* world."

Millie rolled her eyes.

Hal directed his wife to one of the café tables and sat her down. "Dear. Dear, everything is all right."

"I knew Lukey shouldn't marry an Amish girl. I tried to be understanding because I don't want to drive a wedge between us and our boy. But now I learn this? Her father is a convict and she is returning to the Amish! I can't take it, Hal. I tell you I can't take it. I only have one son." She started to cry again.

Charlotte watched their exchange as if she just might fall ill. I can't say I blamed her. I would hate to learn that Aiden's mother was against our relationship. It would break my heart. Perhaps I should be more grateful that the opposite was true.

"No one said that Charlotte was returning to the Amish," I said. "Her family just wants to see her."

Beth rifled through her floral purse and came up with a crumpled napkin. She used it to wipe her nose. "To make her come back, which means my son will become Amish. I'll never see him again!"

Millie put her hands on her hips and stepped in front of Beth. "Pull yourself together. Your son is not going to become Amish, and Charlotte is not going back to the plain life. Even if both those two things were true, you would be blessed to have Charlotte Weaver as a daughter-in-law. I dare you to find a kinder soul in this county. Now, Charlotte's mother is very upset about what has happened with her father and she wishes to see her eldest daughter. That is all there is to it. It has nothing to do with your son or you."

Beth looked up at Millie from her seat at the table with her mouth hanging open. I stopped myself from breaking into applause. *Maami* seemed quite pleased with Millie's speech as well.

Beth sniffed. "I thought the Amish were nonconfrontational."

"*Nee,*" Millie said. "We are pacifists. There is a difference."

Beth rose to her feet. "Hal, I think I would like to go back to the B&B. I'm tired. I need to lie down."

Hal helped his wife to her feet and guided her to the door.

"Can I walk with you?" Charlotte asked.

Beth looked over her shoulder. "No." It was just one word, but it spoke volumes.

When the front door closed after the Littles, Ruth clicked her tongue. "I knew things would not be easy when Miriam Lee Weaver walked onto my farm."

"Ruth Yoder, you need to mind your own business," Millie said not unkindly.

"That's something coming from you."

It was astounding to me to watch Ruth take criticism from Millie in stride.

"Miriam Lee?" Charlotte asked. "You spoke to my sister?"

Millie walked over to Charlotte and led her to the chair Beth had just left. "Sit. Now that we are among friends, we can tell you what we know." She gave Ruth a look as she sat next to Charlotte at the table.

Ruth made a grunting sound and sat across from them, while *Maami* and I perched on chairs at the next table a few feet away.

"What did Miriam Lee say?" Charlotte clasped her hands tightly together on the tabletop.

Millie covered Charlotte's hands with her own. "She said your *maam* sent her to get a message to you. Miriam Lee thought the best way to do that was through our church district. She had heard you and I were friends. She sought me out at Ruth's home where services were today."

"I just so happened to be talking to Millie about our next quilting circle meeting when Miriam Lee came up to her," Ruth interjected as if she didn't want to be left out of the conversation.

Millie shot her a look. "*Ya,* Ruth was there. The message Miriam Lee asked me to get to you was short. Your *maam* wants you to come see her at the family farm."

"When?" Charlotte asked breathlessly.

"Today."

Charlotte's knuckles turned white. "Did she say why? Is it about my father?"

"I can't speculate," Millie said. "But there was something else."

"What?" Charlotte leaned forward.

Millie turned to me. "She wants Bailey to come with you."

Chapter Twenty-Eight

"Me?" I asked. "I would think I was the last person Charlotte's mother would want to see. They have made no secret that they blame me for Charlotte leaving their district."

Millie shrugged. "This is the message Miriam Lee gave us. I have no reason to believe the young girl is lying."

"She wasn't," Charlotte said with force. "It is impossible for Miriam Lee to tell a lie. She is the best one of all the children. The kindest and the most loving." She swallowed hard. "It was not until I saw her at the kettle corn stand at the petting zoo that I realized how much I missed her. How much I missed and continue to miss all of them. Not everything about growing up in that district was bad. There were happy times too." She stood up. "We have to go."

I stood up too. "You want to go now?"

"Yes. I need to know why my mother wants to speak to me. They must blame me for what has happened to *Daed.*" Her voice caught. "That's something I have to face."

"Then let's go." I took a step toward the door.

Millie grabbed my hand. "Bailey, before you leave, I would remind you of one thing."

I waited.

"Take time to listen. You are a woman of action. It serves you well in most things. But going to a strict Amish district like the Weavers', listening to understand will be your best tool."

I nodded, and Charlotte and I said goodbye to the women in the room. The last thing I remember seeing before we left the shop was Nutmeg's orange tail swishing back and forth over the polished wood floor.

Charlotte was as silent on the drive to her parents' farm as she'd been on the way to the petting zoo just the day before. The Weaver farm was on the outskirts of Holmes County, closer to the town of Wooster in Wayne County than it was to Harvest. By buggy, that was quite a distance, which I believed had been a help to Charlotte when she left her home church. If her family had to go into town for supplies, Harvest was never their first or even their second choice. Because of that, she didn't run into her family on the street or in the market. She was sheltered from facing them day in, day out. Maybe that was why she was able to compartmentalize her feelings of missing her siblings and her home.

I glanced over at my cousin, who stared out the window, and my heart hurt for her. I couldn't even guess what she might be thinking as we drove toward her old home.

We were still a quarter mile from the Weaver farm when we saw the line of black buggies that were parked on either side of the Weavers' country road. More buggies were still coming too. As they parked, men, women, and children climbed out of them. Every last one of them dressed from head to toe in black.

It was midday in the summer. Just looking at them in their heavy woolen clothes made my skin itch. I glanced down at my shorts and sneakers. The most inappropriately dressed award went to me.

"It's like a funeral," Charlotte whispered.

I drove to the house, where there were even more buggies. Too many to count. I parked on a spot on the grass.

"The community only gathers like this when someone dies." Charlotte's words were strangled.

She jumped out of the car and ran toward the large white farmhouse.

"Charlotte! Wait!" I got tangled in my seatbelt, which cost me precious time, enough time for Charlotte to disappear into the sea of buggies and people dressed in black.

I finally broke free of the seatbelt and was out of the car. I never felt so out of place in my life, and that included when I moved to Holmes County and only really knew my grandmother. The phrase "stuck out like a sore thumb" was never so accurate.

I remember my best friend Cass telling me when I was nervous to "fake it." I repeated the words to myself as I walked by a group of Amish men smoking and chatting in Pennsylvania Dutch. As I passed, they fell silent. As much as I wanted to, I didn't glance in their direction. Instead, I focused on the farmhouse because I assumed that was where Charlotte had gone.

On the wide front porch, there was a group of women in matching plain black dresses. With their downturned faces, it was impossible for me to pick out any one individual, so I addressed the group. "I'm looking for my cousin Charlotte Weaver."

They stared at me for a long, uncomfortable moment until one of the women in the back spoke up in English. "She's inside." That was it. She didn't tell me to go inside or suggest I knock on the door.

Not knowing what else to do and not wanting to stay on the porch with the women, I went into the house.

This wasn't the first time that I had been to the Weaver farm. I had visited there once before Charlotte left the church district.

The front door opened into a large living room. Instead of couches and typical living room furniture, it was full of wooden folding chairs. Men and women sat on each side of a central aisle. An elderly Amish man with a long white beard stood at the front of the room with his head bowed. He was clearly praying in the Amish language. I hurried to the closest door and went through it. I found myself in a long hallway. There was a break in the floor as if this part of the house had been added after the original construction of the building. That wasn't unusual for Amish homes with large families. As the family grew and evolved, changes were made to the home to better accommodate its inhabitants so that they could remain together but still have some private space.

To me this hallway appeared to be lined with bedrooms. Every last door was closed. I was reluctant to open them. I'd already barged into the house. Barging into someone's bedroom was a little much even for me.

I glanced at the door behind me. I couldn't go back that way. I'd rather be lost in the house than go back and interrupt what was clearly some type of religious service.

As I dithered over what to do, the door that led back into the living room opened behind me. Miriam Lee, Charlotte's younger sister, stepped through the door. When she shut it again, she said, "The ladies of the district told me that you'd be in here."

"Do they usually sit on the porch in a group like that? It's kind of intimidating."

She smiled. "*Nee.* They and the others are here for the prayer meeting. The bishop called it to pray that my father will be released from prison."

"He was arrested yesterday?"

She nodded and turned pale. "*Ya,* in the middle of dinner. In front of our mother and all the children."

I closed my eyes. I had a feeling that the sheriff had timed the arrest to cause the most distress for the family. "Was it the sheriff who came?"

She nodded. "And two other deputies." She paused. "But the deputy that Charlotte is to marry wasn't with them."

I let out a breath. That was one saving grace. I didn't know if the Weaver family would ever be able to get over Deputy Little dragging Sol off to jail.

"Charlotte is with my mother. I will take you to them." She reached out and took my hand in her much smaller one. She led me to the end of the long hallway and through a doorway that opened onto a staircase. The staircase climbed up to a landing with a closed door on it. We didn't stop there because the stairs led to a second landing and another door. This was the door that Miriam Lee opened.

She let go of my hand and went inside. As soon as I stepped into the room, I felt at peace. Compared to the rest of the house, which was stark and severe, this room was colorful and cozy with pieces of colorful fabric laid out on the table, quilts hanging on the walls, and bright bundles of yarn on the shelves. This had to be Josephine Weaver's oasis in the house, her craft room. I guessed it was the one place where she could escape and truly be alone.

Charlotte sat across a table from her mother. Josephine had a piece of needlepoint on her lap, and her fingers moved like streaks of lighting as the needle dove in and out of the fabric.

"Bailey," Charlotte said. "I'm so glad Miriam Lee found you. I'm sorry I ran off like that. I was afraid that . . ."

"You were afraid that someone had died," I said.

She nodded. "It is a lot like an Amish wake out there."

"The community," Josephine said, speaking for the first time, "is treating my husband's arrest like a death. It leaves a hole in the community just like a death would."

"I'm sorry that this has happened. Charlotte and I have been trying to help," I said.

Josephine was probably not even fifty years old, but her blond hair was fading into white. I wondered if the last several days had turned its color even more. I couldn't imagine the worry she must feel. If Sol was convicted, she would be left to raise their children and run their farm herself or possibly worse, a male relative would storm in and take over for her.

"Charlotte told me this, and I am glad to hear it. Please sit." She pointed at a chair, then looked at her younger daughter. "Miriam Lee, you can go now."

The tween's face fell. It was clear to me that she wanted to stay and hear what her mother had to say to me. I guessed it wasn't often that an Englisher came into their home, in shorts no less. I wished I'd had the forethought to stop at home for a pair of jeans before we came out here. In the sea of black Amish dresses, I felt completely overexposed.

Miriam Lee didn't argue with her mother, however, and went out the door we'd just come through.

"It is best that the children don't know about this," Josephine said.

"They have to know that I'm here," Charlotte said. "The whole community knows that I'm here."

"*Ya*, but she and the rest of them don't need to know what I'm going to ask." She looked up at me again. "Sit." She pointed at the empty chair at the table.

I fell into the chair as if I had been shot from the sky. Graceful to a fault, that was me, I thought sarcastically.

"What do you need us to do?" Charlotte asked.

"I want you to clear your father's name."

"That's what we've been trying to do."

"I know this, and I appreciate it." She paused. "But there must be something more you can do. If you had thought of whatever it was, your father would never have been arrested. Do you think that I like all these people from the district in my home? I feel trapped on my own land. I have no privacy in my own home. The only place that I can get away from everyone is here in my little room."

"I am sorry, *Maam*," Charlotte said.

"I know you are, and I know despite everything that you still want to help your family. I was hurt when you left the community. I knew that you dreamed of playing music, but I never knew that you would take it so far as to leave the family because of it. I was hurt, but your father was furious. If it had been up to me, we still would have had some contact with you. It's what I wanted, but your father forbade it. I wasn't even allowed to write you. He wanted zero contact, and I had to abide by his word because he is my husband. Even now with Sol in jail, I have to abide by his wishes."

"But you are breaking his rule now," I said.

She looked at me. "I am, and I am certain that every member of the community knows of it since you came into the house during the prayer service."

"They definitely saw me," I said, remembering how I'd walked right into the middle of the room while the bishop prayed. It wasn't a good move and would not endear me to the community.

"I will deal with any repercussions when they come," Josephine said. "And they will come."

Chapter Twenty-nine

I didn't like the idea of Josephine Weaver dealing with the repercussions of speaking with Charlotte and me.

Charlotte pressed her hands on the tabletop. "We will do what we can to find the real killer so that *Daed* can come home to you and the children."

"*Danki.*" Josephine patted Charlotte's hand. It was just half a second of contact, but Charlotte's face lit up. Her reaction broke my heart. Everyone wanted to be loved and accepted by their mother. Charlotte was no different.

"To help, we need to know a few things," I said.

Josephine widened her eyes. "What are these things?"

"Sol's motive for the murder for one."

"He did not murder that man," Josephine protested.

"I don't believe that he did, but he still has a possible motive that the sheriff's department is using as a basis for his arrest."

She frowned. "I do not know what it may be. They didn't tell us any of their reasons for taking my husband when they were here."

"They believe Jericho is the motive," I said.

Josephine placed her hand over her heart. "My son."

I nodded.

"Jericho is not involved in any of this."

"He's very much involved," I said. "Can you tell us why Sol was so upset that Jericho was working for Wade? The sheriff believes that this was Sol's motive for murder."

She nodded. "It is not much of a motive to me. Sol was upset because Wade was an *Englischer.* He didn't—doesn't want any of his children to spend great lengths of time with *Englischers* because he believes that it corrupts them and causes them to leave the church." She glanced at Charlotte.

"It is okay, *Maam,*" Charlotte said. "I know he believed that after the decision I made, he had to keep the others away from *Englischers.*"

Josephine nodded. "This is the reason."

"What do you mean away from Englishers?" I asked.

Josephine frowned as if she wasn't quite sure that she wanted to bring up the painful family history.

"You can tell her," Charlotte encouraged.

"Charlotte always loved music, and the man who was our bishop when she was a young girl also enjoyed music. He saw a natural talent in Charlotte and encouraged us to let her learn to play the piano. At the time, there was one in the schoolhouse. She was a natural at it and quickly progressed to the organ. We were happy that she was so happy, and she played the piano for church services when they were held at the schoolhouse.

"We didn't see anything wrong with it because our bishop at the time approved of her playing. When that bishop passed on and *Gott* gave us a new bishop, we learned our error. The new bishop believed that the only music in the church should be the joyful voices of the congregation. He got rid of the piano and said instruments were no long allowed at services. He went so far as to order Charlotte to stop taking lessons. She was studying with an *Englischer*. The bishop predicted that Charlotte would leave the church because of our folly, and he was right. Because of this Sol blamed himself when Charlotte left our district."

"But how can you be solely to blame when your old bishop allowed music lessons with an Englisher?" I asked.

"He told us we should have consulted with *Gott* before we agreed. Since we did not, our punishment was that we lost our daughter. This is why your *daed* has been so severe with you. He feels he must be in order to keep the other children from straying. Losing one child to the *Englisch* world is painful enough. To lose all of them would be intolerable. And he blames himself for letting you learn to play. Had that never happened, you would still be with your family; you would still be Amish and part of our community."

Charlotte reached across the table and touched her mother's arm. "You weren't being punished. Even without music in my life, I would have left the faith. That is a decision I know I would have made no matter what. I love you and the rest of the family, but I am in love with Luke Little. He is English and we are set to marry on Saturday."

"I have heard this," Josephine said quietly. "You must realize that in many ways this saddens me because I know that you will never come back. When you are connected to a man in marriage, you must go where he goes. His land is your land. His people are your people."

"Luke is a good man," Charlotte said quietly.

"I have heard this too," Josephine said. "And I thank *Gott* for that."

Charlotte took a deep breath. "I know it is a lot to ask, but you have asked us to help you and I am hoping you will do the same for me."

"I do not know how I can help you."

"You can do that by coming to my wedding. It is Saturday on the square at two thirty in the afternoon. It would mean a great deal to me."

"Your father would not like it."

"I know." Charlotte dropped her gaze to the table. "I sent you an invitation."

"I did not see the invitation. Your *daed* goes through all the mail when it arrives. He always has."

So it was Charlotte's father who'd sent the invitation back unopened. I wasn't surprised.

"Even if you find a way to have your father freed, I cannot believe that we will be at your wedding. It is an *Englisch* affair, and our bishop is strict about us only socializing with other members of the community. He believes *Englisch* friendship pulls members, especially the young, away from the faith."

"I understand," Charlotte said, but since I knew my cousin so well, I could hear the hurt in her voice.

Josephine stood up. "I would like a few minutes to collect myself before I join the prayer meeting." She stepped over to the window and looked out on the buggies. "There are so many buggies here. Not all the people are from our district. Everyone is here praying for our family and for Sol."

Charlotte and I stood.

"I'm praying for him too, *Maam*," Charlotte said.

Her mother turned to look at Charlotte. Josephine's face was drawn. "If that is the truth, I am glad."

"I believe in the same God you do. I just worship him in a different way."

"That is *gut*." Josephine turned back to the window.

Charlotte's lower lip trembled like that of a little child. I grabbed her hand and whispered, "Let's go."

Charlotte and I went back out the door into the stairway. I saw the back of an Amish girl disappearing down the staircase. Miriam Lee had been eavesdropping. Not that I blamed her. Goodness knows, I would be doing the same thing in her position.

Charlotte was too upset to notice. "Bailey, I have to clear my father's name. I don't have any chance of reconciling with my family if I don't."

I squeezed her hand. "We will do it. I promise." Even as I spoke, in the back of my mind I worried that Sol Weaver might be guilty. If we proved that to be true, it would be the end of Charlotte's relationship with her family.

By the time we made it to the main floor of the house, we could hear men shouting.

Charlotte's eyes went wide.

"What is going on? People don't yell at a prayer meeting."

I stepped in front of her and ducked into one of the hallway bedrooms. At the end of the hallway, the door leading into the living room stood open. Through it, I could see a group of men arguing. I grimaced. If I knew another way out of the house, I would have taken it.

"Let's just get out of here," I said to Charlotte. "Stay close to me."

She grabbed the back of my shirt as I stepped through the door.

As one, the Amish men turned and glared at us. The bishop stepped forward and said something I didn't understand in Pennsylvania Dutch. I was certain it wasn't a compliment.

I tried to step around him but another man blocked my way. "You are responsible for this," the old bishop said in English, pointing a crooked finger at me. "You brought those people here."

"What people? I don't know what you're talking about?"

"The camera people," he snapped.

My heart sank. Devon and Z must have been outside. I couldn't think of anything more disrespectful to the Amish faith than recording a prayer meeting without permission. "I didn't bring them here, but if you let me through, I can tell them to leave."

He glared at me. "Go."

Chapter Thirty

The sea of men stepped apart, making just enough room for Charlotte and me to pass through.

As I was leaving the house, I caught sight of Emmaus Linzer, the owner of Linzer Petting Zoo, standing in one corner as if he was trying to hide from sight. It was not an easy task as he was a large man and towered over most of the other men in the room.

When Charlotte and I stepped outside, the group of ladies was no longer on the wide front porch. I guessed they were chased away by Devon and Z, who stood on the road with a camera and tripod. I felt anger boil up inside me. I didn't like everything the Weavers' Amish district had done, especially when it came to the way they'd treated Charlotte over the years, but to be so blatantly disrespectful to a culture's beliefs was unthinkable to me.

I left Charlotte on the porch and marched across the lawn to the road. "What do you think you're doing? Turn that camera off."

Devon pushed her sunglasses to the top of her head. "We don't have to. We aren't on their land. The road is public property."

"What are you, paparazzi now? Turn the camera off."

Devon folded her arms.

"Z, turn it off."

The cameraman looked from Devon to me. Perhaps he was gauging which one of us could put up a better fight if pushed. At the moment, I had anger on my side, so I was the more formidable opponent.

Z pressed a button on the camera, and the red light went dark.

"Z, keep rolling! We need this footage."

"I thought we were making a show about a candy factory. What are we doing out here?" Z asked.

"This is the home of the contractor's killer. It's all connected," she argued.

"It's not proven that Sol is the killer," I said.

"Fine! But he was arrested for the crime. You can't deny that," she shot back.

"I'm taking this down," Z said. "I need to get my equipment off this asphalt road anyway. The sun is beating down and it's hot. The camera and lens could be damaged. I don't think that's something you want to explain to Gourmet Television."

She scowled. "Fine. We probably have enough to give the impression of what is going on here."

"You can't include this in the show. I won't allow it. I do have executive producer privileges and some say. Maybe I don't have as much clout as you do, but this will be an instance where Linc Baggins and the network will listen to me."

She glared. "I wouldn't have had to come out here like this if you were a bit more forthcoming about what you are doing. I have to record something, and we both know that work on the factory is at a complete standstill."

Z removed the camera from the tripod and carried it back to the van. He then came back for the tripod. "Devon, are you coming? I'm going back to the B&B for some AC. It's just too hot out here."

"You'd never make it as a wildlife videographer," Devon said as if that was the ultimate insult.

"That's good because I don't want to be one." He rolled his eyes, and for a second his expression reminded me of Millie Fisher, which was just about the oddest comparison imaginable.

"I'm leaving," Z said. "If you're coming with me, get in the van." He stalked toward the van with his tripod in hand.

I wouldn't be that surprised if Z left Devon there in front of the Weaver farm. If he did, I would be the one stuck driving her back to the village. I didn't want to have to do that.

Devon put her sunglasses back over her eyes. "If I were you, Bailey, I would take a close look at that contract you signed with Gourmet Television. You need to decide whether you're willing to put your career in television in jeopardy for a bunch of Amish." She flipped her yellow hair and marched over to the van with her chin high in the air.

I shook my head as I watched them drive away. I didn't know what was really going on with Devon, but it was more than time that I had a conversation with Linc Baggins. This wasn't what I'd signed up for. If I had to give back the signing money to break the contract, so be it. I would find a way to do it.

Now that the television van was gone, the Amish visitors to the Weaver farm started to pour out of the house and barns. I supposed that's where they had gone to avoid being caught on camera. I stepped out of their way as they walked to their respective buggies. Nothing killed a prayer meeting like a camera crew.

There was a bit of a traffic jam as everyone tried to maneuver their buggies, wagons, carts, and horses down the country road at the same time.

Charlotte was no longer on the front porch. It was just as well since the Amish ladies had come back.

I texted her, asking her where she was. To my relief, she texted back right away. She didn't always do that because having a cell phone was still new to her. More often than not, she left it on the charger in Swissmen Sweets' kitchen.

"We are by the shed phone in the back."

We? Who was the we that she was talking about?

The church members leaving the farm ignored me while I walked around to the back of the house in search of Charlotte. To my surprise, I spotted Jericho Weaver standing with Naz Schlabach under a shade tree. The two young men were having what appeared to be a heated conversation. I was dying to know what they were talking about, and I had to wonder why Naz was there. As far as I knew, he wasn't a member of the Weaver family's district. At least, I would have expected Charlotte to have said something about it if he was.

Jericho shook his head and walked away.

I hesitated, but then decided to stay on my current track and find Charlotte. I didn't think the bishop would tolerate Charlotte and me being on the property much longer.

On the other side of the barn, I spotted the shed phone. I saw two people sitting in the grass by the shed. One was Charlotte and the other was Miriam Lee.

As I drew closer, I saw what the girls were looking at. There was a yellow lab lying on a blanket by the shed with four little yellow puppies bouncing around her. The girls sat cross-legged on either side of the dog, which seemed completely at ease with them. A black lab puppy slept in Charlotte's lap.

Charlotte smiled up at me with tears in her eyes.

Quietly, I sat in the grass with the two sisters.

"This is June Bee." Charlotte nodded at the mama dog. "She's our family dog. We've had her since she was a pup, and I named her when I was maybe thirteen. We got her in June, so I guess you know how I picked the name." She gave a small chuckle. "She had puppies."

"I can see that."

Miriam Lee picked up one of yellow puppies that was asleep on the blanket and set her on my lap. The little pup whimpered, but didn't open her eyes. She settled in the middle of my legs and fell back to sleep. I could feel myself falling a little bit in love with the puppy. However, I reminded myself that I already had more pets than I could handle. There was Nutmeg the orange tabby at the shop, Puff the giant white rabbit at home, and Jethro. Jethro might not technically be my pig, but

I certainly took care of him a lot. I was grateful that he wasn't with me now.

Charlotte, however, was a goner. It seemed to me that she and the one black puppy had bonded. It would be difficult to break them apart. It wasn't lost on me that she was most attached to the puppy that looked different from the rest, just as Charlotte herself was the one who stuck out in the family.

"What's the black puppy's name?" I asked.

"He doesn't have one," Miriam Lee said. "We are not to name them. Their permanent families will name them. They will be for sale as soon as the pups are weaned. Labs fetch a *gut* price, and June is such a *gut maam* that our labs sell for top dollar." She said this as if she was reciting something that she had heard an adult say. I guessed it was her father.

"I do hate it when we take the pups from June Bee each time. She is always so sad for a few days. I spend all the time I can with her, giving her extra love and treats." She looked up at her sister. "Just like you did, Charlotte, before you left."

"I am grateful to you for that," Charlotte said as she leaned over and scratched June Bee between the ears. "*Danki.* You have taken good care of her."

Miriam Lee beamed. Her older sister could not have given her better praise.

I petted the puppy in my lap and reluctantly handed her back to Miriam Lee. Miriam Lee placed the pup next to June Bee's warm belly. The puppy gave a happy sigh in her sleep. My heart melted that much more.

If it was difficult for me to give my puppy back,

it was nearly impossible for Charlotte. She nuzzled the black puppy under her chin and kissed his head.

"Charlotte, we should leave," I whispered. "The prayer meeting is breaking up, and I'm sure your mother is tired and overwhelmed from all the activity."

She nodded but continued to hold the puppy.

Miriam Lee, who had two puppies in her small lap, said, "I heard what *Maam* asked you to do. Will you be able to help *Daed*?"

"You were listening at the door," I said.

Her pale cheeks flushed red.

"I don't blame you. I would have done the same thing in your place."

She smiled down at the puppies. "I know you would. I have heard the stories of how you have caught criminals before."

I raised my brow. The stories about me had even reached the Weavers' conservative district. "We are going to try to help your father," I promised.

"Maybe I can help too," she said. "Because I was with *Daed* that night."

Chapter Thirty-one

Charlotte set the puppy back into her lap and sat up straight. "You were with *Daed* the night that Wade was killed?"

Miriam Lee's eyes were wide with fear. It was as if she was sorry for what she had revealed just a moment ago. However, they were words she couldn't take back. If she wanted us to help her father, then we needed to hear what she had to say.

"What was your father doing that night?" I asked.

"He was looking for Jericho," Miriam Lee said. "He was very angry at Jericho for working for Wade Farmer. He didn't want any of us to have contact with *Englischers* after Charlotte left." She closed her eyes. "I had a friend, Reign, who is *Englisch*. After Charlotte left, my *daed* made me tell her that we couldn't be friends any longer." A tear squeezed out of the corner of her eye.

"Oh, Miriam Lee," Charlotte murmured. "I'm so sorry. I should have thought about how much my decision was going to affect you and the rest of the family."

"There are many *Englisch* contractors Jericho could have worked for," I said. "Why did he choose Wade? Wade wasn't a very nice person."

"I think it was for the money." She licked her lips. "One night, I saw Jericho in his room. He had a pile of money on his bed. All one-hundred-dollar bills. He was counting them and putting them into plastic bags."

My eyes went wide. My first thought was drug money. Could Wade and Jericho be caught up in dealing drugs? It wasn't out of the question. I knew drugs were an issue in rural Ohio, even in the Amish community.

"Was anything else on the bed? Like pills?" I asked.

Charlotte's head turned in my direction. She knew where my thoughts were going.

Miriam Lee shook her head. "*Nee*. Just money."

"Did you ask him about it?" I questioned.

Miriam Lee stared at me as if I had asked her if she had ever been to the moon. "*Nee*, he is my older *bruder*. It is not my place to ask him questions."

Frowning, I turned to Charlotte, who was still snuggling the puppy. "I saw Jericho here a little while ago speaking to Naz Schlabach. I spotted them when I came looking for you," I said to Charlotte. "Is Naz a member of the district?"

Charlotte shook her head. "No, at least, he wasn't when I lived here. I suppose that he might have joined after I left, but the district is very strict. More people leave than join." She paused. "At least that was the case when I was growing up."

"It is still true," Miriam Lee said. "Many young

people leave. When I am in *rumspringa* and have a chance to choose whether I will be baptized, I think that I will leave too."

"Is that because of me?" Charlotte asked.

Miriam Lee shook her head. "*Nee.* But you made me brave enough to think of it."

Charlotte pressed her lips together, and I knew that she had to be thinking that her father was right. He believed that when she'd left the district, she had started a trend in the family. If Miriam Lee left in two years when she entered *rumspringa,* it would confirm his belief. That was assuming he wasn't disconnected from the family altogether and in prison.

"Naz is Jericho's friend," Miriam Lee said. "I did not know him before Jericho started working for Wade. Sometimes he would pick Jericho up for work. My *daed* didn't like it, so Jericho would meet him at the end of the road."

"Why didn't your *daed* like Naz?"

"He is Beachy Amish. *Daed* thinks that they aren't even Amish because they do so many *Englisch* things." She lowered her voice. "Naz has a cell phone." It was as if she was telling a deep dark secret about the young Amish man.

"Beachy Amish. Who else mentioned the Beachy Amish to me?" I thought hard, and then I remembered that it had been Emmaus Linzer. I frowned. I'd seen Emmaus in the Weavers' living room when I left the house. If the Weavers were uncomfortable with Beachy Amish, why was he there? Had Josephine even known that he was present?

I stood up and brushed grass from my backside. One of the puppies thought I was playing some kind of game and tried to catch the blades of grass in his mouth. "We need to talk to Jericho and Naz, and I think I want to speak to Emmaus Linzer too."

Charlotte set her puppy against his mother. He whimpered when she put him down. Charlotte kissed his head and stood up. "If he was my pup, I would name him Licorice."

I cocked my head. "But you don't like black licorice."

Charlotte smiled. "He needs a bittersweet name."

Miriam Lee stayed in the grass. "If you are looking for Jericho, you should try the ice cream social tonight."

"Oh, where is that?" I asked.

She looked up at me. "Linzer Petting Zoo."

I really did need to speak to Emmaus Linzer. I didn't know how yet, but he was involved with this. And I would bet it was tied to Aiden's case at the petting zoo.

Charlotte seemed a lot more like herself on the ride back to Harvest. "When we get back to town, I should catch up with Luke and his parents. I need to put them at ease about my marrying their son."

"Do you feel up to doing that?" I asked.

"If I can walk into my parents' house and face every Amish person in the county who disapproves of me, I can talk to my future husband's parents." She straightened her spine against the back of her seat.

"I'm glad to hear it. I have an idea."

She looked at me.

"What?"

"Why don't I go to the ice cream social alone?"

"What? This involves my father," she said. "And

we don't know that Jericho will talk to you without me there."

"I think he will," I said, but I didn't tell her why I made that assumption. I didn't want to give Charlotte yet another thing to worry about. "Go see Luke and his parents and try to think about your wedding for a change instead of murder."

She wrinkled her nose. "I don't like the idea of you going alone. What if something happens?"

"What could possibly happen at an ice cream social?"

She gave me a look.

"Okay, okay," I said. "I'll call Aiden and ask him to go with me."

"That does make me feel a bit better." She shook her head. "The two of you are going to stick out at a youth ice cream social like a couple of sore thumbs."

"I think that's exactly what we need to do."

Instead of taking Charlotte directly to Swissmen Sweets, I dropped her off at the B&B where Deputy Little's parents were staying. Deputy Little's departmental SUV was parked in front of the large Victorian-style bed and breakfast. It was interesting to me that it was the same B&B where Z and Devon were staying. It was by far the closest lodging to Swissmen Sweets, so maybe that was why they had all chosen that location.

However, the television van wasn't parked on the street or in the small parking lot of the B&B. Maybe Z and Devon were out taping more B roll. At this point, I wondered how much B roll Devon could possibly think they needed.

Since I was so close to the factory, I parked by

the market and walked to my building. I still felt a twinge of nervousness as I stepped into the cavernous space. Part of me expected someone to jump out and shout "Boo!" Aiden's contractor friend was set to meet me there at four, and I was just a little bit early.

My heart sank as I walked from room to room. Would this building ever be finished? I closed my eyes. I'd make it happen. When it came to business, I hadn't failed yet. I'd failed in other parts of life, but never business.

"Bailey's car is in the parking lot, so I'm sure that she is here." Aiden's voice traveled into the main factory room where I stood.

I turned around as Aiden and a middle-aged man stepped into the room. He wore a bright-blue polo shirt that read, BEACHY AND SONS CONSTRUCTION. He was clean shaven and his shirt was neatly tucked into his jeans. My first impression of Jonah Beachy was competence, which is a nice characteristic to see in a general contractor. We shook hands, and he looked up to the solid wood beam that ran along the ridgeline of the roof.

Aiden walked a few steps behind him, letting Jonah take everything in. It still seemed odd to me to see Aiden out of uniform. In all the time that I'd known him, he had been a cop of some type. However, now as a private detective, his wardrobe had changed. He wore jeans and a green T-shirt and carried a pig under his arm.

"You have Jethro," I said.

Aiden nodded and set the little pig on the concrete. "Yes, I went over to Swissmen Sweets to look for you. Clara said that you and Charlotte had gone on an errand." He raised his brow on the word "errand" as if he had doubts about the reason for our excursion.

It was an errand, just a sleuthing one.

"While I was there," Aiden went on, "my mother stopped by and handed over Jethro. She really wanted to give him to you. I was the second choice. She said if I saw you, I should ask you to watch the pig. I guess they are having an alcoholics recovery meeting at the church this evening. Mom didn't want Jethro to get in trouble in the fellowship hall while they were discussing such a serious topic."

Jethro looked up at Aiden as if to say that he would never misbehave. We all knew better. I believed that everyone who lived in Holmes County knew better when it came to Jethro. He was sweet but he could find trouble like nobody's business.

"This is quite a place you have here. I recognize this as solid Amish construction through and through," Jonah Beachy said.

"Do you work with the Amish?" I asked.

"Oh yeah," he said. "Most of my guys are Amish or former Amish. I'm former Amish myself. I left the Amish way when I was twenty-three. I still have a good relationship with my Amish family. I was just at my sister's place yesterday for a family picnic. The Amish are salt of the earth people."

I smiled. "My father is former Amish too."

He grinned. "Well then, I see that we have roots in common. I think we will be able to do a fine job for you. Thanks for emailing me the blueprints. That gave me a good idea of what we are looking at. The plans are excellent. I believe that we can take this job over." He reached into his briefcase and pulled out an itemized estimate. "Here's the price that we are looking at to finish up."

I looked at the final number on the paper, and it was on par with what Wade had planned to charge to complete the building. It included materials cost. "Some of these materials you've listed, I already have. They should be in Wade's warehouse. They are paid for. He was just holding onto them . . ." I trailed off and didn't add what I was thinking, that he was holding onto them to strong arm me out of more money.

"I can contact Wade's warehouse," Jonah said. "If the items are there and you paid for them, there should be no reason why we can't use them. A list of the items you believe he had in storage and vendor names would be a great help."

"I have that," I said. "I can email it to you as well."

"Perfect!" He smiled, and I felt myself calm a bit. The factory was going to be finished. "Do we have a deal?"

I didn't shake his hand just yet because I had one more question. "When is the target completion date?" I asked.

"Realistically, we are looking at early November. I can start in two weeks when I finish my current job, and then we will be working on this place full time until completion."

I bit my lower lip. That was after the planned grand opening in August. I would just have to reschedule it. Thankfully, I'd had the foresight to hold off on any advertising about it in case we ran into a problem. Little did I know that the problem was going to be murder. I glanced over at Aiden.

Jethro strolled around the large room and sniffed every nook and cranny as if he was searching for food. By the looks of him, you would never know that he had been running laps around this very floor just two days ago. Now, he was on his best behavior. However, that was the thing with Jethro. You didn't know if you were going to get a mild-mannered pig or a bacon tornado.

"Can that work?" Aiden asked.

"I think that it has to. At this point, I want the factory to be done right more than I want it done quickly. The last few months have been very stressful."

Jonah nodded. "Aiden told me a little bit of what you have been through. I just hope you don't believe that all contractors are untrustworthy after your experience. Don't let one rotten egg ruin the cake is what I say."

I smiled. "If you can get the job done by early November, we have a deal." I held out my hand.

Jonah grinned and shook my hand. "I'll send over the contract for you sign when I get back to the office this evening. I'll include all the details there."

"Can you include in the contract that we have the option to do the painting and flooring ourselves if money gets tight?"

"I sure will," Jonah said. "I was just about to suggest that you do that." He snapped his briefcase closed and held out his hand to Aiden. "Thanks for telling me about this job, brother." He released Aiden's hand. "You have a good man here. We are all so grateful to have him back in the county. I wish that he was a deputy again. The county felt a whole lot safer with Aiden looking out for us. I always hoped that you would run for sheriff, my friend. The county needs a good man like you. Jackson Marshall is a disgrace and just about the rudest man who ever took a breath of life. He's always been that way."

"Do you know Sheriff Marshall well?"

"Better than most. I grew up with him."

"But I thought you said you were Amish."

"I was. However, I was town Amish and my parents sent me to the public schools up through the eighth grade. Jackson and I were in the same class. I was in school with him every year from first through eighth grade. One of the best things about leaving school early was getting away from Jackson. From what I heard he was even worse in high school. I never went to high school. When I left the church, I got my GED and then went to community college for accounting for a couple of years before I got into construction. Honestly, I don't know why it took me so long to find it. I'd always loved helping my father with projects around our farm. I guess for a long time I thought construction work was too Amish for me. I thought working in an office was the more English thing to do, only I discovered that I hated it."

"Were you Beachy Amish?" I asked.

He chuckled. "You're wondering that because of my name, aren't you? And your assumption would be correct. I am Beachy Amish. I know many Old Order and strict Amish districts don't even think of us as Amish. They think we are too relaxed with our rules." He shrugged. "When I was young, it felt strict to me."

"The person that you are going to speak to at Wade's warehouse is likely his apprentice Naz Schlabach. I understand he's Beachy Amish too. There aren't too many Beachy districts in Holmes County. I just wondered if you might know him."

"Oh, I know Naz. He's quite a character. He's always been an active kid. I thought that one of my nieces might end up marrying him, but she chose someone else. She said that Naz wasn't the marrying type."

"What did she mean by that?" I asked.

"He just isn't a family man or at least that's what my niece said. He told her that he didn't want children. He wanted to focus on his work instead."

"His work for Wade Farmer?"

"Yes," Jonah said with a slight squint of his eye. "It always seemed odd to me that Naz stayed with Wade for so long. He's a talented carpenter. He could have branched out on his own at this point. I know that's what I would do." He pressed his lips together.

After Jonah left, Aiden turned to me. "You seem a lot more at ease."

"I am. I like Jonah and feel he is a good fit for this job. Honestly, I wish I'd hired him from the start."

"I can see that," Aiden said. "What do you want to do now? We actually both have an evening off together."

"How do you feel about ice cream?" I asked.

"I love ice cream."

Jethro hopped to attention. He also was a big ice cream fan.

"That's what I thought you'd say." I hugged him.

Chapter Thirty-two

With my concerns about the construction of the building eased, I could focus fully on solving Wade Farmer's murder. It was amazing how much I'd learned about Wade and Sol Weaver in the last day alone. I didn't have anything that could concretely point me to the actual killer yet, but I felt more than ever that Sol had been falsely arrested. However, I would need a great deal of proof to convince Sheriff Marshall to release Sol from jail.

One thing I knew very well about Sheriff Marshall: he didn't like to be proven wrong. If I was going to challenge him, my accusation had to stick.

Aiden parked his pickup truck in the lot next to the Linzer Petting Zoo barn. His was the only English style vehicle in the lot. The others were buggies, courting buggies, wagons, or tractors. At times, young Amish men would bend the rules and use a tractor to get around since some districts allowed them.

Aiden turned off the engine. "When you asked me to go out for ice cream, I thought you meant going to the ice cream stand in Millersburg. I didn't know that we were going to an Amish youth ice cream social."

"Surprise!" I said with a smile.

"Okay, and how is this related to Wade Farmer's death? Because that's really why we are here, isn't it?"

I quickly filled him in on what I'd learned at the Weaver farm this afternoon.

"I'm glad that Charlotte's mother was willing to speak to her. That's a good sign they may make amends."

"Honestly, I think if it had been up to her mother, they would have done that by now."

"But it's not. It's up to Charlotte's father," Aiden finished for me.

"Right." I nodded and unbuckled my seatbelt.

"I'm surprised that you saw Emmaus Linzer there too."

"Could his case be connected to Wade's death?" I asked.

"I suppose so."

"Do you have any indication where the missing money went?"

"I have an idea, but I want a bit more proof before I take what I've learned to Emmaus. It's going to hurt him."

"Hurt him how?"

"Because the person who took the money is very close to him."

"His wife?" I guessed.

Aiden turned in his seat. "How did you know that?"

"I guessed that she was the person who could

hurt Emmaus the most by her betrayal." I put my hand on the door handle. "We'd better get out. Everyone is staring at us," I said as I looked at the young Amish faces turned in our direction.

Jethro poked his snout between the two front seats. Aiden sighed. "I never should have agreed to take the pig when my mom asked."

"I think that every time she asks me, but what you will find is that you always take the pig. Always."

Aiden laughed. When we got out of the truck, I clipped the leash on Jethro, making sure his collar was secure but not too tight. I didn't want him slipping away from me again on the petting zoo's grounds.

Emmaus ambled over to us. "Bailey! Aiden! And I see that you have Jethro with you. What are you doing here?" Emmaus looked over his shoulder and lowered his voice. "Aiden, are you here because of what we've been discussing?"

"No, actually I'm not. Bailey wanted to check out the ice cream social, and Jethro and I are always game for ice cream. So here we are."

Emmaus visibly relaxed. "That is very good news. I will like to have one day without worrying about it. I'm happy to say that nothing else has gone missing, but I very much want to find what has been lost."

"I understand," Aiden said. "I'm wrapping up the case. Just have to follow up on a few details. I'll be giving you the full report in a few days."

"It would be *gut* if the money was returned too."

"It would be," Aiden said, making no promises.

"*Ya,* well," Emmaus said. "We have ice cream sundaes. You are more than welcome to make your own. The petting zoo is open too if you'd like to go in and visit the animals."

I looked down at Jethro. "I think Jethro and I will pass on that after what happened the last time I was here."

Jethro shivered as if he remembered his close encounter with the aggressive flock of parakeets. I knew it was something that I would never forget.

"I'm glad you could come to the social. I invite all the Amish youth in the county. It doesn't matter what district they are from. All are welcome. I think it's a great opportunity for them to meet people from other churches." He rested his hands on his wide belly like an amiable Santa Claus. "I must say that many Amish courtships begin at my ice cream social. There is romance in the air here."

Aiden took my hand. "Well, it's a good thing that I already found the girl I'm courting."

"Oh, you are courting me, are you?" I asked.

Emmaus laughed and strolled away.

In a low voice, I said, "I hate to know that someone is stealing from such a nice man."

"It is a shame," Aiden said just above a whisper. "And it's only made worse if it's his wife."

"If you think Kelli Anne Linzer is stealing from the petting zoo, what is she using the money for?"

"That's the part I don't know."

"How is she taking the money?"

Aiden looked around as if to make sure no one was listening to us. "She's skimming off the top. She's the one who accounts for how many carrots and treats are sold to visitors."

"It must take quite a long time for her to gather any amount of money."

"Not really," Aiden said. "On a Saturday, the Linzers make close to three thousand dollars in carrot and treat sales alone. If she took a few hundred dollars of that every week, by the end of the month it could be significant."

I nodded as I considered this.

"What's your next move?"

"I want to talk to her about it."

"Does she know that Emmaus hired you to look for the money?" I asked.

"She does."

"How has she acted around you?"

"Completely normal."

I frowned. If I knew that my husband had hired a PI to search for missing money, money that I was responsible for taking, I didn't think I would be acting completely normal. But then again, I never said that I would make a very good thief.

Chapter Thirty-three

Aiden and I made our ice cream sundaes, and if any of the Amish thought it was odd that we were there, they didn't say anything. Not only were we not Amish, but we were in our thirties. We were much older than any of the young people in attendance.

I guessed that one of the oldest Amish youth there was Naz Schlabach. The young Amish man had to be in his mid-to-late twenties if he had been working for Wade for the last ten years. That was also assuming that he went straight to work for Wade when his *rumspringa* began when he was fourteen. I thought he was older. Maybe even twenty-eight. I just couldn't see Wade taking on a fourteen-year-old as an apprentice.

"That is a very interesting sundae you made," Aiden said.

"What?" I was perched on a wooden fence bar, eating ice cream and keeping my eye out for a chance to speak to Naz. As of yet, I had not spotted Jericho Weaver.

"You have mint chocolate chip and butter pecan ice cream doused in hot fudge and marshmallow, and you topped it off with fresh blueberries and chopped nuts."

I licked the back of my spoon. "Don't forget the caramel sauce and whipped cream too."

"It's just a lot," Aiden said. "I thought that being a candy maker, you would be better at putting flavors together."

I looked at his sundae. Vanilla ice cream, hot fudge, and whipped cream. Boring.

"I am excellent at putting flavors together," I argued, "and one way that a person acquires that skill is through trying new combinations. Admittedly, not all of them work, but the ones that do can change your life."

He knitted his brow together. "Change your life?"

"Sure," I said, holding my dish up to him. "Taste it."

He waved at me with his own spoon. "No, no, that's okay."

"Do it!" I ordered, but my command came with a smile.

"Fine." He dug his spoon into my dish and put the spoonful into his mouth.

"Well?" I asked.

After he swallowed, he said, "It's not bad. The blueberries bring a tart burst that counteracts the sweetness."

"Exactly. Personally, I think the mint chocolate chip wasn't the best choice, but the rest of it is a winner. I might make a fudge based on this now."

"You can call it kitchen sink fudge," Aiden said.

"Not funny. If I made a real kitchen sink fudge, you would never be brave enough to try it."

"Want to bet?"

I didn't answer his question because just then a young Amish man rolled up to the ice cream social on a scooter. It was Jericho Weaver.

"Bailey?" Aiden asked. "What is it?"

"Jericho is here."

By this time, Aiden and I had been at the social for over an hour. We'd both eaten more ice cream than we should, and I shuddered to think how much Jethro had eaten off the ground. It seemed like every third Amish teen dropped an ice cream cone on the ground, and Jethro was there for cleanup duty. If he kept this up, Emmaus really was going to hire him to clean the grounds when the petting zoo closed at night.

"The ice cream line is almost nonexistent now. I'm going to wait until he goes there to talk to him."

"Do you want me to go with you?" Aiden asked.

"Not at first. I'll wave if I need you to come over. To be honest, I don't know if he will talk to me."

"What do you plan to ask him?"

"I have so many questions. When Charlotte and I spoke to him before, he seemed to think it was possible that his father could have killed Wade Farmer. I want to know why. I want a better reason than stopping him from working for Wade. And I want to ask him about the money."

Aiden nodded. I had told him about the piles of money that Miriam Lee had seen her brother counting on the bed.

I handed Aiden the remains of my sundae. "You can finish this."

"Umm, thanks."

By the time I reached the sundae-making tables, Jericho was already there, scooping out chocolate ice cream from the cooler on the table. At this time in the evening, the ice cream was easy to scoop because so much of it had been eaten or melted. Chocolate was a popular flavor too.

When he was satisfied with the amount of ice cream in his bowl, he moved down the table and looked at the toppings as if he was taking each one into careful consideration.

"I think the blueberries would be a nice tart punch with the chocolate. Add a little marshmallow fluff to that and you'll have a real winner."

Jericho jumped when he heard my voice and almost dropped his bowl.

"Careful there. I think you got the last of the chocolate ice cream, so if that hits the ground, the only one who is going to enjoy it is Jethro, who has had more than enough sweets for one night, believe me."

"What are you doing here?" Jericho asked in a sharp voice.

"Waiting for you," I said honestly. "You might have heard that Charlotte and I were at your farm earlier today. I saw you there but didn't get a chance to talk. When I saw you, you were talking to Naz Schlabach. Are the two of you still working together?"

He set his ice cream bowl on the table. "That's none of your business. I wish you would just leave us all alone. You already ruined my family by taking Charlotte away from us. Don't make it worse by hurting the rest of us too."

"I'm not trying to hurt any of you." I ignored

the part about taking Charlotte away from them because even if I told the Weavers until I was blue in the face that Charlotte had left their district of her own accord, it would not matter. I was still to blame in their eyes

"Charlotte cares about all of you, and I care about Charlotte. I want to help. Your mother asked Charlotte and me to help find out who killed Wade."

"We already know who did it. It was my father. *Maam* just doesn't want to accept the truth. She also doesn't want to accept that we will all be a lot better off with *Daed* in prison."

"What do you mean by that?" I asked.

"I don't feel like ice cream." He walked away from the table.

As I followed him I could feel the Amish youth around the property watching us. "Jericho!"

He turned around. "What?"

I caught up with him. "Why did you say that about your father?"

"Because it's true. He's not a *gut* father. He's not loving. He does not hit us if that is what you're thinking, but he's unkind in other ways. He wants to control everything that happens under his roof. If he weren't there, we would have space to breathe. I need space to breathe."

"Why don't you leave?" I asked. "You are of age."

"Where am I to go? I am not sweet like Charlotte. No one is just going to welcome me into their home. I could not leave until I could pay my way."

"Is that why you had so much cash stashed in your bedroom?"

His mouth fell open. "How—"

"It doesn't matter how I know," I said. The very last thing I wanted to do was get Miriam Lee into trouble with her brother. It was clear to me that he had some of the same anger issues as his father. He might not like how his dad treated him, but I could see him going down the same bitter road himself.

"There is nothing wrong with me saving up money that I earned."

"I never said there was," I replied quietly and then I looked around. We were the center of attention at the ice cream social. However, at this point, I didn't think Jericho even cared. "But how did you earn that much money?"

"I work as Wade's apprentice—I told you that."

"He must have paid very well."

Sweat gathered on his upper lip. "I don't know what you are getting at. I've worked for him for a couple of years. I'm a saver. There is nothing wrong with that," he repeated.

"I'm just surprised that he was paying you so well when he claimed that he was struggling with money."

"This is ridiculous. I'm leaving." He marched back to his scooter, climbed onto it, and kicked his way back onto the road.

For a moment I wondered if Aiden and I should follow him in Aiden's truck. We would have no trouble catching up with the scooter. However, I decided against it because it would be a little too threatening for my taste. I didn't want to terrify Charlotte's brother.

I looked around the ice cream social for Naz, but he must have left while I was talking to Jericho. I wasn't surprised, and I kicked myself for not interrupting him earlier when he was talking with his friends.

Aiden and Jethro walked over to me. The little pig waddled a bit more than usual. I grimaced. "How much ice cream do you think he ate?"

"A good gallon's worth, I would guess." Aiden looked down at him. "I really hope he doesn't get sick in my truck."

I hoped not too.

"Looks like your conversation didn't go all that well."

"It did not. The only thing I learned is that Jericho doesn't deny having all that money in his room. He claims he's saving up so he can leave the Amish for good."

Aiden nodded. "That's not unusual for a young Amish man who's leaving the faith."

"But he said that he got the money from working for Wade as an apprentice in the construction business. I would bet my new factory that he was lying."

Chapter Thirty-four

Monday morning, I went to the shop at my normal time. Charlotte seemed to be especially quiet, and we moved quickly through all the tasks on our list before the shop opened at ten. The blueberry-and-cream fudge had been popular at the Blueberry Bash. After we gave out all the samples we had, we sold out of the flavor in the shop.

I made a fresh batch and decided to add it to our regular summer menu when blueberries were in season. Fresh local blueberries were truly the key to the recipe. I had tried it with frozen once, and the fudge was far too watery. No one liked a watery fudge. I certainly didn't.

Maami stepped into the kitchen where Charlotte and I were working. "My, the two of you are very quiet today. I'm more used to hearing chatter and laughter when I come down the stairs in the morning."

"We both have a lot on our minds." I glanced at Charlotte, and she gave a slight nod. I knew that she must be thinking of our conversation with her mother and Miriam Lee. She must also be worrying about the wedding, and the fact that Deputy Little's parents still were not thrilled that he was marrying a former Amish woman whose father had been arrested for murder. I guessed she wasn't the person they had conjured in their heads when they were thinking of their future daughter-in-law.

"It was so very nice to meet Luke's parents yesterday," *Maami* said. "I know they seemed a bit surprised by everything going on in your life, but they must be nice people to have a son as *gut* and kind as Deputy Little."

Charlotte and I shared a look. Charlotte had confided that when she went to the B&B after I dropped her off there Sunday, Beth Little refused to come down and see her. She claimed she had a headache. Hal came down but he didn't say much. Finally after an hour, Charlotte gave up and walked back to Swissmen Sweets with her head hung low. It made me want to march over to the B&B right then and there and give both of the elder Littles a piece of my mind.

"Luke has taken a vacation day today," Charlotte said. "He and I are going to show his parents the county. We will go to all the towns. He says that they want to see everything. He was planning on picking me up at eleven. Is it all right if I go?" She didn't ask with a great deal of enthusiasm. I could think of about a million things that I would rather do than spend the day with the elder Littles, such as swim with sharks and get a root canal.

"*Ya*, of course," *Maami* said. "His parents are never in town, and they came all this way to meet you, the woman who will be marrying their son. This will be a *gut* time for them to get to know you.

I know they have reservations because of your family, but Deputy Little is not marrying your family. He is marrying you, and he could not find a better bride."

Tears came to Charlotte's eyes. "*Danki*, Cousin Clara. You are too kind to me."

"Don't be silly," *Maami* said.

Charlotte nodded, then turned her attention to the tray of chocolate-covered pretzels she was sprinkling with crushed nuts while the chocolate was still warm. She cleared her throat. "I know Emily doesn't usually work on Mondays, but she said she would come in today if you need an extra set of hands."

"It should be slow today after the busy weekend," I said. "As far as I know, there are no bus tours scheduled to stop by, but sometimes they surprise us. I'll call Emily's shed phone and leave a message asking her to come in after lunch. It should be quiet until then. She's good about checking the phone. If she doesn't, her husband's *grossmaami* will. I think she waits all day long for that thing to ring."

Maami smiled. "When you're older things like that become amusements, but I know she is happy to have her grandson, Emily, and their two little girls living with her at the Christmas tree farm. Those little ones keep her young."

Charlotte and I shared a glance.

I swallowed. "When Emily comes in, I'm going to run a few errands myself."

My grandmother gave me a look. "I hope these errands don't have to do with Wade Farmer."

"Not directly," I said.

Maami shook her head as if she knew better.

Deputy Little came to pick up Charlotte right at eleven, and they headed to his parents' bed and breakfast to collect them. I reminded Charlotte to just be herself, and they would love her.

I was loading the candy counter when Emily Keim came in; with her was her eldest daughter, a lovely blond replica of her mother. "I hope it's okay that I brought her. My husband's *grossmaami* is watching the baby, but both of them can be a bit of a handful for her."

I waved at the young girl, and she waved back.

I signed that I was happy to see her. She beamed and signed the same back. Hannah had been born deaf and had had a difficult start to life, one where she had been separated from her mother by a forced adoption.

It took years for Emily to find the little girl and get her back. Now that she had, Emily's husband accepted Emily's eldest daughter as his very own. I had seen him many times with her and the baby, and he always treated them the same.

Emily got Hannah settled at one of the café tables at the front of the shop, and I said and signed goodbye as I headed out the door.

On the drive to Charm, I made a phone call that I'd needed to make for the last several days.

"Baggins," Linc answered his cell with a bark.

If someone who didn't know him saw Linc on the street, they would give him a wide berth. He was a squat, gruff man with a tad more body hair than was the norm. However, he was a person who really cared about his job and really cared about making quality cooking and baking shows for his channel, Gourmet Television.

"Hey, Linc. It's Bailey."

"Bailey! How the heck are you? Found another dead guy, I heard, and messed up my production schedule because of it."

"I'm sorry about that, Linc."

"Aww, I should have been expecting something like that would happen if you were involved," he said as if it wasn't a big deal.

I wrinkled my nose at his statement. I didn't want to be known in the television world for messing up production because I found dead bodies. It wasn't a good look.

"I know you've been in contact with Devon, but I'm calling because I need to tell you that the building opening is delayed until November. I'm so sorry. I know this show is important to you, but the circumstances are way beyond my control. I was able to find a new contractor, but he just needs more time for the job. I guess what I'm asking you is to tell Devon and Z that the show has to be postponed or canceled."

There was a long pause on the other end of the line, and I began to sweat. I waited for him to say that he needed his advance money back or to yell that I'd signed a contract that was binding. He said none of that. Instead he said, "I already pulled the plug on it."

"What did you say?"

"I already canceled the production. I knew that it was on life support anyway since you were so behind, but as soon as I heard about the dead guy, I called Devon and told her that the show was over."

My chest tightened. That was three days ago, and in that time, Devon had continued to shoot, insisting that I had to allow her to because she needed footage for the show, a show that had been canceled. She went to the Weaver farm and recorded the prayer meeting, and she wasn't even on the job any longer. What was she doing? Did Z know the show was canceled?

"If you are worried about the advance money and the contract details, we can talk about it. I met with the executives; we might be able to deduct the money from your earnings from *Bailey's Amish Sweets*. You just need to give me some time to figure all that out. But don't sweat it. We will sort it out, and I think we can still do a special episode of *Bailey's Amish Sweets* from the factory, but I think a whole series is out of the question at this point. The executives would nix that in one second."

"Thank you, Linc," I murmured. "That's so very kind of you."

"Well, you have one of our top-rated shows, so we want to do well by you. I guess it's not your fault you keep finding dead people." And just like that he ended the call.

Chapter Thirty-Five

The new candy shop in Charm was as charming as I expected it to be. Many of the buildings along the main road were small businesses run by Amish companies. In the last several years, abandoned shops had been bought up and renovated. Swiss German Candies was in one of those buildings, and that surprised me. I had wrongly believed that Wade worked only on new construction. It also made me wonder why an Amish family would hire an English contractor. I would have thought that they would know someone in the Amish community who could revitalize a building.

I parked at the far end of the long street so I didn't take up any of the parking spots in front of the businesses. Owning a shop myself, I knew how important it was to keep parking spaces open. If a visitor couldn't find a good place to park, they might keep driving, which meant potential sales were lost.

I got out of the car, and the air around me

smelled like fresh baked bread. There was a bakery at the opposite end of the street. Its front door was open, letting out tantalizing smells.

I walked by a wood worker and a quilting shop. I realized that I needed to get out of the candy shop more and explore the county. There were so many lovely nooks and crannies in Holmes County that I didn't even know about. Maybe now that Aiden was back in the village, he and I could take a bit of time off to explore here and there. That was if our schedules would allow it. Both of us worked constantly, and now I was taking on the factory and Aiden was starting a new PI business. It seemed to me that we were always missing each other even when we were in the same town.

The outside of the candy shop looked as if it was ready to open in a matter of days. There was a large handwritten sign in the window that read, COMING SOON.

Perhaps Swiss German Candies' project had not been delayed as terribly as Russell's or mine had.

When I went to the door, I expected it to be locked, but to my surprise it opened easily.

A young Amish woman sat at a card table looking at paint swatches that were scattered across the table. All around her was a construction zone. The inside of the building had been ripped down to the studs. I could see the beginning of wiring and outlets, but the space was far from finished. The outside of the building might have looked like it was ready to go, but the inside was a disaster.

The woman gasped and placed her hand against her cheek. She stood and knocked her metal folding chair to the wooden floorboards below her feet. "You're Bailey King!" She blushed and then ran out of the room through a doorway and disappeared.

I stood in the middle of the gutted candy shop and wondered what I should do. Clearly, I had scared the young woman. How did she know my name? I had never seen her before and had never been inside this building in my life. There was always the chance that someone I didn't know recognized me from television, but this woman was Amish. I guessed that wasn't the reason she knew me.

I hesitated, and just when I made the choice to follow her, a young man with a curly blond Amish beard stepped through the same doorway through which she had disappeared.

"Hello, can I help you?" he asked in a pleasant voice.

"Maybe," I said. "I just walked in to learn more about the shop. My name is Bailey King."

"I'm James Klum. I know who you are, and my wife does too. You will have to forgive Lydia. She is a big fan of yours."

I raised my brow. "A fan? She watches television?" I asked.

"*Nee,* my wife would not do that. She's Amish," James said. "But she has wanted our family to have a candy shop for as long as she could remember. She was inspired by you and the success of Swissmen Sweets since you took over."

"I didn't take over. My grandmother, Clara King, is still very much involved in the business."

"I have heard that, but you grew the business. When Wade Farmer was working for us, he spoke often of the candy factory and what an undertaking it was. I believe he thought that he'd bitten off more than he could chew, taking on that project as well as the other smaller ones like ours." He looked around at the bare room. "Not that we believe this is small. This is the biggest thing we have ever done. I'm doing it for my wife. This is her dream."

James's last comment surprised me. It was not typical that an Amish man would support his wife's business so openly. My surprise must have shown on my face because he said, "We are Beachy Amish, so roles are a little bit different in our community. We're not nearly as strict as many other Amish groups."

"Oh, I just recently met a Beachy Amish man. Do you know Emmaus Linzer?"

"Of course! He's in our district. He's a very nice man. Our children love his petting zoo and ask to go there all the time." He paused. "Let me go find my wife. She would like to meet you now that she's recovered from the shock of seeing you here."

I wasn't so sure that was true, judging by the way she'd run away from me just a moment ago.

He left the room.

While I waited for James and Lydia to reappear, the front door opened, and Naz Schlabach stepped into the shop. He held a set of blueprints in one hand and a tape measure in the other. "Oh, Bailey, what are you doing here?"

I could be asking him the same thing. However, before I could, James returned, and Lydia followed behind him.

She stayed close to her husband and had almost a look of fright in her eye, as if she wasn't sure what I might do.

Thankfully, Naz was there to break the awkward

silence. "I just came by to give you the updated plans. I wanted to see if you have any more changes before I take over this job next week. I'm really looking forward to handling this challenge alone for the first time."

"You're going to take on this construction job?" I asked.

He nodded. "I can't work for Wade anymore." He paused as if out of respect to his former employer. "I'm so sorry that he's gone. He truly taught me everything I know about construction and about business. This is a chance to move on, though, as scary as it is. Truthfully, I would have worked with Wade forever if he were still here."

That was interesting to hear. The general consensus seemed to be that Wade was a tough boss and very demanding of all his employees. Naz was the first one I'd spoken to who had said he wished Wade was still alive.

"It's very kind of you to let us have another look, Naz," James said as he took the rolled blueprints from the young man's hand.

Lydia stepped forward. "It's so nice to meet you, Miss King. I have been following your career in the newspapers. I'm so very excited about your candy factory." Her voice trembled slightly.

I smiled at her. "It's nice to meet you too. I'm sure the village of Charm will be excited to have this candy shop." Some of my anxiety about the rival candy shop fell away. James and Lydia seemed to be nice people. There were multiple cheese and quilting shops in Holmes County, and none of them seemed to suffer from the competition. There was no reason there couldn't be more than one candy shop.

"We hope so." She looked at her husband. "James has been so kind to do this for me. He has put a lot of himself into the shop. It's really been my dream since my *grossmaami* taught me to make candy when I was a young girl."

The last of my nervousness about the new shop evaporated. "My grandparents taught me how to make candy when I was young too."

James squeezed his wife's hand. "I have done it for both of us. Opening your own shop is a great idea, and you make the best candies."

Lydia blushed. "I don't make anything as fancy as what Bailey does. She worked in New York." She said "New York" as if she were talking about another planet, which in a lot of ways it was.

"How did you hear about our shop?" James asked.

I glanced at Naz. "It was actually through Wade Farmer. We have, or had, the same contractor until . . ." I trailed off.

James's brow furrowed. "And what was your experience with him?"

"Okay to start."

He relaxed. "But not okay after that."

I shook my head.

James glanced at his wife. "We had the same experience." He then looked at Naz.

Naz smiled. "Don't feel bad talking about Wade in front of me. I've just been learning how he was treating our clients. He told me that we stopped working on your jobs because people weren't paying."

James's face flushed. "That is not true."

Naz held up his hands. "I know that now. I've learned what was really going on since he passed. I didn't know he was asking for a larger advance from all our clients."

"All?" I asked.

He nodded. "There are at least eight projects that were put on hold because Wade asked the clients for more money." He swallowed. "I know because I've been getting all the angry phone calls. People are either asking me to come out and finish the work Wade started or they want their money back."

I raised my brow. "Are you responsible for paying them?"

He shrugged. "I don't believe so. I wasn't an owner in the business, just an employee. However, I can understand why everyone is so upset. I feel that I have to apologize since I worked for him, but none of us on the crew knew what he was doing." Naz grimaced. "He just told us that he couldn't continue with any of the jobs until he got more money. He led us to believe that the clients weren't paying him the money that was already owed. It wasn't until after he died that I realized that wasn't true. Instead, he was asking for money for work that he hadn't completed yet. Knowing that now, I feel awful that I didn't have more of an idea what was going on, but ever since his wedding was called off, Wade was erratic and very angry. None of us wanted to do anything that might upset him even a little bit. He was a hothead as my *grossmaami* would have said."

I was in full agreement with that assessment.

Naz sighed. "I'm doing what I can by taking on some of the unfinished jobs. Unfortunately, I can't take them all on by myself."

"We are grateful that you will be working for us,"

James said. "We very much want the shop open by fall."

Naz nodded. "We will make it happen." He removed his tape measure from his tool belt. "Let me take some measurements, and the three of you can chat about candy." He walked into the next room.

Lydia watched him go. "He's a nice young man. I thought that when he came here with Wade the first time."

"I'm sorry to hear that you had a bad experience with Wade too," I said.

"As am I." James nodded. "*Ya*, Wade was fine to work with at the start. His work is second to none, but then he just stopped, saying that he needed more money than we were prepared to pay without seeing any progress."

"We are just so grateful for Naz," Lydia murmured.

"Did either of you go to the Blueberry Bash in Harvest on Friday?" I asked.

"We were there," James said without seeming overly concerned about the question. "But we didn't stay long as we had work to do here. We've put everything we have into this place. We didn't have to start from scratch like some businesses, but we ripped the building down to the studs. We've done much of the work ourselves with family and friends, but when it comes to the electrical and some other details, we need help. That's what we hired Wade for."

"Naz is going to do that?" I asked.

"He is," James said.

I had never heard of an Amish electrician, but I knew many Amish contractors built English homes and businesses. All those places have electricity. It would make sense that some of the Amish contractors, at least, would learn the skills of an electrician in order to provide that service during construction. Also, most Amish businesses that were in the main part of towns like Harvest, Charm, and Berlin had electricity so that the buildings were up to code.

Then I remembered that Naz was Beachy Amish too. "Is Naz a member of your district? I thought I heard he was also Beachy Amish."

"*Nee*," James said. "I will have to ask him which Beachy district he is a member of."

"I'm glad to see that you have a plan," I said. "I've also found a new contractor to finish the candy factory. My job was at a standstill too, but now I'm hoping to hold my grand opening in November."

"Perhaps," Lydia said in her soft voice, "we could have a joint event featuring our two shops?"

"I would like that," I said.

She blushed.

James held up the blueprint. "Would you like to see the plans for the shop? Maybe you can let us know if there's anything we've overlooked."

I agreed, and James rolled out the blueprint on the card table. The plan they had was lovely, with equal space given to retail and to the kitchen area.

"It looks to me like you have everything in order. It will be a lovely shop," I said.

"Thank you again for coming," Lydia said. "I hope you will come back when we open."

"I will, and I think a joint candy event would be a great idea."

She beamed.

James and Lydia were such nice people. It was hard for me to believe that they could have hurt a fly, let alone shot Wade Farmer in cold blood. I said goodbye and let myself outside.

If I removed the couple from my suspect list, I was just left with Russell and Charlotte's father. And I had to include Jericho, too, due to his odd behavior. He seemed to have a real problem with his father. Perhaps, he'd framed Sol just to get him out of his life.

I started down the long sidewalk to my car, but I'd just taken a few steps when the door opened behind me. "Bailey!"

I turned to see Naz hurrying down the sidewalk toward me.

"I'm glad that I caught you. Ever since what happened on Friday, I have felt bad."

"You mean Wade's death?" I asked.

"I do feel bad about that. *Ya.* Wade was a grump, but he was a great craftsman and contractor. I learned so much from him." He was quiet for a moment. "What I meant was how Wade treated you that day. I should have spoken up. I'm sorry I didn't."

I shook my head. "There is nothing to apologize for."

His face broke into a smile. "*Danki.* I have been thinking about that the last several days, and it's nice to finally be able to say it."

I nodded and started walking again in the direction of my car. Naz walked with me and kept talking. "I'm really looking forward to working with the Klums. They are a nice couple. It's going to be quite a change for me after working for Wade all those years."

"How long did you work for him?" I asked.

"Almost ten years. Wade seemed to go through tradesmen quickly because he was a hard man. We all thought that when he was married, he would soften up a bit." He shook his head. "When the wedding fell through, he was even worse."

"When did that happen?"

He thought for a moment. "A month or so back."

That was about the same time Wade had stopped working on my factory, and I was willing to bet it was the same time he'd stopped working on Russell's and the Klums' jobs too.

"Did he tell you why the wedding was off?" I asked.

"*Nee.* He would never share anything so personal. I didn't even know the name of his bride."

This surprised me. I'd have thought that Wade would have said his wife-to-be's name at least once. "How did you know the wedding was off then?"

"I heard him on the phone canceling his flight to the wedding."

"Where was it supposed to be?"

"I don't know." He shrugged and changed the subject. "I guess you must be looking for a new contractor too. I'd love to take on your job, but it's a little bigger than I am able to handle on my own."

I nodded as we reached my car. "I understand. There are also a lot of hoops I have to jump through since it's a factory. There are local and FDA rules that must be followed if I'm to ship the candies and sell them in a wider area. I've actually already found a new contractor, Jonah Beachy. He will be calling you about any materials of mine that might be in the warehouse."

"Oh, I know Jonah," he said in a careful way.

"I happened to see you yesterday at the prayer meeting at the Weaver home."

"Oh, you were there," he said in mock surprise. Naz had to have known that Charlotte and I were there. Everyone at the meeting did.

"Why were you there?"

"I was just comforting the family like everyone else. I have worked with Jericho for a couple of years. He's a friend. I wanted to support him."

The angry conversation I'd witnessed when I walked by didn't seem all that supportive.

He pointed his thumb behind him. "I have to get back to the Klums, but it was nice chatting with you," he said while backing up. "Have Jonah give me a call!" He ran down the sidewalk as if he was afraid I might chase him.

Chapter Thirty-six

On the drive back to Harvest, I called Devon to tell her I'd found a new contractor and asked her and Z to meet me at the factory. The part about finding the new contractor was true, and I hadn't said he was going to be there.

Devon said she and Z would come. She seemed to have completely forgotten how mad I was at her when she'd tried to film the prayer meeting yesterday.

As I expected, they beat me to the factory. They were just across the street in the B&B, so they had a lot shorter distance to travel.

"There you are," Devon said. "What took you so long?"

"Hi to you too," I said. "I told you I was on my way."

Z was attaching his camera to a tripod. "Fine. You're here. Where is the new contractor? We want to get this meeting on tape."

I folded my arms. "I've already met with him. He's not coming today."

Devon threw her hands into the air. "What? You met with him without telling us? It's our job to get this on film for the series."

"That's the funny thing about it," I said. "There is no series."

Devon sputtered. "Wha—That's not true!"

Z looked up from working on the tripod and gave us his full attention for the first time.

"I had an interesting conversation with Linc Baggins today. He said that he canned the new series and told you three days ago."

"I—I—" Devon wasn't able to get her words out.

"What?" Z exploded. "It's canceled and I'm still here? Who is paying my traveling expenses?"

Devon held up her hand. "Listen, Z! The time you're putting in here will pay off. Think of the show we can create with this Amish murder. We could sell it to a really important network or even get a streaming deal."

"No way. I didn't sign up for that." He quickly removed the camera from the tripod and put it in its case.

"You can't quit!"

"I'm not quitting," he cried and then pointed at me. "From what she said, I was already fired!" He furiously packed up his gear. He zipped his bag closed, stood up, and slung the heavy equipment over his shoulder. "We can't just stay here because of your obsession with true crime. That was never the assignment," he snapped. "And now there is no assignment, and I have to figure out how I'm going to get home since it looks like I have to pay for my own flight!"

"True crime?" I asked.

Z narrowed his eyes at Devon. "Yes, that's what

she really wants to be producing. She took this job because she read about your history with the sheriff's department here. She thought that she could make a show on the side about the crimes in Amish Country. But I don't think even Devon would have predicted that there would be an actual murder on site."

"You never said anything about this," I said to Devon.

"If I did, would you have let me be the producer?"

Probably not.

"You took this job under false pretenses. Did Linc know your real intentions here?"

She folded her arms. "Linc knows I have a passion for true crime. Gourmet Television is part of a conglomerate of networks. One of those is a true crime channel. That's where I really want to be. I thought I'd get my foot in the door at Gourmet Television and then transition to the station I really wanted to be on."

This explained Devon's desire to go with me to talk to witnesses about Wade's death and why she would morbidly record the prayer meeting for Sol Weaver. She had claimed that it was because of the candy factory series, but now I knew better. It was never about that for her.

"There is nothing wrong with having ambition," Devon said.

I agreed with her to an extent, but I believed that she should have been a little more up-front about her intentions. She'd said she was interested in the case because of the factory. That had been a lie. She was interested because she thought it would help her career.

In many ways, I understood Devon better now, and as hard as it was to admit, I saw a lot of myself in her. When I was her age, I did whatever it took to advance my career as a New York City chocolatier. I put in the long hours and did all the extra things that I thought would help me.

"That's true, but you can't force your ambitions on me," Z said. "I like working for Gourmet Television, and this is where I want to stay. Now, I don't even know if they will keep me after the stunt you pulled." He marched out of the factory carrying every last piece of camera gear.

Devon stared after him with her hands on her hips. "I don't need you anyway. You sleep too much," she called after him, but since he was already outside the building, I doubted he heard her. That was probably for the best.

I frowned at her. "I think it's time for me to leave."

"But we could still make a documentary about the murder. I would cut you into the deal. True crime is huge! Think of all the money you will make!"

"No," I said and walked out of the factory. She could find her own way back to the B&B and back to New York for that matter.

Instead of walking to Swissmen Sweets, I continued on to the side street where I had parked my car after my trip to Charm.

A quick search on my phone showed me where Wade's workshop was. It was in Millersburg on the outskirts of the town. By the look of the map, there wasn't much else on the road where it was, so it would be easy to spot. Naz had told me to have Jonah call him to see which of my materials were at the warehouse, but I thought I would rather take a look for myself. Besides, I wanted to finish the conversation with Naz that he had so abruptly ended.

However, I was driving there on a whim. There was no guarantee that I would be able to get inside the warehouse or that Naz would even be there.

The drive to Wade's workshop was peaceful. It was another gorgeous summer day with bright sunshine. I knew farmers across the county were watching the skies and waiting for rain. It hadn't rained in a week, and in Holmes County, that was a long time to wait.

I was grateful that the workshop was on a paved road—many of the roads weren't in Amish Country. The building was simple to find, as it was a large bright-blue pole barn. In front of the pole barn sat a trailer I assumed Wade had used as an office.

The whole setup was pretty basic, but the grass was trimmed and the walk was swept. I had to wonder if those activities were some of the last that Wade had done before he died.

There was a handwritten sign over the trailer's door that read, PERMANENTLY CLOSED.

I couldn't help but wonder who'd made that sign. Naz would be my best guess. He said that he had worked the longest for Wade.

Just in case someone happened to drive by the barn, I parked my car behind the trailer so it would be out of sight from the road and from the pole barn itself. I got out of the car, expecting to peek in the windows and leave. It was unlikely that I would see anything with my name on it. However, if there were a lot of building materials in the pole barn and some of them were mine, it would save me a lot of money completing the factory.

Thick shades were pulled down over all the windows, so my plan to sneak a peek was a bust. I sighed as I walked back to my car. On a whim, I tried the door, and to my surprise the doorknob turned.

I pushed it open.

Wade wasn't Amish, so I expected to find electric lights in the workshop. However, I couldn't find the switch by the door, and with all the shades pulled tightly closed over the windows, it was difficult to see.

I took a few steps into the building with a tingling feeling on the back of my neck as if someone was watching me. I peered around but didn't see anyone. As I took another step forward, my foot caught on a piece of metal and I went tumbling forward. I threw out my hands and caught myself on a cart that had dozens of boxes of nails stacked on top of it.

Two boxes fell from the cart and burst open on the concrete floor, sending roofing nails everywhere.

I froze as I stared at the mess I'd made. I stayed there for a moment and listened. I half-expected an Amish worker to appear and ask me what I was doing there. I thought it likely that someone was in the shop because the door was unlocked.

No one came. My eyes finally adjusted to the darkness, and I spotted the shape of a floor lamp a few feet away from me.

I reached over to turn on the lamp. It gave a weak light, but it was enough to keep me from tripping over something again.

I picked up one of the empty boxes and started to collect the nails. It took me several minutes to grab all the ones I could see. I was sure I'd missed some because they'd scattered in all directions and probably rolled under the nearby furniture and supplies.

I stood and set the last nail box back onto the cart. Out of the corner of my eye, I saw three nails sticking out from under the desk. I could have ignored them, but I hated to leave a mess behind.

I bent over to pick them up, then felt around under the desk in case there might be even more nails there. I was praying that I didn't find any spiders with my fingertips. There were no nails or spiders, but I felt a piece of paper. I pulled it out.

The paper turned out to be a printout from a computer. In fact, it looked like a computer coupon. At the top it said, "Use this code for fifteen percent off. Find the love of your life through Heart and Soul Inc."

I frowned. What an odd flyer to find in a pole barn. It was probably nothing, but I folded it into quarters and stuck it in the back pocket of my jeans just as the front door opened. I ducked under the desk.

"How did these nails get all over the place?" I heard a man ask.

I'd missed more than a few, I guessed.

"I don't know. I haven't been in here for days," said a voice I thought I knew. I wished that I could peek over the edge of the desk to see who it was, but it was too great a risk.

"Well, you can clean it up."

"You're not my boss."

"I am now," the first man said. "I was Wade's second-in-command."

My eyes went wide. The first man speaking was Naz, and I realized that the second voice belonged to Charlotte's brother Jericho. I should have expected that it would be the two of them who had access to the warehouse.

"We don't even know if we can work here anymore," Jericho said.

"We will be able to. We have nothing to worry about any longer. He assured me."

Who was *he*?

"He can't control everything," Jericho said.

"He can control a lot more than you can," Naz snapped.

"I just don't know why my father had to take the blame for this. You don't know the strain it's put on my family."

"Do you want to take it?" Naz's voice was harsh. "Someone had to, and you said yourself that your *daed* is a cruel man."

"*Nee*, I don't want to take the blame. I'm just thinking of my *maam*. It's hard on her. She asked that Bailey woman to look into the murder."

My whole body tensed at the mention of my name.

"And you don't know for sure your father didn't kill him. He was very angry at Wade. Just let it be. That is the best way to keep us out of it."

"But my *daed* wouldn't do it. He's not capable of that."

"That's what all killers' family members say."

My leg was bent at a strange angle under me and had fallen asleep. The urge to move was overwhelming, but I stayed where I was. A sharp pain tore up the side of my leg, and I squeezed my hands together to keep from crying out.

Footsteps passed the desk, and I saw two sets of work boots go by me. A door somewhere in the building opened and shut. It was my one chance to move.

I stretched out my leg and bit my lip. It felt like thousands of pins were being jabbed into my muscles all at the same time.

Slowly, I stood up and hobbled to the front door. I must have looked ridiculous.

I opened the door just as Naz came into the room. Jericho was no longer with him. I closed the door behind me as if I had just come in.

Naz pulled up short. "Bailey, what are you doing here?"

"Oh hi, I hope it was okay that I let myself in. The door was unlocked."

He frowned.

"When I saw you in Charm, it got me thinking about my factory build. I was in Millersburg running errands, and thought I'd stop by on the chance that you were here. I thought it might be good to see for myself if any of the candy factory building materials are in this warehouse. Then Jonah can send one of his guys over with a truck."

His face cleared. "Let me check the ledger." He moved over to the desk where I had been hiding just moments ago.

My leg was still throbbing, but with every passing second the pain was fading away. However, walking was still a bit tricky because I didn't have feeling in my right foot. I stayed where I was for fear of bringing attention to it.

"Actually, your insulation is here."

My eyes went wide. "For the whole building?"

He nodded. "According to this you paid for it too."

"Can Jonah grab it for me? I know this is Wade's business, but if I paid for it . . ." I trailed off. The thought of paying for that expensive insulation twice turned my stomach, and if I could tell Jonah I had the insulation on hand, my estimate from him might drop dramatically.

"Jonah doesn't have to worry about it. I know he's busy, and the sooner I can sort through everything and get the materials that aren't Wade's out of the warehouse, the better. I'll have it delivered to your factory site tomorrow. Actually, it would be a big help to me to know which materials in here are going to a particular job and what can be used for something else," he said with a smile.

"I know this might be a personal question, but are you authorized to give it to me? Are you Wade's heir?"

He shook his head. "I don't think he had one. He didn't have a will either as far as I know. I have proof here the insulation was yours and paid for. I don't see why you can't have it." Naz shook his head. "As for the stuff that no one's paid for, I don't know what is going to happen to all that. It might have to be sold to pay off any debts Wade had. I'm happy that's not my job to do. But again, I can deliver your insulation."

I twisted my mouth. I wasn't sure if it was right to take the insulation even though I had paid for it. I guessed that everything in the pole barn had to be inventoried and accounted for after Wade's death. However, I knew I wasn't going to get back the money I'd spent on it, and I didn't want it to get lost in the confusion of settling Wade's estate. "If you could deliver it, that would be great."

"Was there anything else?" Naz asked in a cheerful voice.

"Is Jericho Weaver still working here by chance?" I asked.

"*Nee*," Naz lied to me. "He found work somewhere else." His eyes bored into mine. "If that's all, I'll see you tomorrow with the delivery."

I had been dismissed.

Chapter Thirty-seven

On the drive back to Harvest, my mind buzzed over the conversation I'd heard between Jericho and Naz. It sounded as if they might know who the killer was, and neither of them thought it was Sol Weaver. However, they'd both agreed to let Sol take the blame. Perhaps I could see Naz doing that, but Sol was Jericho's father. How could he let his own father go to prison? Did he really want Sol out of the Weaver home that badly?

Then I thought about what Aiden had said about the sheriff convincing Sol to confess to the crime. Had that happened yet?

I knew why Sheriff Marshall had arrested Sol so quickly. The Amish were very protective of their members, and Sheriff Marshall would have been afraid Sol might flee and hide somewhere in the community or possibly leave the state and hide in a community somewhere else. It was easy for the Amish to disappear. They had no social security numbers, credit cards, or cars to trace. Sol could have just vanished if the sheriff hadn't caught him first.

I needed to know what was going on with Sol and check that he was all right. Personally, I didn't care for the man, but he was Charlotte's father.

At a stop sign, I reached for my phone on the passenger seat. I was about to call Aiden when it rang in my hand.

My best friend's face appeared on the screen. Cass Calbera's hair was dyed in blocks of black and purple, and she wore all black as part of her uniform as the head chocolatier at JP Chocolates in New York City. However, Cass didn't have to be in uniform to wear black. She always wore black. She was so committed to the hue that she'd made me promise she could wear black to my wedding someday, "assuming Hot Cop ever proposes," as she said. Hot Cop was Cass's name for Aiden, not mine. She should probably change it to Hot Private Eye now.

"Hello, Best Friend Who Never Calls," Cass said into my ear.

"I call you," I said.

"Not as much as I call you. I know Hot Cop has moved back to Harvest, and you must be occupied, but at least shoot me a text now and again."

"Sorry, it's been a little crazy with the factory and the film crew."

"I'm sure it has," she said, sounding appeased. "How is that all going? Jean Pierre is thrilled to watch the new series."

"There's not going to be a series," I said.

She must have heard something in my voice because she asked, "What happened?"

"It's kind of a long story."

"I have six minutes before I have a Bat Mitzvah consultation. Talk fast."

As quickly and concisely as I could, I told her about the last several days. When I finished my story, I heard nothing.

"Are you still there?"

"I'm digesting," she said.

"Do you have time to digest with the Bat Mitzvah consultation and everything?"

"Not really, but I need a second to think this through. So did Charlotte's dad kill your contractor?"

"That's the thing. I don't think he did, but the sheriff is set on the idea."

"Well, we know the sheriff is a selfish man and will do anything to make his own life easier. Even railroad an innocent man. I can spare three more minutes. I sent one of the under chocolatiers out to meet with the family and give them a list of the options we can provide. Tell me about the dead guy."

I wondered in the last few years how many times Cass had used the phrase "tell me about the dead guy." I guessed it was more than I wanted to count.

I quickly told her what I could. "He was supposed to get married this spring and travel with his new bride, but he never did."

"Who was he marrying?" she asked.

"That's the thing. No one seems to know, but I found something interesting under his desk today."

"You broke into his place of business?" she asked.

"The door was unlocked."

"Go on."

An empty Amish schoolhouse with a small parking lot came into view as I drove down the country road. Since it was summer, the schoolhouse was empty. "One second. I have to pull over to get something from my pocket."

I pulled into the lot and parked the car. Then I reached into my back jeans pocket for the coupon. "Under his desk I found this online coupon offering fifteen percent off on a matchmaking website called Heart and Soul."

"Heart and Soul?" Cass asked with shock in her voice.

"Yeah, have you heard of it?"

"Bailey, everyone who doesn't live under a rock has heard of it. I can't believe you haven't," Cass exclaimed. "I swear, when you moved out to Ohio, you moved to another planet entirely. You know nothing about current events any longer."

"I never knew about current events," I corrected. "It doesn't have anything to do with where I live."

"Okay, that's a fair point." She sighed.

"Tell me what you know about this website."

"It's a huge catfishing scheme. Men looking for love send money to be matched with a beautiful woman on the other side of the world. At least they think that's what's happening. The deeper they get into these online relationships, the more money the guys are asked for. As time goes on, more and more money is requested."

"Do you think that's what happened to Wade?" I gasped.

"Well, you said he had a wedding coming up that never happened."

"How much money do these guys send?"

"Thousands, and in one case a million dollars."

I gasped. "I can't believe they would do that without meeting the woman in person."

"Some people want love that badly I guess. It was a pretty smooth operation. One victim said that he even video chatted with his match countless times. He realizes now it was likely a paid actress. It's a complete catfishing scheme."

"When did the news break?" I asked.

She thought for moment. "I think it was early May."

The same time Wade had stopped working on my factory and his other projects.

"If Wade was one of these victims, would he have gotten his money back?" I asked.

"I doubt he stood a chance of that. The whole company disappeared when the news broke. The website was deleted and the messages that went back and forth were obliterated. The FBI suspects that the company is running out of Eastern Europe, but since it is in a different country, there is very little that can be done to retrieve any of the money these men spent."

I had a twinge of sympathy for Wade. How hurt and betrayed he must have felt. He was made to look like a fool and might have lost thousands of dollars in the process. Now it made sense to me why he wanted so much money from his clients. However, the question remained: How much money had he lost? And how much of that money had actually been his clients' funds?

Chapter Thirty-eight

Back in Harvest, I texted Aiden and asked him to meet me on the square. It was a beautiful summer afternoon, but dark thoughts gathered in my head. I was surer than ever that Sol hadn't killed Wade. I had newfound sympathy for Wade, too, knowing that he'd been cheated out of money and had likely died heartbroken. No one deserved that.

I was sitting on a bench facing Juliet's church. The white steeple shone brightly in the sunlight, and the purple front door gleamed with a fresh coat of paint.

I heard someone moving through the grass behind me. I glanced over my shoulder to see Aiden walking toward me wearing khakis and a blue polo shirt. When he was a sheriff's deputy, I had always thought that he was most handsome when he wore his uniform. However, now I thought he was more handsome than he'd ever been.

"Do you know you have a roofing nail in the cuff of your jeans?" he asked.

I leaned over and plucked the nail from my jeans. "Oh wow."

"How did it get there?" he asked as he watched me closely.

"I had a bit of an adventure this afternoon."

He gave me a look. "Oh?"

I quickly told him about my trip to Wade's workshop.

"You shouldn't have gone there alone."

"I wasn't expecting anyone to be there."

He gave me another look.

"Is there a way to find out if Wade was one of the guys who were tricked out of their money through that dating website?"

"I can make some calls. When I was in BCI we worked closely with the Cleveland office of the FBI on several cases. I have a friend there who might be able to tell me whether Wade Farmer was listed as a victim. If my friend doesn't know, he will be able to direct me to the right person."

I nodded. "That would help. Honestly, I think that's what really happened, but having proof would be nice."

"I don't think it will be enough for the sheriff to open a new case. He will say it's unrelated to the murder."

"On the surface it appears to be, but I just don't buy that."

"I don't either."

"How's the petting zoo case?"

He sighed and ran his hand through his thick blond hair. He had let it grow a little longer than when he had been a sheriff's deputy and it curled around his ears. I had an urge to tug one of those curls, but I kept my hands to myself. "That case is all but wrapped up. I confronted Kelli Anne about it this morning, and she confessed that she did take the money."

"Wow, she just came right out and said it?"

He nodded. "It helped that I had hidden a battery-operated camera in the office and caught her skimming money from the carrot sales. There wasn't much she could argue with when I had it on tape like that."

"What did she use the money for?" I asked.

"I don't know. She claimed it was to benefit the petting zoo and to help her husband. She had no way to prove that."

"Now what happens?"

"Nothing. Emmaus doesn't want to press charges against his wife." He shook his head. "He paid me for solving the case, and I almost felt bad for taking his money because I wasn't able to recover his lost funds. If Emmaus doesn't want to pursue the case, there is no reason for me to press the issue." He dropped his hand from his hair. "But it does make me frustrated that the case doesn't have a neat and tidy ending. Most cases don't though." His shoulders drooped. "I'd hoped when I decided to be a private detective that I would be able to see every case through to the end. There were so many times as a deputy or as a BCI agent that I was pulled off a case because of politics, money, or time and didn't get to see it through. That was the most difficult part of working in the system for me. I'm disappointed to find it's the same working outside of the system too."

I linked my arm thought his. "We're a lot alike in that way. I want to see through everything I start."

He wrapped his arm around me, and for a moment I forgot about construction and murder and Charlotte's upcoming wedding. I was just in that quiet moment with Aiden.

"I have been thinking about us a lot the last few days."

"Oh?" I sat up straight, and the peaceful feeling I had vanished.

"When all of this is over, we need to have a serious talk about our future." He looked at me with his chocolate-brown eyes. "A very serious talk."

There was a sharp pinch in my chest. What was wrong? What did he want to talk about? And what was "all of this?" The murder? Or the construction project? Because the construction job would go on for several more months as the building was completed and fine-tuned.

He touched my cheek. "Don't look so worried. This is all good news. You're the love of my life, Bailey."

Relieved tears came to my eyes. "And you're mine."

It wasn't often that Aiden and I sat down and really spoke of how we felt about each other. We were both so busy, and if we were honest with each other and ourselves, we were both workaholics. It wasn't easy to navigate a relationship, but we always found a way to come back together. Even after he'd moved away to work for BCI, we hadn't taken a break or anything. We'd stayed together, though I wasn't saying it had been easy.

I pressed my hand over his on my cheek. "We'd better move. Your mom is probably watching us with binoculars from the steeple of the church, thinking you're about to propose."

He dropped his hand. "We wouldn't want her to think that."

No, we wouldn't, I thought sadly.

Chapter Thirty-nine

The next morning, I quickly completed my duties at the candy shop and left *Maami* and Charlotte to handle sales. Deputy Little's parents planned to rent a car and travel to Columbus for some sightseeing. Charlotte was relieved to go back to stirring chocolate and pulling taffy.

While my grandmother and Charlotte worked at the shop, I hurried to my car with the intention of going to the petting zoo to speak to Emmaus before it opened. However, I hadn't yet made it out the door before I heard a familiar voice call my name.

"Bailey!" Juliet waved to me from the square.

I wasn't the least bit surprised to see she had Jethro tucked under her arm.

"Bailey, what are you doing leaving the shop at this time of day? Shouldn't you be making candies?"

I tried not to overthink how Juliet knew my schedule so well. "What can I do for you, Juliet?" I asked as if I hadn't already guessed.

"You're the sweetest girl. You're always willing to help out. You will be a great addition to the young mothers club at our church when you have a little one of your own." She shook her head. "I hope it's not too long. You don't want to be the oldest lady in the group!"

This was not the conversation that I wanted to have with her so early in the morning—or ever. Also, that group sounded like my worst nightmare. Rather than waste time, I asked, "Do you need me to watch Jethro?"

She hoisted the pig into my arms. "How did you know? I have a garden club and social committee meeting today at the church. I just can't have Jethro underfoot. I have lovely refreshments planned for both, but can you believe some of the women aren't comfortable eating when there is a pig in the room? I never heard of such a thing."

"Maybe they are thinking of farm pigs and not Jethro."

She put her hands on her hips. "I should hope they are. In any case, there are some contentious topics scheduled for the meetings—I want to replace the lilac bush behind the church, for example. It's half-dead, but any proposed change to the gardens sends these women into a spiral."

"I have some errands to run, but Jethro can stay at the shop with *Maami* and Charlotte. Nutmeg is there. The two of them could get in a good nap."

"Oh no," Juliet said. "He wants to spend the day with you, and he loves to run errands. He told me so."

"He *told* you?" I squinted at her.

"We are very connected. Sometimes, I feel that we are the same person."

They certainly had the matching polka dots down.

I agreed to take Jethro because the truth was, I didn't have time to argue with Juliet about it, and I knew that she wouldn't give up until I gave her the answer she wanted.

On the drive to the petting zoo, I had a vision of a repeat of Jethro's visit to the parakeet cage. If I could help it, I wasn't going to let that happen again.

It was still two hours before the petting zoo was to open, and the parking lot was empty save for a handful of buggies that I guessed belonged to employees.

Sol's kettle corn stand stood cold and empty. I wondered who would be making the corn that coming Saturday.

I was surprised to see one automobile parked behind the large barn. It was a sheriff's department SUV. My first thought was that it must have been Deputy Little. Perhaps Aiden had told him about the case, and the deputy had decided to check it out. However, I was soon corrected when I saw the sheriff walking to the car with Emmaus following a few feet behind him. I was still sitting in my car, but I could hear their voices through the open window.

"Everything goes through me now. Your wife knows how it works."

"I understand," Emmaus said. His typical smile was gone. "But I don't think we want to continue this in the future."

"That's interesting because I've noticed six violations since I pulled into your parking lot this morning. That's before the tourists have even arrived. I'm sure that number triples when they are here, doesn't it?"

Emmaus hung his head.

"Just think of it as an arrangement that benefits us both. You keep your zoo. I keep my job." He climbed into the SUV and drove away.

The dust settled around Emmaus's feet. I had never seen a man look more dejected.

"Emmaus?" I asked as I got out of my car.

He jumped. "What are you doing here?" He stared at Jethro on his leash. "And you brought that pig again?"

"I just wanted to talk to you. I know Aiden was working a case for you."

His skin flushed when I said Aiden's name. It had not been the reaction I was expecting.

"He was, but that case is closed, and I have paid him. There is no more to be said about it."

"Was that Sheriff Marshall who was just here?" I asked as if I didn't know.

"It was."

I waited.

He frowned at me. "I have much work to do to prepare for opening."

"Why was the sheriff here?"

"My wife made some mistakes, and now, we will have to continue with them. We are trapped."

Trapped? With the sheriff? Was that what he was implying?

Emmaus fast walked to a side door that led into the petting zoo barn. "I must go."

"I just wanted to ask—"

He closed the barn door in my face.

Disheartened, I drove back to Harvest. I decided to approach the village by a different route than I normally took in order to drive past the candy factory. I was surprised to see a wagon filled with insulation parked at one end of the building. I hadn't realized that Naz would make the delivery so early in the day.

I parked by the wagon, tucked Jethro under my arm, and hopped out.

Naz had the wagon backed up to the open delivery bay door at the end of the factory. He and Jericho were working together. Jericho would throw a thick bundle of insulation to Naz, who was standing below the wagon. Then, Naz would carry it inside.

I waved. "Hi. This is so great! The two of you bringing this by makes my life so much easier."

Jericho didn't respond, but Naz smiled. "I'm glad to hear it. It's my goal to get Wade's affairs settled as quick as I can so I can move on to my own business."

I nodded and then glanced at Jericho. "I thought Jericho didn't work with you anymore."

Naz frowned. "I just paid him for the day. It would take me much longer to move all this insulation by myself."

"Oh right," I said, feeling a tad uneasy. "It's nice to see you, Jericho. You should stop by the candy shop before you leave Harvest to see your sister."

Jericho threw another bundle, and Naz caught it. There had to be a hundred more on the wagon.

"Let's take a break," Naz said.

Jericho waved and sat on the mountain of insulation that remained in the wagon.

"Let me show you where I put them," Naz said,

"and you can tell me if that works." I followed him into the building, where there were twenty bundles in a pile lined up with military precision.

"This is great. I'm sure Jonah and his guys will know what to do with it."

He nodded. "After we unload this wagon, I have to go to Swiss German Candies to start the job there, but we can come back tonight and start dismantling that scaffolding. I know where Wade rented it from, and it's costing you money sitting there not being used. Jonah uses his own scaffolding."

"That would be great, and it's very kind of you to offer. I was wondering how I was going to get rid of it."

"It's no trouble at all. Like I said, I'm just trying to get Wade's business settled."

I thanked him and continued on to Swissmen Sweets.

Late in the afternoon, I heard my grandmother and Charlotte speaking in the kitchen.

"Sometimes bridges can't be mended on this side of heaven. The hurt is too deep," *Maami* said.

"I know I hurt them, and now they've been hurt even more by *Daed's* arrest. They believe it is my fault. I was the one who put this all into motion."

"Perhaps that's true," my grandmother said. "But they have hurt you too. You can't let the past hold you back from the future. That is not what *Gott* wants for you. You are to be married to a *gut* man. *Ya*, he is not Amish. All I care about now is that you follow *Gotte's* will for your life. I truly believe that your marriage to Deputy Little is part of it."

I stepped back from the kitchen door. Whatever I needed to grab out of the kitchen could wait.

"Did you speak with Emmaus at the petting zoo this morning?" Aiden asked when he met me at the shop after we closed that evening.

I had to admit it was pretty nice to have my boyfriend walk me home from work. I wrinkled my nose. "Jethro and I both did."

"Of course."

"How did you know?"

"He told me that something you said made him think, and he told me what happened to the money."

I stopped in the middle of the sidewalk. "What? What happened to it?"

"His wife gave it to Wade."

"Are you kidding? Why?"

"It seems that Wade could guarantee the safety of Emmaus and the petting zoo."

"From what?"

"From government interference and fines for violations."

I started walking again. "That's what Sheriff Marshall said when he was there." I quickly told him about everything that had happened when I went to the petting zoo that morning.

"It fits with what I surmised."

"And what is that?"

He took a breath and looked around as if to see if anyone was listening to us. He was spooked. I'd never seen Aiden spooked before, even when someone held him at gunpoint. "I have always wondered how Sheriff Marshall has been able to stay in power all these years. Why is he reelected time after time?"

"The last election, no one ran against him," I said.

"Yes, in that election, because I think the community believed it was impossible to oust him."

"What's your theory?" I stepped over a crack in the sidewalk.

"I think he's been protecting important business people in the community who have committed violations. He ignores those violations in exchange for their loyalty and money."

"Like extortion?" I asked.

He nodded. "And bribery."

It was my turn to look around. "That was a big statement to make about the county sheriff. How does it work?"

"From what I gather, Wade was the middleman. He was the one who delivered messages from the sheriff to the business owner and took the money. He then passed that money on to the sheriff."

"How did they move the money?" I asked.

"I haven't been able to confirm anything, but I think they did it through fake bank accounts in order to launder it. I'm guessing Wade hired Amish men to deposit the money into bank accounts under false names. The Amish don't have social security numbers, so it's much easier to make up a false identity. If that was the case, they'd probably use night deposit boxes, and when the money cleared, they'd take it from the bank with a debit card. Wade probably then took his cut and passed the rest on to the sheriff." He swallowed. "It's only a theory. If I could get one of the Amish men to corroborate the story, then I might be able to approach the DA with what I know. I have to be careful. Sheriff Marshall is a master at covering things up."

"Do you think this has to do with the murder?"

"Yes. I spoke to my friend at the FBI, who put me in contact with the agent on the Heart and Soul case. He said that Wade was one of the victims. He lost fifty thousand dollars."

"Fifty thousand!"

Aiden nodded.

"I know he does a good business, but where did he get the money?" A light dawned. "You think he used the bribery money."

"Exactly," Aiden said. "When he realized his bride was a hoax, he was feverishly trying to restore that money so that the sheriff didn't find out."

"But he might have found out." I paused. "And killed him."

Chapter Forty

Aiden and I agreed that the only way to get to the bottom on this was to talk to two of the Amish men who might actually know something, Naz and Jericho, who just happened to be taking down the scaffolding at my factory that very night. The irony of its being the place where Wade had died was not lost on me.

As we stepped into the candy factory, we heard the sounds of drills and tools in the big room. We found Naz and Jericho taking down the scaffolding piece by piece.

Naz climbed down one side. "Hi, Bailey, this should just take a few hours to bring down."

"I appreciate it," I said.

He smiled and then looked at Aiden.

"This is my boyfriend, Aiden," I said.

"You used to be a deputy," Naz said.

"That's right," Aiden replied.

"Well, it's nice to meet you." Naz waved his wrench at Aiden. "I'm going to get back to work."

"Can I talk to you for a moment?" Aiden asked.

Naz wrinkled his brow, but then shrugged. He and Aiden walked to a corner of the room.

Jericho kept working. His red hair shone in the sunlight coming in through the windows. It was only eight in the evening, and this early in the summer, the sun would be up for another hour at least.

"Hello, Jericho," I said.

He glanced at me but said nothing.

"I know that you really care about your family. You don't want your father to be in prison. Aren't you the eldest son?"

He snapped his head in my direction. "*Ya.*"

"If your father doesn't come home, won't you be responsible for the family?"

He paled.

Just then, Naz stomped away from Aiden toward the scaffolding, shaking his head. "You know, we're doing this as a favor to you. You can't come in here and accuse us of knowing something about Wade's murder. We don't know anything. We just worked for him—that was where it stopped."

Aiden stepped forward. "One of the bank ATM videos shows you removing money from an ATM in Berlin. The money removed was in the name of Anton Swept."

"I don't know what you are talking about. I'm Amish, and in those cameras every Amish man looks the same."

"No, I'm sure it's you," Aiden said.

Sweat gathered on Naz's lip. "We're leaving. You can take this down yourself."

"No one is leaving this room," a deep voice boomed. Sheriff Marshall walked into the candy factory with his hand on the hilt of his gun. "What's going on here? I happened to be passing by and heard shouting."

"You just happened to be passing by?" Aiden asked dubiously.

"I don't want to hear one word out of you, Brody," the sheriff snapped.

"I'm sure you don't want to hear the way your bribery scheme worked. Is that how you got elected in the first place?"

The sheriff narrowed his eyes at Aiden. "No. My first three elections, I won handily, but I knew by the fourth, my popularity was beginning to dwindle. Acquiring power and keeping it are two very different things. It's difficult to acquire power, but it's not nearly as difficult as keeping it. Humans are finicky creatures. The person they believe is their hero one day becomes a fool the next. By working with Wade, I secured my place. It was impossible for anyone to beat me in elections, and those who might have tried—like you, Brody—were too afraid to attempt it." He cleared his throat. "Now, if you want Bailey to remain unscathed, I'd drop the subject. With Wade gone, there's no trail or proof of what's been done in the past."

"Is that why you killed him?" I asked. "To erase the trail? Or was it because he double-crossed you and lost fifty thousand of your extorted money on a scam."

The sheriff's eyes bugged out of his head.

"It doesn't matter what you do, Marshall," Aiden said. "My friend at the FBI has tied Wade to a catfishing scam. They will start to investigate his movements and his murder. All of it will lead back to you."

Sheriff Marshall removed his gun from his belt.

"You may be right. There might be no way out for me at this point." He raised his gun. "But that doesn't mean I'll let you walk away." He turned the gun on me. "Until you showed up in the county, everything was going smoothly. Over the last few years, you've made a joke of my department and disrespected me as the sheriff."

"Perhaps if you'd had more respect for the Amish, that wouldn't have happened." I tried not to stare at the barrel of the gun.

"The only value the Amish bring to this county is tourism. People who don't live here think the Amish are just so quaint and charming. The tourists don't know what they're really like. Not like I do. And you have to admit, you know exactly what I'm talking about. There is no reason to bellyache that Sol Weaver is sitting in jail. He was no saint."

It was true that not all Amish were good. That was because no matter how they might have been raised, they were still human. Not all humans were good. That was something that had been made apparent to me in the last few years. The corrupt sheriff standing in front of me was living proof of that.

Aiden stepped in front of me. "Let Bailey and the young men go. You can have me. Use me as a bargaining chip. I don't care."

The sheriff laughed. "Let the young men go. Don't you know they are in on this? They killed Wade Farmer, not me. You might be able to arrest me for the other crimes, but not for murder."

Jericho, who was still on the scaffolding, cried out and jumped from the structure onto the sheriff. He bounced off Sheriff Marshall's broad shoulder, but the blow was enough to startle the sheriff and make him drop the gun.

Naz dove for the revolver and scooped it up. He pointed it at each of us in turn.

Jericho moaned on the concrete floor and held his leg. It was possible he'd broken it.

"You killed Wade, Naz?" I asked.

Naz pointed the gun at the sheriff. "He talked me into it. He told me how much money I was losing because Wade stole not just from him but from me too. He lost all that money, my money, on a woman who wasn't even real!"

"Naz," the sheriff said as he struggled to his feet. "You're right. Why don't you and I leave here together?"

"*Nee*," Naz said. "I know how you police are. You will twist my words and confuse me. You'll make me think this is all my fault like you have with Jericho's father. It's all your fault, not mine."

While Naz and the sheriff argued with each other, I kept an eye on Aiden. He had his cell phone in his hand and pressed to his thigh. I was willing to bet he'd called the authorities and they were hearing all of this.

But I wasn't sure they would get here in time.

Naz raised his gun, pointing it at the sheriff. "What is one more murder?"

There was a piece of scaffold pipe just at my feet. Slowly, I bent down and picked it up. I held it behind my back.

Aiden and I made eye contact. He shook his head slightly. I nodded.

Before he could shake his head again. I jumped forward and hit Naz on the back with the pipe. The gun flew from his hand. This time, Aiden was there to scoop it up.

Epilogue

Charlotte, who stood in the middle of the gazebo wearing a simple white dress that she had made herself and delicate flowers in her hair, looked into Deputy Little's shining eyes, and said, "I do."

A black lab puppy named Licorice, a gift from her family, sat at her feet. The service was short, sweet, and simple, but perhaps too long for the young pup, because it fell asleep before Charlotte and Deputy Little shared their first kiss as husband and wife.

Most of the village was in attendance, but the most notable guests were Charlotte's parents and siblings, who stood at the edge of the square. They never came any closer, and when the ceremony ended, they piled into their buggy and drove away. However, they had been there in support of their daughter, and that was all she'd ever wanted.

The only one who had not been among them was Jericho. Charlotte's brother was sitting in jail awaiting trial for the bribery scheme. Aiden didn't believe he would serve much time because he'd told the DA everything that he knew about Sheriff Marshall and Naz Schlabach's involvement in the bribery and Wade Farmer's murder. Even so, I doubted Jericho would rejoin his family when he was released. This might be a case where it would be best for everyone if he did leave the Amish way.

The reception was a supremely casual cookie-and-cake reception in the church's fellowship hall. As the maid of honor, I didn't have to make a speech or even stand in a receiving line. At my first chance, I stepped out of the back door of the church for some fresh air.

"I thought I would find you out here," Aiden said as he walked out of the church with Jethro on his leash. The little pig had a giant pink-and-white polka-dotted bow around his neck.

I smiled. "Just catching some air."

He took my hand in his. "I have a hankering for chocolate. Let's walk over to Swissmen Sweets."

I chuckled. "Aiden, there is a ton of chocolate in the church right now."

"The candy shop chocolate is better."

"It is the candy shop chocolate in the church."

"Besides, Jethro needs to walk off some of those cookies he ate." He looked down at the pig. "Right, buddy?"

Jethro scrunched up his snout at Aiden.

"Fine." I said, allowing him to lead me away. When we reached the candy shop, I unlocked the door, and we went inside. Jethro bumped noses with Nutmeg, who was sleeping in his cat bed.

Aiden tugged on Jethro's leash. "Stay with me, buddy."

The pig sat on his haunches next to Aiden.

I raised an eyebrow at Aiden. "Is something going on here I don't know about?"

"Nope. But I would love something sweet to eat," Aiden said with a smile. "I'll be a customer and you give me a candy sample."

"Oh-kay, but we don't have much in stock because most of it is at the wedding."

"I like all candy."

I shook my head and went behind the domed counter. There were a few pieces of blueberry-and-cream fudge left on a plate. I pulled it out from the tray, set it on a small paper plate, and placed it on the top of the counter. "Here's your treat," I said with a bright smile.

"Looks delicious! I have a treat for you too." He bent down and pulled the bow loose from Jethro's neck. As he did, a small ring box fell into his hand.

"Aiden?" I felt tears coming to my eyes.

"It just seemed fitting to have Jethro play a role."

"Aiden?" I whispered.

He looked at me with those chocolate-brown eyes that I'd melted into on so many occasions. "I remember the first time I saw you in this very spot at this counter. You almost choked on a piece of fudge."

I laughed through my tears, and Jethro snuffled at Aiden's feet.

"I knew then I wanted to get to know you better. I wanted to know everything about you. What I didn't know was how deeply I would love you. I do love you with my whole heart. Bailey King, will you marry me?" He opened the ring box. The diamond inside sparkled.

I nodded, unable to speak. He took my hand

over the counter and slipped the ring onto my finger.

I smiled at him. "Let's keep this between us for a few days. It's Charlotte's day."

He squeezed my hand. "Whatever you want, fiancée."

Jethro looked up at us with the biggest smile on his piggy face.

RECIPE

Bailey's Blueberry-and-Cream Fudge

Ingredients

1 cup fresh blueberries
½ tablespoon cornstarch
1 tablespoon of lemon juice
¼ cup of sugar
24 oz white chocolate chips
¼ stick of unsalted butter
14 oz of sweetened condensed milk

Directions

1. Make the blueberry sauce. In a small saucepan add blueberries, sugar, lemon juice, and cornstarch over medium heat.
2. Stir continuously and smash the blueberries until you have a thick sauce like a puree.
3. Using a fine mesh strainer, push the puree through into a bowl and set aside.
4. Make the fudge cream. Over a double boiler, add the white chocolate chips, sweetened condensed milk, and butter.
5. Stir continuously to blend and until all the chocolate is melted.
6. Line a 9x9 pan with parchment paper.

7. Pour ⅓ of the white chocolate mixture into the 9x9 pan.
8. Pour ⅓ of the blueberry sauce on top of the chocolate in the pan.
9. Using a knife, swirl the white chocolate and blueberry sauce together.
10. Repeat steps 7-9 two more times.
11. Place in the fridge to set for at least three hours.
12. Cut into pieces and enjoy. The fudge can last for a week in an airtight container.

Please read on for an excerpt from
DATING CAN BE DEADLY,
the newest book in Amanda Flower's
Amish Matchmaker Mystery series.

Chapter One

"Do you see him?" Lois asked, standing on her tiptoes, trying to look over the line of people paying for their tickets to enter the Holmes County Fair. "He said he would meet me at the ticket window."

"How would I know if I've seen him?" I asked, holding my quilting basket tightly to my middle so that it wouldn't get jostled in the crowd. "I've never met him. And neither have you."

"I've seen his picture on the app," Lois said.

"*Ya*, but you told me that pictures can be misleading on the dating app. People post a picture of themselves taken when they were much younger or use someone else's picture altogether," I said.

Lois touched her hair. The purple-red spikey tufts on the top of her head didn't move. She told me once she had to use three different styling products to get it to hold. I didn't know how she did it. I had never used a styling product on my hair. I knew what it would look like every day. I would twist my long white hair into a bun at the nape of my neck and finish the look with a white Amish prayer cap held in place with hairpins. My clothing choices were as simple. I always wore a plain solid colored dress, usually navy blue, and sturdy black walking shoes. Knowing what I was going to wear every day took a lot of angst out of my life. At least it took out the angst that I observed when Lois tried to choose her outfits.

Lois Henry was my dearest friend in the world, but she was as far from Amish as a person could be. She had that wild hair, she loved bright clothes with multiple patterns, and she never met a piece of costume jewelry or a container of eye shadow that she didn't like. The massive patchwork purse over her arm held everything in the world or so it seemed. Lois's purse was the stuff of legend; she could pull just about anything out of it at any time, including a brick.

She always wore makeup and did her hair, but today, she'd gone all out. Her hair was as hard as concrete—not even the thick August humidity was going to take it down—and she wore a purple leopard-printed jumpsuit.

There was quite a range of fashion at the fair, from the plain Amish to the *Englisch* teenagers in shorts so short that the inside of their pockets hung below the hems, but even in that crowd, Lois stood out.

"Virgil would never lie about his pictures on the app. He's an upstanding man. Why do you think I'm meeting him here? I don't have time to waste on deadbeats. I'm sixty-eight years old. Chances are he will be my last husband."

"Whoa," I said, as if I were telling my horse Bessie to slow down when she was pulling my buggy.

"Whoa. Why are you talking about marriage at all? You haven't even met him yet."

"Millie, when you know, you know."

I folded my arms. "When you know, you know? Could this be how you ended up being married four times already?"

"Listen," Lois said. "I'm not one of those slow burn people like you."

"What are you talking about?" I wanted to know.

"Uriah? Need I really say more? The two of you have been dancing around each other for months since he returned to Harvest. I don't have time for that. If I want to be able walk down the wedding aisle under my own steam and without the aid of a walker or cane, I need to get Virgil locked down."

I rubbed the spot between my eyebrows because I could feel a headache forming there. I loved Lois dearly, and I didn't want her to end up in another bad marriage. She'd had three. Her only good marriage had been to her second husband, who left her widowed.

Lois sucked in a breath. "Oh, I see him. He's as handsome as his picture."

I stood on my toes, trying to see. "Where? Where?"

"Millie, stop that; you'll make a scene," Lois hissed.

"*I'll* make a scene?" I asked, but I stopped trying to look over the crowd.

Lois put a hand to her heart, and the late morning light sparkled on the bright gemstones of her many rings. "He's standing by the ticketing booth, waiting for me just like he said he would. Isn't that the most romantic thing?" She turned to me. "How do I look?"

"Colorful," I said.

"Perfect. Now, you have to leave."

"Leave?" I asked.

"You need to get to the quilt barn to show your quilt. You don't even have to buy a ticket. You go in as one of the presenters through the other entrance."

"I know I can do that, but I want to be with you when you meet Virgil."

"You can't be," Lois argued. "Shoo. Shoo." She waved me away.

"You're shooing me?" I asked.

"Yes, I don't want Virgil to think that I brought a friend because I didn't trust that he was who he said he was."

"You might trust him, but I don't. I want to see him and make sure he's deserving of you." I adjusted the heavy quilting basket on my arm.

"Please, Millie." She looked over her shoulder. "Let me meet him alone. I will come to the quilt barn where you'll be, and we can bump into each other all natural like."

I frowned. "Fine, but I don't like having to wait. Don't take too long making your way to the quilt barn. I need to see him."

"I won't. Go!" She peered over the heads of the people in line again.

Shaking my head, I stepped out of the ticketing line and walked a little way down the chain-link fence that surrounded the fairgrounds until I reached the vendor and presenter entrance.

"Good morning, Millie," a large gentleman in overalls and a bucket hat said. "It's going to be a hot one today. Are you sure you're going to be able to stand it in the quilt barn with no AC?"

"Sal, you know I don't have air conditioning at home. I will do just fine," I said.

"If you ask me all those non-Amish ladies are going to melt right into the concrete slab. They aren't built for this." Sal grinned. "That might be good for you though, right? You can't win the quilting competition if you aren't present for the judging. One of you Amish ladies will be a shoo-in."

"Let's hope that everyone is present for the judging, so that the best quilt wins."

He shrugged. "If you say so."

I went through the entrance and left Sal to greet the next person in line.

On the fairgrounds, there was the heady smell of manure, hay, and fried food. It took me back to my childhood when my family would come to the fair. To my left, there was a line of games. Everything from a basketball hoop to a ring toss to a water pistol shooting competition. I walked down the line of booths, which were doing a good business by the looks of it, and the game operators shouted in their loud voices for me to come give their games a try. At the end of the games was a trailer that had been transformed. One end was like a normal trailer, but at the other end, the sides and the roof of the trailer were made of chain-link fencing to form a cage of sorts. "Axe throwing is good for the soul" was emblazoned on the side.

A young *Englisch* man stood in the trailer holding a hatchet over his head. He took one step forward and flung the hatchet. The blade dug into the wooden target. "Great job!" the game operator said, and the young man inside jumped up and down in excitement at hitting the bull's-eye.

I shook my head. I remembered when the fair's most dangerous game was darts. The axe throwing seemed to be a bit extreme.

Ahead of me was the horse barn and horse show paddock. I turned right there and passed the line of food stands. My stomach growled. I promised myself that I would get a corn dog just as soon as I could break away from the quilt barn. I wondered if there were any blueberry desserts at the fair. I loved blueberries.

The quilt barn was actually the barn where all the craft judging would be held, including flower arranging, needlework, photography, and other artwork. However, the quilt competition was the premier event in the barn. It even rivaled the cattle judging that would happen three barns away.

The building itself was a white pole barn on a concrete floor. It was made of metal, so it was a little bit like walking into a hotbox. All the windows and doors were wide open, and three huge industrial fans circulated the humid air. I was glad I had left my large black bonnet at home.

Presenters were set up all over the barn displaying their work. Quilters hung their prize-worthy quilts on giant mobile walls that could display every inch of the quilt to the public. For judging the quilts would be taken down off the walls and closely scrutinized.

"Millie!" Raellen Raber waved at me from the other end of the large barn.

I waved back. Raellen was a member of my quilting circle. We went by the name of Double Stitch. The group had five members, but Raellen, Iris Young, and I were the only ones who were entering the fair's quilting competition this year.

I was making my way to Raellen when an *Englisch* woman stepped in my path. "Observers aren't supposed to be in the quilt barn yet, just presenters." She had short, bobbed blond hair and wore jeans and a checkered shirt. She held a list in her hand. There was a large purple ribbon on her chest that said, "Judge."

"I'm a presenter. My friend over there"—I pointed at Raellen—"is going to help me hang up my quilt." I showed her my basket. "She's a presenter too."

The woman pressed her mouth into a thin line. "What's your name?"

"Millie Fisher."

She consulted the list. "Your name is on here," she said somewhat reluctantly.

"I'm glad to hear it. May I ask your name?" I nodded at the ribbon. "Judge?"

"Tara Barron. I'm the head judge for the quilting competition and do not abide any foolishness in my barn."

I looked down at my Amish garb. I was a sixty-eight-year-old Amish widow. What foolishness could I get into? I wanted to ask her that. Then I thought of all the tight spots that Lois and I have gotten into over the years and kept my mouth shut.

Tara looked over my shoulder at someone else coming into the barn. Her face paled slightly, but when I turned to see whom she was staring at, I couldn't tell. There had to be forty people behind me hurrying here and there to get ready for the various contests.

"Good luck," she said with a sniff and walked away from me.

I didn't for a second believe she meant that.